CHRISTMAS
at the ISLAND
HOTEL

CHRISTMAS
at the ISLAND
HOTEL

A NOVEL

Jenny Colgan

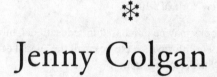

WILLIAM MORROW
An Imprint of HarperCollins*Publishers*

HarperCollins books may be purchased for educational, business, or sales promotional use. For information please email the Special Markets Department at SPsales@harpercollins.com.

Originally published as *Christmas at the Island Hotel* in the United Kingdom in 2020 by Sphere.

FIRST EDITION

Designed by Diahann Sturge

Library of Congress Cataloging-in-Publication Data has been applied for.

ISBN 978-0-06-291128-5
ISBN 978-0-06-291140-7 (hardcover library edition)

20 21 22 23 24 LSC 10 9 8 7 6 5 4

To the front line staff, all of you, who got up and went to work every day whilst the rest of us had to stay indoors. You were, and are, the glue that holds the world together. Thank you.

Prologue

Day and night the great tankers plow the freezing water of the North Atlantic.

Vast up close—two, three hundred meters, filled with cars and rocking horses and teddies and barometers and valves and bonnets and tea—they are nonetheless still dwarfed by the scale of the ocean.

Coming in from the west, they cross imaginary lines in the water that the comfortable and landbound hear about only as they fall asleep to the shipping forecast: Rockall, Hebrides, and, over the north of Fair Isle, Mure, the tiny island between Shetland and the Faroes, home to 1,500 souls (in a good year).

The southwesternmost tip contains the village and the port, and the sailors—from the Philippines, often, and Thailand, the great seafaring nations of the South Seas—are about as far away from home as they can ever get. They look out, often, on the little point of light marooned in the ocean, eyes starved of diversion from the endless dark waves.

You cannot be a seafaring man if prone to melancholy—you will live away from your family, in close quarters with other men, for nine, ten months of the year, so a positive attitude is best. But even the most sea-hardened occasionally gets a little mournful for home, particularly when he pulls up the binoculars, sees the colored houses of Mure crowded higgledy-piggledy on the wharf, along with the soft gray of the café, the pink of the pharmacy, the black and white of the old Harbour's Rest hotel.

There is no deepwater harbor on the island. None of the great container ships will ever land there. But more than a few like to mark Mure's passing, as it is the last spot of land they will see before Bergen, and the cottages and buildings cluster together, heading upward from the waterside, in a cozy, haphazard fashion, as if leaning against one another for warmth on the bare island with its vast, empty pale yellow beaches and low-bending rushes.

Sometimes through the binoculars, on a clear day in the summertime, you can see the children wave.

But now, in the pitch black of an early winter's morning, it looks like a tiny pinprick of comfort in a world gone dark, as they chug past, the huge ships making light work of the slapping waves, the motion so familiar as to make walking on land a difficult adjustment for the men.

The island is so small that, at twenty knots, it doesn't take long for it to disappear behind you, for Apostil or Danilo or Jesus to go back to checking the radar and the fax machine, and to move on to North Uist, to the vast rich fjords of Norway, leaving the quiet island marooned once more under the cold stars, where, in the MacKenzie farmhouse, at the very southernmost tip of the island, the early-morning fire is going and the coffee is heating on the stove, and Flora MacKenzie is currently in the middle of having a furious stand-up argument with her younger brother, Fintan.

"COLTON'S BAR," SHE repeated. "Absolutely not. I mean, I understand it, but also we sound like a saloon where girls wear hot pants and fringing and cowboy boots and ask 'How y'all doing' and we have a mechanical bull."

"Nobody said anything about a mechanical bull," grumbled Fintan, breathing in the scent of the coffee and the fresh rolls warming in the oven. Then he looked up. "Hmm," he said. "Mechanical bull."

"Do I have to take that coffee off you?"

Fintan rolled his eyes. "Anything but that."

"Look," said Flora practically. It had only been a year since Fintan's husband, Colton, had died of cancer. Fintan had good days and bad days. This was not shaping up to be a good day. There weren't many good days.

Colton had left him the Rock: the hotel he had always dreamed of opening on the island, and it was finally coming to fruition. But there were a million and one little details and he wasn't enjoying that side of things in the slightest. The hotel had been useful: it had kept Fintan phenomenally busy and helped keep the grief at bay—sheer exhaustion was his friend when it came to sleeping alone in a very big bed. Plus, they had bookings for Christmas Day. They had to open, and quickly.

Flora technically had nothing to do with it.

But somehow, as she already had catering experience running the Summer Seaside Kitchen down on the shore, she couldn't stop poking her nose in. Also she was meant to be on maternity leave, which, as far as Fintan (and not just Fintan) was concerned, was leaving her with far too much time on her hands to interfere.

"I think Rogers's Bar is fine," said Flora. "Just not so on the nose, you know?"

Fintan pouted.

There was a commotion at the entrance to the kitchen. Fintan was staying at the farmhouse, as was their brother Innes and his family. Innes's daughter, Agot, five, was marching into the kitchen in her nightie, a serious look on her face, a thin wail rising behind her from the corridor.

"*Bug*glas Booker is awake," she said with a sniff. "I think he's a bad baby, Auntie Flora. He is very cross."

"Douglas," said Flora for the nine hundredth time. "His name is Douglas."

Agot and Fintan gave her a similarly dry look.

"What?" said Flora. "She watches *Hey Duggee* on TV all the time."

"Duggee is a very good dog," said Agot loudly. Then, "I'm not sure about *Bug*glas."

She marched over to the retired sheepdog Bramble, and the two of them went outside to examine the vegetable garden. Agot had a very strong resistance to actually eating vegetables, but she liked watching them grow, and there were still a few very late rhubarb stalks.

"She's doing that on purpose," said Flora, heading out. "She can speak perfectly well."

"She is," said Fintan. "And yet you somehow let it rile you."

Flora headed toward the back room, even though the baby was

barely crying, thinking Agot was ridiculous, and then she realized she was mentally having an argument with her five-year-old niece, which was a waste of time if she'd ever known one, but it didn't matter, because by the time she got there, Joel was already with him, and Douglas had fallen silent.

He looked so like his father—black eyes and already, at five months, a shock of black curly hair—it was actually hilarious. Almost everyone who met him had felt the urge to put a pair of glasses on him.

She stood in the doorframe for a moment, watching them both. Douglas didn't smile much—he was not at all a smiley baby; his little face was grave and serious, as if he had been born knowing all the mysteries of the universe, which he would gradually forget as he grew older. He also shared his father's serious demeanor; he was watchful and careful. For a long time Flora had thought that Joel was like that because of his difficult upbringing—he had been in and out of foster homes since he was very little. She was coming to think, however, that in fact Joel's demeanor was innate, as never was a baby boy smothered with so much love and affection as Douglas, coming in to a home with three uncles at close quarters and his grandfather Eck, who worshipped him and did much of the babysitting duty. Then there were his adopted American grandparents, Mark and Marsha, who sent giant care packages of ridiculously expensive baby clothes imported from France, via New York, which were frankly a little too good for the muddy farmyard and changeable climate of a small, very northern Scottish island, but Flora made sure he was dutifully photographed in them all anyway. The Bookers were just like that.

Joel didn't fuss him or sing to him. He just lay down on the bed next to him, and the two of them eyeballed each other. It was the oddest thing, as if something intangible flowed between them through eye contact alone. Joel's large hand would reach out so Douglas could clasp a finger, and they would commune. Flora didn't even know how to ask anyone if this was normal behavior. Sometimes Douglas would flap at Joel's heavy gold watch and Joel would let him. Usually, after fifteen minutes of this, they would both be asleep, the long body gently cradling the tiny one.

Flora was supposedly on maternity leave, Isla and Iona running the café perfectly well, somewhat to Flora's annoyance. But it was Joel, her workaholic boyfriend, who appeared to have taken it most to heart, and she couldn't help occasionally feeling just a little jealous. Which was, of course, completely ridiculous. Everything was great. Fine. Great. I mean, Douglas cried at her but was totally calm with Joel, but she didn't mind. Not a bit.

Chapter 1

W ell, which is the best one?"

Isla Donnelly's mother, Vera, was looking at her over the old teapot with the flowers and the chip in the top.

Isla, staring at it, realized something she had never quite put into words before: she hated that teapot. It was the stupidest thing she could imagine, hating a teapot. It was possibly because her mother treated it like a precious heirloom she needed to be more careful with rather than just a dumb crappy teapot. She sipped her tea.

"I don't know, Mum," she said again, trying not to get riled, which wouldn't help.

"So, the MacKenzies need someone up at the new posh hotel."

Vera Donnelly sniffed loudly. She didn't think much of the new hotel. Not the kind of thing Mure needed in her opinion, and Vera had a lot of opinions. Too fancy, too expensive—who wanted that kind of thing?

Regardless, it was set to open this Christmas, and Flora had offered to help Fintan by moving one of her café staff up there.

Isla sighed. She was, in fact, indeed quite terrified, but she would never tell her mother that. Not good to give her the ammunition.

"Well, one of us will stay and take over more of the running of the Seaside Kitchen and one of us will go up to the Rock."

Isla and her best friend, Iona, had worked in the Summer Seaside Kitchen for years, and neither was looking forward to getting separated. Isla in particular was very much the shyer of the two and absolutely dreading being without her cheeky chum.

"Yes, but which one is the *best job*?"

"I don't know."

Vera carefully picked up her treasured teapot and daintily poured herself another cup of tea. "You know, I just don't want them taking advantage of you," she said. "That Flora treats you like a scullery maid."

"I'm just learning on the job," said Isla, who adored Flora and didn't quite have her mother's expectations for her. She knew it was difficult being Vera's only child. She hated constantly adding to her disappointment. "What are you doing today, Mum?"

"It's *Homes Under the Hammer*!"

"You know there's a choir rehearsal tonight . . . You should go to that."

Isla's main goal was to stop herself being Vera's only area of attention.

"Bunch of busybodying old gossips. No thanks!"

Isla put on her coat and pulled her tam-o'-shanter down over her unruly dark chestnut curls, which pinged out every which way—unusual on the island, where people had fair or red hair, depending on whether they were descended from Celts or Vikings. There had once been a rumor of Spanish invaders making it as far north as Mure, which would have made more sense of her dark eyes, although the pale skin, lightly freckled in the summertime, was purest Scotland, to Isla's eternal chagrin.

"Bye, Mum," she said.

"Aye well. Good luck then," said her mother grudgingly as she left, and Isla reminded herself that her mother loved her and wanted the best for her, even when it felt unpleasant.

A nor'wester was blowing down from the arctic circle straight into Mure and made walking in a straight line quite difficult, but it wasn't far to the little Seaside Kitchen, down two cobbled streets and on the seafront.

The little café was always warm: the baking ovens through the back never really quite cooled down, and on freezing winter mornings it was cozy even before she lit the golden lamps that, together with the cheery spotted tablecloths and the pretty pictures on the wall, made the café so inviting. Iona would already be brewing up coffee, and together they could make a start on the scones, pies, tarts, and cakes for the day, while Mrs. Laird popped off the freshly baked bread. The coffee machine would hiss and grind in a comforting fashion, and the day could begin. And it wouldn't be long before the first chilled worker arrived, fresh from milking or a fishing boat or waiting on the earliest ferry of the morning.

Chapter 2

Two hundred miles to the east, the expensive sheets of the bed were ruffled and crumpled. A pale figure was lying on them unconcerned and snoring heavily. The thick scent of stale beer was in the air.

A short man with an exceedingly tidy haircut entered the vast room, paused in front of the bed, and coughed loudly. Nothing happened.

"*Ahem,*" said the man.

There was an unpleasant hacking cough from the bed, followed by a snorting and some grunting. A large arm grabbed the shiny coverlet and pulled it over.

"Go away, Johann," came a very croaky voice, muffled beneath the covers.

"Johann has been sent away," said the man.

There was a pause in the room.

"Huh?"

The young man who emerged from the covers had fair hair sticking up in every conceivable direction, a very tiny amount of stubble, and a confused look in his round blue eyes, which became markedly rounder as he registered whom he was talking to.

"Pappa," he said, and there was a notable tremor in his voice.

He clutched the covers round him. The man staring at him looked disappointed. Again.

"Uhm," said the boy, whose name was Konstantin. "I mean, hello. Good to see you. You don't normally . . ."

He glanced around at the large, lavish suite. There were pillars in the corners, gilt on the cornicing, and vast, ancient mirrors lining one wall.

Unfortunately there were also underpants and socks on the floor, empty bottles, books scattered everywhere, a snorting, piglike dog called Bjårk, who hadn't woken up yet but had left muddy paw prints all over the wildly expensive rug and black-and-white tiled floor, and at least four towels.

"I don't normally come here, no," said the boy's father, whose name was also Konstantin. There had been Konstantins, in fact, all the way back to the early seventeenth century, when they had first become dukes of Hordaland and the grand castle had been built on the beautiful Forgalfanna peninsula. Titles in Norway had been theoretically abolished. Of course, everyone still knew. An unbroken line. Which, the older Konstantin reflected sadly, was about to be broken when he kicked his dissolute only son down the 118 curved marble steps of the grand entrance hall. "Because it's a revolting pigsty."

"That's Bjårk's fault."

The hairy creature didn't stir.

"Do you recall what happened last night at the state banquet?"

Konstantin screwed up his face. "The snowball fight," he said finally. "Yes, wasn't it brilliant?"

He remembered the palace windows blazing light as they ran about outside, exhausted, freezing, and soaking, but laughing their heads off.

"It was *not* brilliant," said his father. "You hit the archbishop on the ear."

"Well, he should have joined in."

"You put snow down the neck of my financial adviser."

Konstantin shrugged. "He's an old stick."

His father shook his head. "No. You behaved like a thug."

"We were having fun!"

"And worse than that, you behaved like a bully to people older and weaker than yourself."

"With a *snowball*."

But the older man wasn't stopping now. "This is after the ice races."

"I accidentally tripped up—"

"The entire professional team."

"They were in the way!"

The boy pouted out his lower lip and suddenly looked a lot younger than twenty-four. His father shook his head. "You know, if your mother were still with us, she wouldn't have stood for this."

The boy pouted more. "That's not fair," he said, but now his voice was quiet and sad.

"We were too soft on you . . . afterward," the man went on. "I didn't want to upset things . . . didn't want to make you study too much or get a job or work hard. And look at you now. Twenty-four years old and in bed in the middle of a Tuesday."

He shook his head sadly.

"I got it wrong. I got it so wrong."

He turned round, his younger years at Sandhurst still apparent in his gait. Konstantin stared after him, stricken.

At the door, his father turned round one more time. "I'm tempted to disinherit you."

"You wouldn't! For a snowball? Don't be silly, Pappa, you can't mean that."

"This is a big job. And you do nothing, you learn nothing, you work at nothing except drinking champagne and playing with that fat idle hound of yours."

Konstantin frowned and covered Bjårk's ears.

"Be as mean as you like to me, but don't upset Bjårky."

"It's all a joke to you, isn't it?" said the older man. "All a joke. And I am going to fix that."

And he opened the heavy white door with its gilt handle and let it slam behind him.

KONSTANTIN SAT UP in bed, Bjårk snuffling underneath his hands. It would blow over, wouldn't it? Surely. His father was always getting these ideas into his head, insisting he should go to college or into the military, or get a job, and nothing ever came of it in the end. The much-loved only child who'd come along late in life, whose mother had died when he was fourteen . . .

Mind you, there was no Johann. That was odd. He looked at the grandfather clock in the corner. No breakfast either. Normally he needed four strong cups of coffee and some excellent rye bread thickly spread with *smør* before he could even think about a steaming-hot bath and a read of the sports pages. His paper wasn't even here. He frowned and reached over to ring the bell. But nobody came.

Chapter 3

Flora caught up with Fintan and they walked through the lobby of the Rock hotel. It had felt like it would take forever to get finished, but it was done: sound and warm and dry and very beautiful. And Christmassy, even though it was only November. The tree wouldn't arrive for a few weeks, but the staff had already put up the great scalloped green hanging boughs tied up with tartan ribbon, their scent filling the air. There were bowls full of oranges studded with cinnamon cloves, the great log fire at the entrance was lit, and gentle music was playing in the background.

Originally a large mansion built for a wealthy local family, the Rock had been converted by the brash American developer Colton Rogers, with absolutely no expense spared. There was also no taste spared, in terms of what an American thought a Scottish hotel was supposed to look like, which meant tartan carpets, lots of open fires, muskets and giant stag heads on the walls, and a library full of old hardback books that had been bought from an aristocratic book dealer down Kirrinfief way, without Colton reading a single word of any of them.

It was a little kitsch, maybe, but Flora couldn't help admitting to herself that she rather loved it. It was just so warm and cozy all the time, which in the winter on Mure meant a lot. And being done up for Christmas put it in its absolute prime.

There was underfloor heating, towel warmers filled with fluffy towels, and great deep tubs in the bathrooms, and the hot water never seemed to run out. The kitchen was pristine and full of the latest equipment, Flora noticed enviably, ready to churn out bread and pastries, high teas and fresh lobster, buttery scones and creamy Cullen skink, sumptuous cranachan. And behind the bar, forty-five different types of whisky waited tantalizingly, together with a menu of delicious local cocktails.

Flora and Fintan looked at each other. Flora was excited by all the possibilities; Fintan's shoulders were slumped, his entire countenance a mask of misery and defeatism.

"It's never going to pay its way in a billion years," said Fintan bitterly. "We should just get rid of it.

"Colton didn't leave me a fortune," he went on anxiously. "He just left me this place. We'd tear through the money in five minutes."

Colton had donated the bulk of his considerable fortune to medical research; he'd left the hotel and his house to Fintan, but Fintan couldn't bear to live in the vast echoing house by himself, so Joel and Flora were renting it, while Fintan stayed back at the farmhouse.

"And I don't know how to run a hotel! I don't even know what VAT is!"

"It's like a very complicated puzzle the government sets you for fun, but if you get it wrong you go to jail," said Flora, but Fintan wasn't listening.

"I already can't get staff! And how am I going to tell them what to do? What if the people here want to leave because they hate me? What if nobody comes? How much would we have to charge? I should sell it. I should sell this whole place."

Flora stood, warming her hands in front of the fire. There was a skeleton staff, all of whom seemed great. They just needed a chef and a bit of help in the kitchen. Fintan was panicking.

"But it's all Colton's," said Flora softly. "It was his dream. It's exactly how he wanted it."

Flora eyed the huge antlered stag head above the fireplace and reflected that, for better or worse, it certainly was that.

He sighed. "It's all that's left of him. How could I sell that?"

His voice was anguished. Flora didn't know what to say.

"Well, how would you feel if you did sell it?" she tried gently.

"We met for the first time on the lawn," said Fintan bitterly. He now appeared to have completely changed his mind about selling it and was somehow blaming Flora for implying it. "We got married out there, or did you forget?"

Flora stayed silent. She understood Fintan's bitterness and grief. She had just slightly hoped that he might get a bit more excited about moving forward, find energy in working on the new project, in making it as wonderful as Colton always hoped it would be.

Fintan, however, was still fuming at the world, specifically the Rock hotel section of it, the amazing boutique property that was now, technically, his to do as he liked with. To most people, Flora reflected, a little glumly, it would have been a wonderful legacy. But Fintan seemed determined to have none of it.

She tried to help. "We'll just need to charge a lot of money," said Flora. "Get the right people in."

"Rich nobbers."

Flora shrugged. "There are plenty of nice rich nobbers."

"Are there, though?" said Fintan, looking cross.

"Well, you married one for starters."

"Yes, but he . . . he was a one-off."

Flora smiled sympathetically as they walked on to the dining room, which had cozy soft leather banquettes at the windows, comfortable tweed chairs, and wide dark oak flooring. There was paneling along one wall with expensive, terrible oil paintings of stags and Bonnie Prince Charlie. It was completely empty and still.

Flora looked around. "So many tables," she said, half to herself. The Seaside Kitchen had twelve tables, at least two of which were permanently occupied by knitters who worked with the Fair Isle companies. Then there was the mums and babies group who spent copiously on the organic purees she put together each morning with whatever she had on hand, plus a long line of extremely hungry fishermen, farmers, hikers, bird-watchers, and holidaymakers who wanted sausage rolls and haggis pies and hot soup. She knew her clientele back to front and was fond of all of them. That she could manage. But this . . . even though it was technically a boutique hotel, it was still an awful lot of doing. Was Fintan up to it?

As if hearing her thoughts, Fintan let out a great sigh. "All I ever wanted to do was make cheese."

Flora looked at him. His handsome face was so tired; he'd lost too much weight. He was still in the throes of such a strong grief.

It made her vow to appreciate her own situation more. Especially when she remembered how much she'd worried about

Douglas before he'd arrived. And after. She had been told by the other mums she met around the place that this wasn't uncommon at all. People who desperately wanted to be parents, who had fantasies about how perfect it was all going to be, had a very difficult time of it, when their baby wouldn't sleep or eat, or wasn't the perfect heavenly dream they'd expected or read about in magazines or looked at in advertisements. And new mums didn't lose their baby weight by "running about after the baby" like celebrities said they did. Was it just possible, she'd heard one mother muse, that those celebrities might in fact be talking out of the cracks of their arses?

Flora had by no means lost her baby weight but was filing it very far down on her list of "Current Things to Worry About." He wouldn't mention it in a million years, not being an idiot, but Joel thought it suited her; it made her so pretty and rounded and soft.

With Joel, there had been some worry. But as with some reluctant parents in cases of accidental pregnancies, or those who had slightly (or in Joel's case, extremely) ambivalent fathers, the force of the extraordinary rush of love that babies brought with them could knock them over, take them completely by surprise, and Joel was the worst of the lot.

From the second Dougie had arrived, Joel had behaved like a man poleaxed by love. Flora complained he had never once appeared so gaga about her, but she didn't really mind, she supposed. He had been so worried about whether he would take to parenthood—he had been a foster child, moved around from house to house, never once finding a home—that he had been mute and difficult and anxious all the way up to the birth itself

(an unusually speedy process that Flora found increasingly difficult to remember anything about), but as soon as the squawking
gawky, tiny, blood-, shit-, and goo-covered alien—or, counter-
point, the most beautiful miracle ever in the history of human
existence—was placed on Flora's stomach by the midwife, Joel had
been hit by a lightning bolt.

And any ups and downs Flora felt after the birth—and there
were absolutely loads of them, notably how it feels to become a
mother when your own mother is no longer around to share it
with you—were somehow balanced out by Joel's extraordinary,
all-encompassing love for the baby and for her; and finally, her
doubts about whether he was, with his difficult past, capable of lov-
ing at all were set aside. She knew she was lucky. She didn't even
know where the resentment came from. So she ignored it, hoping
it would go away. She was so lucky.

"I'm just so miserable," said Fintan again.

Flora looked at him. Time was running short. She'd hoped
and hoped and hoped that he would perk up, come back to himself for long enough to consider taking the job on. But he was
listless and sad and nothing could motivate him. If it was ever
going to happen, she knew, there was only one person who could
do it.

"Okay," she said finally. "Well, I suppose I could help out a bit."

"We've been through this! It's called *interfering*."

Flora gave him a big-sister look.

"And I thought you were on your fancy maternity leave."

Flora chose to ignore him. "Look. You love doing all the food
and stuff, right? That's your area. Best of everything. We have a

little money. And even if we lose it all, well, we never had any to start with, right?"

Fintan shrugged. "But this is Colton's dream."

"And his dream was to have the absolute best of everything, right?"

Fintan nodded.

"Well. You go do your part. Find the best chef, get the best local ingredients, make sure the food is amazing. Let me handle the rest."

Fintan stared at her. His entire demeanor changed. Flora could tell he really didn't want to accept, but also that he really, really needed to.

"Yeah, I'm not going to do *much*," she said. "But I've got experience with hygiene regs, fire checks, all of that now. I can help you out when Joel has got Dougie."

She didn't dare even hint that she might quite like having a project while Joel and Dougie were carrying on their massive love affair.

They both looked around. The dining room still seemed huge. But Fintan's face showed something she hadn't seen for a long time: a tiny bit of hope.

Chapter 4

So it was that Flora came to be interviewing her own staff at the Seaside Kitchen. They were doing a brilliant job during her maternity leave and the place was as bustling and jolly as ever, she observed, not without a touch of envy, and young Malik, who'd been drafted in to help, seemed competent and popular too.

Flora sat the girls down.

"I feel like Paul Hollywood," she grumbled. "Not necessarily in the good way."

The girls looked at her expectantly, Iona cheerful, Isla terrified. Flora smiled encouragingly.

"The Rock needs kitchen staff, and the Seaside Kitchen needs looking after just as normal till I get back."

Iona frowned. "By 'looking after,' do you mean making too many giant custard creams and then secretly eating them by yourself by the cold storage?"

"Uhm, no," said Flora, blushing.

"Do you mean going behind the larder to snog your boy-friend?"

"I . . . I do not mean that," said Flora, biting her lip a bit. "And this is insubordination."

"Well, not if I'm going to be management. Is Isla going to be management too?"

"I think I'm going to regret this," said Flora. They were just young girls, after all. Maybe this wasn't a good idea.

"You were right about the big custard creams, though," mused Iona. "We should do more. Bourbon creams and jam sandwiches, people loved them, and they're easy to do, you just need the molds. Markup's good. Oh! And pumpkin spice."

"What?" said Flora, carefully pretending she knew what Iona meant.

"We need to get pumpkin spice."

"Uhm, what is that?"

Iona looked unsure for a moment. "I don't know *exactly*. But it's what you have to have on your coffee this time of year. Instagram says so."

Flora blinked. "Instagram?"

"Yeah. You have your pumpkin spice latte and post it on Instagram."

"And it makes your coffee taste of pumpkin?"

"I don't know." Iona started scrolling through her phone. "It's just what everyone's doing, that's all. And people take pictures of the biscuits."

"Do they?"

Flora had noticed, in the last year or so, people taking pictures of themselves more and more outside the pretty pale-gray-painted frontage of the little harbor café but hadn't thought much of it;

customers were customers, and tourists did tourist stuff, and even if these days it meant all of them lining up in the exact same angle to take exactly the same photograph, well, she didn't really think about that very much.

"We need an Instagram page."

Iona was quite pink in the face now, and Flora realized she was entirely serious and also that she'd thought about this a lot and hadn't just been cutting sandwiches the whole time.

"We need to show off how lovely it is here and have people come in and link and make sure that tourists come even if it's just to see us. And—"

Flora frowned. "Hang on . . . have you been having these brilliant ideas all this time?"

Iona looked perturbed and didn't say anything.

"Am I a terrible boss who never listens to anything?"

"You never asked," said Iona.

This wasn't at all the way Flora had predicted the morning turning out.

"Also, I think we should do organic baby food for the mothers group. The markup is—"

"Okay, okay, you've got the Seaside Kitchen," said Flora, smiling. "Just turn us into millionaires by Christmas, please."

She looked at Isla, who was standing there quietly.

"Are you happy to come up to the big house?" she said. "I know it's not as glamorous a job, but there's lots of opportunity to learn in a bigger kitchen, try out different skills, cooking as well as baking . . ."

"Does she have to wash pots?" said Iona.

"Everyone has to wash pots," said Flora. "That's how small businesses work."

Isla looked at Iona a bit sadly. "It'll be hard to be separated," she said quietly. In fact, she was gutted to be leaving her best friend. She didn't like things changing. She wasn't very good at it.

"You'll be great," said Flora.

"I don't know if I have good ideas like Iona."

"That's not really how you should approach a job interview!" said Flora, then, when she saw Isla's face fall, "I'm kidding! I'm kidding. I've seen you work your socks off here for three years. I know how good you are. I'm lucky to have you both and you're both getting raises."

"And a marketing budget," said Iona.

"*Iona!*" said Flora. "I am intensely cross with you for not telling me all this before."

"Take it up with management," said cheeky Iona. "Oh no, that appears to be me!"

Flora shook her head. "Okay, Isla," she said. "You come with me. I'll talk you through it up at the hotel. And the calls have already gone out for other staff. It's going to be fun!"

Isla was already working out what to tell her mum.

Chapter 5

Konstantin was perturbed. There was no breakfast. Not delivered, and not in the great dining room. He ended up heading down to the kitchen, where normally Else would pet him and find a tidbit to eat. After his mother had died he had been so spoiled and coddled by the kitchen staff (beyond even if they'd been allowed to refuse him, which they certainly were not) that he had been a lonely, podgy boy. When his father sent him off to boarding school at fifteen, hoping this would straighten him out, it had gotten better and worse all at once. Worse because he was initially unbelievably miserable. Better because the enforced sport and meager rations had gotten rid of the flab immediately. And then worse again as, to try to make himself popular, he had done his best to get in with the worst gang in the school. Since his father was extremely busy trying to keep up with ceremonial duties, as well as manage his own grieving, he hadn't always been able to keep on top of his absent son's behavior too.

Having an unusually large stipend, even for a boarding school boy, allowed him to become accepted into an unruly gang of reprobates who liked to take weekends in Montenegro, Gstaad,

Monaco, and Biarritz. They would stay in the flashiest hotels and see just how much they could get away with, which, as a group of northern white aristocrats, turned out to be an awful lot. School hadn't been so bad in the end. He'd stuffed up his exams, of course, but these things happened. There wasn't much incentive to take exams when you already drove a nicer car than the head teacher ever would.

And being an excellent shot, a good and brave horseman, and a tremendous skier took work, didn't it? And effort. His father never recognized *that*. Though when he'd been tapped to join the national ski team, the discipline and expected hours were, quite simply, unbearably dull—not to mention the nutritional requirements—and he hadn't attended any practices at all.

So now Anders, his father's personal secretary, had taken him aside and was talking to him, but every word of it was going in one ear and out the other.

Anders was doing his best to explain yet again. "We've found a job for you, and you're going to be beginning in a week."

Konstantin screwed his face up in a charming appeal that had always worked like gangbusters with the palace staff. "Yeah . . . noooo."

"I'm afraid it's your father's orders," said Anders.

"He's not the boss of me!"

"I've been asked . . ." Anders was not a cowardly man, but he hadn't been looking forward to this in the slightest. "I've been asked to inform you that all of your credit cards have been stopped as of this morning, your phone contract has been canceled, and you'll be leaving in five days. Your tickets are in this envelope."

Konstantin gawked in astonishment. *"What?!"*

"Your horses have been restabled and . . ."

Konstantin immediately looked around for Bjårk, who lumbered over—he was frightfully overweight. "You're not taking Bjårk Bjårkensson."

His face grew grave. Now he was listening.

"He stays with me."

"I'm not sure whether that will be possible."

"You can't banish me and not him! He behaves worse than I do!"

As if to prove this, Bjårk slinked over to the breakfast table and, disappointed to find it empty, let out an almighty fart and disappeared underneath, snuffling for crumbs. His large hind end started shaking the exquisite rococo legs of the gilt table, and Anders rushed over to steady it before it crashed onto the parquet. He rolled his eyes.

"Well, I'm not going anywhere," said Konstantin.

"You aren't today," said Anders. "Your father has impounded your cars. But next week, I'm very much afraid that you are."

Konstantin blinked. This couldn't be happening. It just couldn't. Gradually, the meaning began to sink in.

"You took my *phone*?!"

Chapter 6

On the rare occasions Fintan had the funds and free time to go to Glasgow, he had absolutely loved it. He adored the wet, majestic city with its vast sandstone tenements, the glittering straight roads like he imagined they had in New York, and the expensive Merchant City district with its designer clothes shops and mysterious-looking restaurants.

He loved the people marching down from Buchanan Street, every shape and size, from every corner of the world. Students, tourists, businessmen. It felt like the center of the world. He loved the Glasgow girls, with their tans and long eyelashes and brightly colored clothes, often inappropriate for the weather, and who cared a jot for that? They yelled, they laughed, they looked like stunning tropical birds compared to the duller colors of home.

But most of all he loved the men. Or rather, a certain type of dangerous, slender, short-haired man, who might give you a glance here or there, or walk boldly up Sauchiehall Street hand in hand with his boyfriend. The city smelled of opportunity and excitement and sex, and Fintan had loved it ever since his mother had first brought him there, a wide-eyed and extremely confused fifteen-year-old, to do the Christmas shopping, loading everything into the little prop plane that would take them home again. It had been quite the adventure. They had eaten oysters at Rogano and looked at the beautiful Glasgow School of Art. Fintan had never seen anything like the variety of shops and things to buy and had been paralyzed by choice. His mum had bought him a discounted Tommy Hilfiger sweatshirt and he had worn nothing else for a year. And he had sworn he would go back, be a student there, make his life in the city.

But he hadn't. His mother had gotten sick and he'd had to look after her, and then the farm had really needed all hands on deck, and that dream had gotten away from him. Of course, he had discovered a new love of food and cooking when Flora came back from London. And then he'd met Colton and fallen in love, and everything had changed in the very best way, and for a short time he'd been the happiest man in the universe and firmly believed that everything had turned out for the best.

That had not lasted long.

And now here he was, trudging the damp shiny pavement of the old place again, the leaves wilting beneath his feet, umbrellas overhead, pipers trying to make money on the corners of the huge stone buildings. He didn't raise his eyes to look in the extravagant shop windows; he didn't glance at men walking into coffee shops who might glance back at him. He just thought over his life, of the ways he had and hadn't taken, the other roads and other doors.

HE ARRIVED AT the employment agency in a very low mood indeed. Flora had suggested, at the beginning of the year when things were very bleak, that he take a little of Colton's money and go lie on a beach somewhere, and he'd gone to Cancún by himself and drunk cocktails under a palm tree and cried himself sick. It had not been entirely successful.

People did keep telling him not to worry, that it took a long time. The problem was they'd say that with their heads tilted and a sad face on, and he knew they meant it and he knew they were concerned. But then they went on and bought one of Flora's sausage rolls, or patted the next dog they saw, or went to the library and exchanged the latest novels. But he was still here, stuck in his misery. They did two minutes a day and thought they were being helpful, when it was all he could do to not snarl at them, to not feel enraged at the way they carried on with their totally normal lives, now made even more perfect by being able to mentally pat themselves on the back for doing a good deed to poor wee Fintan.

Grieving set his teeth on edge. And more than this, it was dull. So dull. To be missing Colton every second of every day, to wake up every morning and remember the whole sodding thing again, to know, because he'd been told, that it would never go away, not entirely, and that this was just how it was now, and oh, by the way, loads of people lived like this so he might as well get used to it.

He didn't want to get used to it, he thought, kicking a pile of leaves with unusual savagery, so that a passing taxi driver eyed him warily. He didn't want any of this. He didn't want to be going to some lousy chef agency. He wanted to be lying in his and Colton's vast bed in the mansion—before it turned into a hospital bed, before that bed was donated to a hospice on the mainland. Way, way back, even though it was only a year or so. He wanted them to be lying there, going through CVs, laughing at things together, then going to the kitchen to make French toast and those hideous vitamin things that Colton would gulp down with a wince and a shudder. Fintan had assumed it was because he was being Californian about things.

It wasn't.

But no. He was out on his own, doing a job he didn't even know if he was suited for. It was all right for Flora, he thought. Her life had worked out absolutely fine. She had her boyfriend, had a baby, had the house even. Fintan couldn't bear to live in his mansion, had made Flora rent it. But he still resented them being there. He wanted it bricked up like a shrine, kept exactly how it had been when they had been in love, with nobody else walking through it, no babies laughing or fires crackling. Every time Flora changed something, he winced. Flora, aware of this, tried to tiptoe around the place, so as a result, nobody was particularly happy with the arrangement.

He arrived at the large red sandstone building. Happy Hospitality was the name of the company. He snorted to himself. Whatever.

Chapter 7

The young recruiting agent was pretty and enthusiastic.

"Well!" she said. "You are quite the conundrum! Lots of our chefs want to work with their own kitchen . . ."

Fintan stared ahead stonily, ignoring the cup of coffee the receptionist had brought him.

". . . but the location is quite . . ."

"It's far away, aye," he said shortly. "It comes with accommodation."

"Yes, but often people aren't sure whether they want to uproot their entire lives . . ."

"Is that so?"

"But we do have a *few* people for you to meet!"

The woman smiled brightly and buzzed in the first person, a morose bearded man with a bright red nose and trembling hands. Fintan internally sighed. He had thought that recruiting a chef to a state-of-the-art kitchen, with a mandate to build a creative menu using whatever local ingredients he or she wanted to source, would be enticement enough. Mure had an embarrassment of riches in that regard: shellfish—oysters, lobsters, and crayfish—all pulled from the ice-cold water each morning; rich green vegetables that kept their flavor from the soil; samphire glistening like emeralds along the wide beaches; careful crops of wild mushroom; venison from the mainland, rich and dark as chocolate; elderberry and juniper gin, distilled on the island; rhubarb to beat the band.

As well as luxury accommodation on a beautiful island . . . He'd thought it would be a dream come true. But now, in the city, burnout followed burnout: old chefs who'd seen it all; tourist hoteliers, whose limit was scampi and chips or chicken in a basket. Time-servers and bedraggled kitchen casualties who he wasn't entirely sure just weren't after the free room and board. Being a chef was a punishingly difficult career, with high rates of drink and drug taking. Not everyone got out of it unscathed. And the people Happy Hospitality had lined up for him were hardly the cream of the crop.

He'd hoped he might find someone with as much passion as he had, who could see the amazing potential of the little island at the top of the world. But he sat through interview after interview with little light. The idea was that he would talk to everyone, then the ones whom he liked would cook something in the kitchen set up in the offices. But so far he wouldn't let anyone he'd met make him so much as a sandwich.

"I'm not sure this is going to work out," he said, as he and the recruitment agent took a break. He tried the coffee this time. It really wasn't bad.

She nodded. "I do realize . . . It's just the location . . ."

"Yeah, you said," said Fintan. "The location is amazing, actually."

"We do have a couple more people for you to see," said the woman.

Fintan glanced at his watch. The plane didn't leave till the evening. He didn't have anything else to do; there was nowhere he wanted to go, nothing he wanted to see. The bright lights of the shops and gay clubs and restaurants had no appeal for him anymore. It was, he reflected once again, so dull being so joyless.

"Okay, bring it on," he said.

The woman glanced at her watch worriedly. The next interviewee was late. Rather late. Bordering on very late. "I'm sorry," she said finally.

"I thought you had a couple of people for me to meet."

"I know, but the last one just pulled out. Apparently one of their friends was in earlier . . ."

Fintan's brow furrowed. "What does that mean?"

The recruitment agent's lips twitched. "Oh, nothing," she said.

"What?" said Fintan, then he gradually realized. "What, because they'd met *me*?"

"I couldn't possibly say," said the agent, whose name was Marian and who thought it was a fiendish disappointment Fintan was gay, because she had a terrible soft spot for handsome angry men. Although that had brought her nothing but grief in her life, she reflected, so this was something of a lucky escape. Regardless, word had already gotten around and nobody wanted to work for a misery guts in a place where, if you were lucky, the thermometer might hit 12 degrees Celsius in July.

Fintan folded his arms. "For fuck's sake," he was saying crossly, just as the door burst open.

"*I am late!*" announced the tall, very skinny man standing in the doorframe. He was wearing a rather grubby T-shirt and jeans. His arms were completely covered in spiky tattoos, and he was unshaven and looked none too clean. His accent was heavy.

Fintan internally sighed. So the whole day would be completely wasted. No decent chefs would ever want to come with him. Flora had tried to cut down on everything he had to do, and still he hadn't managed to properly handle the one thing—the kitchen— that he was meant to love, that he was meant to be looking after.

"Yes, thank you, Gaspard," said Marian primly. Her lips thinned. She liked sullen men, not ridiculous ones.

Gaspard came in anyway and threw himself insolently onto a chair. "So. A keetchen. In the ocean."

His accent was so French as to be absurdly comic. Fintan wouldn't have been at all surprised to learn he came from Basing- stoke and was putting it on.

"I thought you were back in Marseille," said Marian, flicking through the CVs.

Gaspard gave a shrug. "Eet ees feelthy like wild dogs on street. Also, there ees wild dogs on street."

"I've heard Marseille is nice."

"Not my Marseille."

He had two days' stubble on his cheeks and really did look in profound need of a bath. He also sat sullenly, his arms folded, as if furious at being in a job interview situation—which indeed he was—as Fintan attempted to explain what was going on up at the Rock. He looked around even as Fintan was still talking.

"You want me to cook *ou quoi*?"

Fintan was caught mid-spiel. "Well, I'm just trying to explain what—"

"*Oui, oui,* but eef you hate what I cook, then this ees a waste of everyone's time, *non*? Eet ees pointless talk talk talk, bleh bleh bleh."

Without waiting for an answer, he stood up and stalked into the small kitchen.

"Maree-ong!" he shouted. "You have *nuzzing*! *Nuzzing* ees here!"

"You know this guy?" said Fintan.

Marian nodded.

"Is he a dick?"

"Uhm." Marian truly didn't want to be unprofessional.

Fintan, reading her face, groaned.

"But," said Marian, to the sound of a gas burner being turned up high and popping loudly, "he can cook."

Chapter 8

Fintan went in to watch what Gaspard was doing. What Gaspard was doing was having a cigarette out the window, in blatant defiance of the fire regulations and the many signs posted around the walls.

"What are you doing?" said Marian.

"Sweating the onion," said Gaspard. "Nobody does eet properly. They do not leave eet long enough. They rush rush rush. And so, *dégueulasse*."

He shook his head sadly and leaned back so far out the window, Fintan thought he might fall out.

Fintan couldn't help himself. His lips twitched ever so slightly. Gaspard tossed his cigarette out the window and went back to the pan without washing his hands. Hearing Marian's anguished sigh, he theatrically returned to the sink and did so. Then he added some finely chopped bacon, reduced some white wine he had already sampled straight from the bottle, and gave Marian a big telling off on terroir, explaining that if you bought wine for cooking that was worse than your normal wine, you were an idiot, and if you bought that wine for both cooking and drinking, you were also an idiot, and so what was she? Finally he added some cream to the sauce, quickly seared some scallops in another pan with fennel, and served them all the lightest, most delicious lunch Fintan had had in some time, particularly after ferreting around in the back of the cupboard and finding a slightly more acceptable bottle of wine.

"*Tiens*," Gaspard grumbled, throwing his food down like a lanky bear.

He disappeared after Marian insisted on his leaving the building for another cigarette.

"I'll take him," said Fintan.

"Are you sure?" said Marian. "He's a pig. And he doesn't last long in jobs."

"So why did you show him to me then?"

"Because we were . . . a little short on CVs."

"Well," said Fintan, as Gaspard rolled back in, shouting at the top of his lungs what were patently obscenities in French down his phone. "You've got him off your hands."

"For now," said Marian, glumly collecting the plates. "See you in a week, Gaspard."

Chapter 9

The following week, Isla walked up the steps of the hotel somewhat tentatively.

She'd been to the Rock before, normally to help waitress at parties. But that was different; then she was just in and out the back door in a black skirt and a white shirt, handing round haggis canapés and refilling people's glasses, except for Wullie Stevenson, who wanted his filled a tad too often, even by Colton's generous standards.

She'd never really thought of it as anything other than the big house, the hotel. She'd never considered that one day it might be a place where she worked every day.

Nervously, she fiddled with the zip of her padded jacket. Would she be able to handle such a big job? Flora seemed to have confidence in her, but wasn't it just that Flora was so distracted with the baby and that grumpy boyfriend? And Fintan being so miserable that he wouldn't even care?

Isla hadn't always lacked confidence. Not when her dad . . .

Well. There was no point thinking about that now.

The huge oak doors were propped open and a bright fire was

burning in the grate. The receptionist, Gala, was a beautiful American girl, a niece of a colleague of Colton's who was supposedly on work experience and had gotten rather more than she bargained for, but she was friendly enough.

"Isla! Yeah! Sure! Got your name right here!" chirruped Gala.

Isla glanced around. Beyond the welcoming hallway with the flickering fire, the restaurant was sitting cold and empty and the kitchen lay cold and bare. There were so many chairs to fill, so many mouths to feed. Flora kept saying it was just a bigger version of what she was already doing and that there'd be a boss in place, but she wasn't sure. Not at all.

She passed on through the heavy oak doors at the back of the restaurant into the kitchen. It was huge! State-of-the-art burners and grills, walk-in freezers, a wood-burning oven for bread—wow. Colton had stinted on nothing. Lines of shelving with butter, eggs, flour, everything she could conceivably need, tidy and neat and brand-new.

Well, maybe, she thought. Maybe she could make this work. Her dad would have been pleased. Roddy had adored his only child. Lost in a fishing accident, the industry as dangerous as ever it was, his death had broken everyone's hearts. Especially his daughter's. It had turned her mother's heart hard as flint, everyone said.

ISLA WAS FIRST, but it was a day of arrivals at the Rock, and Flora somehow found herself turning up to help Fintan welcome the new chef. The servants' rooms on the very top floor of the house had been repurposed to be as comfortable as possible for seasonal staff; Gala had already taken the best one on the corner.

Fintan had gone down to the dock to meet Gaspard off the ferry. Isla found him and looked up at him shyly; she was slightly terrified of him.

"Hello? I'm Isla? In the kitchen . . ."

"Oh yes, hello." He sank into his traditional sullen silence in case she started to talk about Colton or asked him how he was doing, something he was tired of and normally discouraged.

"I am a bit worried," said Isla in that quiet way of hers, "that they might not be very keen when they arrive."

Sure enough, it was an absolute pig of a day. Hail was blowing into their faces; Isla was barely visible inside the zipped-up hood of her puffer; Fintan had an expensive overcoat and a cashmere scarf, but the tips of his ears were bright pink.

He smiled ruefully. "It's not Antigua."

Isla pulled open her bag.

"I brought hot chocolate," she said, "to kind of welcome them if they'd had terrible journeys. Would you like some?"

Fintan was about to say no—he ate rarely these days and never really felt hungry—when he felt how cold his fingers were, even inside the leather gloves he was wearing.

"Okay," he said.

She poured him out a cup of the most delicious frothy hot chocolate he'd ever tasted, sliding in a couple of marshmallows for good measure. He warmed his hands, then took a sip of the rich, not-too-sweet goodness. It tasted like Christmas and home and warmth all at once.

"Oh my," he said. "That's fantastic."

Isla smiled. "We've been perfecting it in the café for years. Have you not tried it?"

"It's not very good for you."

Isla didn't say anything, as she disagreed with him thoroughly and thought a delicious, satisfying milk-based beverage on a cold day probably didn't do anyone any harm. She caught sight of the arriving ferry bouncing on the gray sea.

Fintan stared out at the waves pounding against the dock that had been the background noise to almost everything he'd done for so long that, like most people on Mure, he couldn't even hear it anymore. He took another sip. It really was good.

"We need to serve that in the bar," he said.

Isla nodded. "You could put a shot of whisky in it and have it like Irish coffee," she said. "Only better."

Fintan nodded back. "It would be better," he said. "I should write that down."

Isla pulled out her phone. "Hot chocolate with booze," she said into it. Fintan looked at her.

"You talk to your phone?"

Isla flushed instantly. She hated anyone singling her out for anything. "Uh, yeah," she said, quietly. "When I have to remember something but I don't want to take my gloves off."

"That makes a lot of sense," said Fintan.

The ferry started to churn in reverse, backing up, and they fell once again into a watchful silence.

GASPARD HAD SPOTTED the lean, confused-looking boy in the corner of the bar in the nearly empty ferry. November was not what you'd call peak season for island hopping in the far north of Scotland, and there was barely anyone on board: a few farmers with Land Rovers stowed downstairs; those who had come back

from the market enjoying a wee dram at the bar; a clutch of ladies who'd been shopping and to a show in Glasgow, giggling and
cheerful and dressed up, albeit with their fleeces pulled back on
over the top, now that they were heading into the real world again.
And a well-built blond-haired boy looking sulky and completely
out of place.

"Hey," Gaspard had said. "You live in thees end of world? Huh?
You can tell me about it?"

Konstantin shook his head miserably. "I've been banished," he
said in neatly clipped English with just the trace of an accent. "I'm
being punished."

"Me also," said Gaspard. "Except I have done notheeng wrong.
Notheeng!"

He marched up to the tiny brass bar and rang its heavy ship's
bell, which was really only for decoration, as the barman's face
made perfectly clear as he straightened up from the shelf where
he'd been putting glasses away. Gaspard had made several questions about the wine, none of which the young barman could
understand or answer, then pointed at one bottle and took the
whole thing. After seeing Konstantin looking increasingly miserable, he grabbed another glass and bade him sit down and tell
him the whole sorry story, fueled with the terrible wine, which
didn't taste quite so bad by the time they got halfway down the
bottle.

The long and short of it was, by the time the boat churned
into Mure Town, as the sun was falling over the horizon and the
gleam of bigger ships was the only light to be seen, both of them
were a) great friends and b) completely roaring drunk.

FINTAN WAS STRICKEN as they arrived.

"*Voilà!*" yelled Gaspard, turning into the wind, where hail had started and spiked into the face like daggers. "Welcome to hell, *non?*"

Konstantin lurched off the ferry, the difference in the motion between sea and land and the frankly rough wine having a predictable effect. As Isla watched him, horrified, he wobbled over the gangplank and threw up heavily over the side.

"Oh Christ," said Fintan.

Chapter 10

Gaspard kept up a constant slew of loud questions as they walked to Fintan's Land Rover, Isla silent by his side. Konstantin had come via some kind of client of Joel's, and Fintan was utterly dismayed. What kind of young lad got drunk on his way to his first job?

And Gaspard was looking like he was hell-bent on proving why he couldn't get a job anywhere except at the tail end of nowhere, because nobody wanted to work in the islands, and nobody wanted to work for him. Fintan felt bitterer than the acidic wine sloshing in the men's stomachs. This whole enterprise—Colton's pride and joy, the dream of his life—was going to fail. Fintan was going to fall flat on his face.

"So you have cellar?"

"You can't stay here if you drink," Fintan said steadily.

"I 'ave not 'ad one seengle drink on this soil!" protested Gaspard noisily. "Not one! It was my final celebration of life as a free man."

"This isn't prison," said Fintan gruffly.

"Oh yes, yes it is, actually," said the young man, who up until now had been very green and quiet. Suddenly he straightened up and shouted, out of nowhere, *"Stop!!"*

Assuming he was going to be sick again, Fintan did so. And immediately, Konstantin turned and started running toward the boat, which was filling up, ready for the return crossing.

"Well, he didn't last long," observed Isla.

The small party watched him with consternation, waving his arms and shouting, charging down the hill to the men putting away the gangway. *"Waaaiiittt!"* he yelled.

"I hate this job," said Fintan despondently.

"Me also," said Gaspard, pulling out a cigarette and lighting it, somewhat miraculously, in the full force of the oncoming wind.

"I FORGOT MY dog!" Konstantin panted to the tall, kindly captain of the ferry, who had been very unimpressed with both of the men coming to work on Mure; he took as keen an interest as everyone else in the success or failure of the Rock.

"Did you now," said the man. Grudgingly he opened the rope that blocked off the gangway and Konstantin, slightly fuzzily, ran into the hold, where Bjårk was filling his traveling box a little snugly.

"Bjårk! I am so sorry. I am a terrible, terrible man," he said. "Well, so everyone else says. I was probably just having a bad day," he added, kneeling down.

Bjårk, as it happened, was happily in the process of forgiving him, as he wanted out and, ideally, a snack, and then perhaps another snack. Indeed, Konstantin felt in his pocket and found a packet of crisps that had been on the bar and that he'd completely forgotten was in there. He opened them up, sniffed them—they were a flavor he was not familiar with—and passed them all on to Bjårk, who didn't care either way.

The captain had come down to the hold and was staring at him.

"You give crisps to your dog?" he said incredulously. "The dog you didn't even remember you had?"

He shook his head and felt sorry for Fintan. Konstantin returned a haughty stare. He was used to everyone being nice to him and fussing over him. Being cross with him wasn't really done, unless of course it was his father.

Instead he hauled Bjårk, who didn't want to leave the huge raft of fascinating smells coming from all over the boat, down the gangplank with every ounce of dignity he could muster, which, given he was half drunk, splashed with water, and heaving a large, hairy beast whose muzzle was covered in crisp crumbs, wasn't much.

FINTAN AND ISLA stood watching them approach. Gaspard was delighted and waved cheerfully.

"Hey! Monsieur Chien," he shouted cheerfully. Bjårk wagged his tail in return.

"Okay. Now we can go," said Konstantin stiffly, arriving back and slightly peeved that nobody was making a move to carry his ancient leather suitcase for him.

"But . . . but . . ." Fintan started to stutter.

As he did so, the dog walked up to him and licked his palm. Bjårk smelled, inexplicably, of shrimp cocktail. His tongue dangled cheerfully.

"We don't have room for a dog!"

Isla gave him a side-eye. Colton's two dogs, ridiculously expensive deerhounds, lived around the place perfectly happily, and everyone quite liked having them around, even though they were trained to tear you limb from limb on hearing a key word that Colton appeared to have taken with him to the grave and Fintan was terrified of saying by accident one day.

"We absolutely didn't say dogs were allowed. Obviously we wouldn't offer you a job like that."

"Okay fine," said Konstantin, bored now, who made to turn round and catch the ferry back.

Isla gave Fintan a hard stare.

"Okay," said Fintan finally. "Okay. We'll sort it out later."

And the very strange party made their way in silence to the Land Rover.

Chapter 11

It didn't help that Flora liked almost anyone who came with a dog attached. Back at the hotel, she had found the whole thing patently hilarious, to Fintan's fury. She looked Konstantin up and down. It was very unlike Joel to make this kind of request for anyone, and it had been very hush-hush. So she knew absolutely nothing about the younger boy except that he was Norwegian and, by the look of things, a bit of a drip. He stood tall in the doorway with his blond hair flopping over his eye, gazing at the Rock as if it were the worst place he'd ever seen.

"Okay, Isla, can you show Konstantin where he's going to be sleeping and take him round the kitchen? And is it Gaspard . . . ?"

But Gaspard had already disappeared. From the back of the long corridor, Flora could already hear the *whoosh* of a burner being turned on. She frowned. Fintan had mentioned he was "temperamental." It appeared to be rather worse than that. Crazy, drunk, and covered in tattoos seemed about the size of it. Fintan himself looked absolutely disconsolate and desperate to get away, even though he should be settling everyone in and leading his new team. Oh lord. This was like herding cats. She felt a sudden wish to be at home, snuggled up with Dougie and Joel in front of some ideally really, really terrible television. She had a bad feeling about . . .

"Oh, hello! Cooee!!"

Flora turned round slowly. There was Pam, who led the Outward Bound group.

Flora would never like to say she had a nemesis. But had she had a nemesis, it would have been Pam, who had never quite forgiven her for, years ago, getting off with her boyfriend. For like two seconds. Actually, Flora suspected, correctly, that Pam found it slightly more annoying that Flora had never given it a second thought afterward, not once she and Joel had found each other.

Pam's baby, Christabel, was strapped to Pam in a woven homemade baby wrapper that looked oddly confrontational. She was red of face and had her father Charlie's heavy eyebrows and a permanent frown.

"Hello," said Flora, smiling at Christabel at least.

Pam blinked, and her voice took on an instant pitying demeanor. "Oh, Flora. Where's little Douglas?"

"He's at home with my dad," said Flora. "Ten minutes down the road. I'm just going home."

Pam smiled sympathetically. "It's so hard to be apart, isn't it? Such a shame you can't have him with you. What a shame you don't get any maternity leave."

"I'm on maternity leave now actually. Just popped in."

There came the sound of loud swearing in French from the kitchen, and Fintan immediately headed off in the opposite direction, shouting, "Flora, can you see what that is?"

"You know," said Pam, "I never put Christabel down. Never! It's called attachment parenting? It's how our ancestors would have done it in the old days."

Before catching scrofula and dying at thirty-two, Flora almost said, but managed not to.

"We're always together, she and I. Mummy and baby! How it's meant to be."

Christabel screwed her face up crossly.

"Of course it's different with girls."

"Is it?" said Flora, genuinely curious, then annoyed with herself that she'd fallen for it. She knew she should always keep her distance. The problem was Pam was the only person she knew with a baby, and she would have loved to have asked her lots of things—like was it normal to want to get away from your baby sometimes, and was it all right to be a bit resentful of being knackered all the time? But Pam was obviously having an absolute ball.

"Oh yes. Girls and their mums. It's a special thing."

Flora thought about her own mum, who had died far too young, and smiled ruefully.

Pam was now talking to the baby.

"Poor little Douglas doesn't get to spend time with *his* mummy, does he?" said Pam in a baby-waybe voice, bouncing Christabel's fingers up and down. "Poor ickle baby Douglas."

"Is there something you want, Pam?" said Flora, realizing too late she'd betrayed her frustration, which in Pam's world she'd totally chalk up as a win.

"Oh. Yes! Dinner for the Outward Bound sponsors. But, Flora, these are . . . these are important people. Sponsors and people coming from the mainland. You know, the Seaside Kitchen is all very adorable and so on, but these people . . . they'll be expecting something quite good?"

Flora tried to breathe in through her nose and out through her mouth. The most annoying thing about this was that they needed a soft launch, a chance for the kitchen to run through its paces before they opened properly at Christmas.

"Well, we have a new chef, so we'll have a menu for you to take a look at."

"Oh, *good*," said Pam, clapping Christabel's little fingers together. "Not that you're not, you know, wonderful, at what you do. But a real chef . . ."

There was a bang from the back of the kitchen. Gaspard marched into the main hallway. Despite the fact that there were brand-new whites ordered in for him with his name on them, he was wearing a pair of filthy old checked trousers with a packet of cigarettes clearly hanging out the back of them.

"Your fridge—no good. Your oven—no good. Your cupboards—no good. You need to change—*poof!*—everything."

Pam blinked. "Yes, I'm sure that's true."

Gaspard stopped. "'Ello, tiny baby," he muttered in a soft voice much different from anything Flora had heard so far. "Ah, she is very sage."

"She isn't," said Pam crossly. "She's pink, thank you very much."

Christabel, however, was cooing loudly in Gaspard's face. She had her father's pale coloring and round cheeks.

Pam was waving her hand in front of her face. "I'm sorry, I don't like smokers near the baby?"

Gaspard gave her a long look, then glanced at his hands as if he had a lit cigarette there he hadn't known about (it was, to be fair, always possible). As he backed away, Christabel started to bawl.

"So," said Pam fussily. "Send over the menus, please, we'll be thirty."

Gaspard blinked. "'Ow can I send over menus?"

"Just. Tell. Us. What. You're. Making," said Pam, speaking very loudly and clearly as she liked to do when speaking to foreigners. "We'd like one full turkey and all the trimmings, one vegetarian option, and one gluten-free."

Gaspard stared at her, then looked at Flora as if to clearly say, *What in the hell do you expect me to do with this woman?* Flora felt caught between a hard place and, well, the Rock, she supposed.

"We'll get you something as soon as possible," she said to Pam, who looked skeptical as she turned around.

"Of course, obviously we'll be expecting a big discount," she said, "seeing as it's for charity and you're just basically having a test run. You should probably do it for free," she added pointedly.

"I think for everything to be great for your charity you should buy good produce," said Flora smoothly. Pam's family was one of the richest on the island. "Which costs money, I'm afraid."

"Produce, which all mysteriously comes from your farm," said Pam.

Flora put her best smile on again and hustled her out the door.

"I am not doing turkey," Gaspard was already threatening, within earshot.

"It's Christmas!" said Flora. "Please! We'll never hear the end of it. Please do turkey at Christmas."

"Turkey is 'orrible! Is huge dry chicken! Huge dry unhappy chicken!!"

"I'm sure they're not—"

"Do not eat unhappy animals!! Is unhappy! That is why"—he paused for emphasis—"so many fights at Christmas."

Flora looked at him. "What are you talking about?"

"People, they are so sad, they fight at Christmas, boo-hoo. Everyone sad. Is all *EastEnders.*"

"That's a fictional television show."

"Christmas Christmas Christmas, fight fight fight."

"You're saying people fight at Christmas because turkeys are unhappy?"

"*Exactly,* yes."

There was a pause.

"So what would you . . . ?"

"*L'oie.* Goose. You have goose at Christmas. Delicious goose."

"And geese are happy?"

"You know geese?"

"I do," said Flora, who was terrified of geese; she'd been taken to a wildlife park on the mainland as a child and one had nearly broken her arm.

"Geese, they are fierce! They are strong! They hate everyone. *Cacar!!*"

"That's not the sound a goose makes! They honk!"

"A goose, he has an 'appy life. *I 'ate you,* he say. *Cacar! Everybody move.* Happy goose."

"Not foie gras."

"*Oui,* foie gras! 'Appy, 'appy goose, something to eat, yes, please."

"No," said Flora. "No foie gras, it's cruel."

"Okay," said Gaspard, not in the least bit perturbed. "Free-range goose."

"Thank you."

"Cacarrrrr!!"

"Honnnnkkkk!!"

I like him, thought Flora.

Chapter 12

It had happened the previous month. Entirely with Joel in mind, Colton had left a large bequest to a fostering charity on his behalf. This was embarrassing enough in itself, but they'd also asked him to speak, which he did, about his own childhood and his new life in Scotland, with a baby, and Colton's hotel.

Afterward, Joel had found himself next to a portly short Norwegian man.

"You have a new baby?" the man had asked him.

Joel nodded.

"How's it been?"

Joel half smiled, which was more or less as demonstrative as he could ever get in company. He had been up with Dougie at four, giving him a bottle as Flora slept, happy as Larry. He'd reminded himself to get started on Colton's Christmas lights—Colton had likewise requested that the island be made more Christmassy, a responsibility that fell on Joel as his foundation's lawyer—and looking round at the smart room he was in in London, with a huge, chic silvery tree and cutting-edge modern baubles, he made a mental note to remind himself again. Unfortunately, someone had just offered the possibility of him showing off pictures of Douglas, which made it immediately fall out of his mind again.

He whipped out his phone to show pictures of the little dark-eyed baby boy.

"Oh, he's . . . he's amazing." The man smiled sadly, then he sighed miserably. "Ah. Then they grow up."

"You have children?" said Joel, who was of the unshiftable view of new parents: that their children would of course be different.

"A son," said the man. "Layabout, more like."

He blinked.

"He needs a job, in fact."

There was a pause.

"What kind of job?" said Joel carefully. He wasn't crazy happy about bringing on board people's privileged children. They tended to take up more time than was strictly necessary and be frankly horrified that they were expected to work every single day, that people might occasionally tell them that what they had done wasn't wonderful and perfect, and that they couldn't just get immediately promoted.

"Oh, anything," said the man. "He should really start at the bottom. He's never held a proper job. Have you got anything an idiot can do?"

Joel smiled. "Probably, but I'm sure you wouldn't want to . . ."

But the man took another swig of his wine and was warming to his theme. "No, do it," he said. "Get him cleaning floors, washing pots. I insist! I'll sponsor the charity too if you do it. Yes. This is it."

And Joel could hardly refuse that. And so it was arranged.

NOW, ISLA STOOD in the kitchen, looking at her watch. It was time for the new kid Konstantin's shift to start—everyone else was there, but he hadn't shown up yet. Which was not ideal, considering he only lived upstairs. Gaspard was late too, but she kind of expected that. Still, it was frustrating.

The double swing doors that led to the dining room suddenly burst open and two people came through: Gaspard and a plain, doughy-faced woman.

"Thees is Kerry. She is my sous chef."

Isla frowned. "Does Fintan know?"

Gaspard shrugged. "I don' care. I need more help. Ees beeg job."

Kerry was already tying on a cap round her head. Isla tried to smile hello, quite excited about the possibility of a female friend in the kitchen to take Iona's place, but Kerry returned a stony look.

Gaspard looked around. "Where is my boy who cleans pots?"

"I don't think he's up yet," ventured Tam, a stolid redhead from one of the most northern farmsteads who absolutely didn't care what job he had to do in this hotel as long as it didn't involve walking up and down the side of a hill in the pouring rain all day for the next forty years like his father, three uncles, three brothers, and nine cousins were all doing. He would scrub the floor with a toothbrush if it meant not wearing nine jackets and getting sewn into his underwear.

"Well, go get him!"

Tam frowned. "Where is he?"

Gaspard shrugged. Isla sighed.

"You know?" demanded Gaspard.

Isla flushed bright red. She didn't like being picked out to do anything. "Same place as you, in the roof—"

"Go! Get him!"

"But—"

"Feerst thing in my kitchen." Gaspard flexed his arm, and all his tattoos stood out. His face suddenly looked rather menacing. "We say '*Oui*, Chef,' okay? You are in a real kitchen now, leetle girl! Ees real job, not pretend! Okay? You understand? Not pretend?"

Isla froze.

"*OUI*, Chef!"

She had absolutely no idea what he was talking about as everyone stared at her.

"*Come on,*" he snarled.

And then he paused, until he drew out of the utterly humiliated Isla a rather half-hearted "Wee, Chef!"

He nodded curtly, and Isla scampered off up the stairs, feeling wretched. It had been all right being shy in Flora's kitchen. Iona could pick up the slack for noisiness, and Flora was kind enough that she never noticed. Isla even spoke up from time to time. It wasn't impossible, when she felt comfortable.

But when it came to strange foreign men yelling at her, or, like now, asking her to do something utterly preposterous like go up to a strange man's bedroom . . . her face was absolutely flaming and she wanted to burst into tears, and the thought of how it would be to burst into tears on your very first day in a new job was so awful she couldn't face thinking about that either. So she bit her lip incredibly hard and went past the corridors leading to the Rock's twelve boutique rooms, all beautiful, and up a hidden staircase to the old attic rooms, which in their day had housed the servants. And now, she supposed, still housed the servants. All were open except for one at the very end of the hallway. She pulled herself together and knocked loudly.

There was no answer. She tried again, harder.

"Hello?" she said. Then, louder: *"Hello?"*

She touched the door, which, to her horror—she had been hoping to turn back and say she hadn't found him—started to creak open. It was too late now; she was stuck there and would have to hope for the best.

"Uhm . . . Chef sent me upstairs to . . ."

There was still no sound of movement from inside the room. Curious, she pushed the door farther and glanced inside. The bed was completely unmade; possessions were strewn everywhere. But the room was empty of people. And the window was flying open.

She frowned. Surely he wouldn't have made his escape; they were three stories off the ground. And it was only a job, not prison, whatever he thought. She blinked. Had he gone?

Isla found herself going to the open window, her heart beating quickly. She was struck suddenly by the most horrifying thought: What if he'd fallen? Tried to climb out and slipped on the wet pipes?

It was freezing in the room. The wind blew right in off the sea, and there were little flecks of rain bouncing off and around in the maelstrom. The curtains were dancing; papers were jumping off the desk.

Slowly she advanced.

"Uhm . . . Konstantin?" she said, the odd consonants taking shape in her mouth.

As she moved there was a sudden flurrying noise and a *wouf!!* as a massive, hairy something exploded in her face. She screamed and dropped her phone.

"What?" came a voice.

Shocked, she'd fallen back a few paces and tripped, sitting heavily down on the unmade bed. There was little space in the room for anything else. A bemused-looking figure with rumpled hair appeared at the window, standing as if in midair, only half his body visible. Isla was so shocked she could barely speak. With his white shirt and pale skin, she thought for one terrifying moment she was looking at a ghost.

"Oh," he said, eyes wide. "Santa got my letter!"

He had a slightly flat, barely traceable Scandinavian accent. Isla jumped up as if the covers were hot.

"Wh-where . . ." she stuttered. Konstantin showed her that the window of his room let out onto a flat gable—dangerous, unfenced off, but wide enough for his big dog to stand and, she could now see, have a gigantic pee.

"I don't think you can let your dog pee on the roof."

His face puckered. "Well, he cannot fly, so you see I have no choice."

Isla blinked. He shivered and jumped back in through the window, encouraging his clearly overweight dog to do the same behind him, even as he scrabbled and whined for help, and Konstantin ended up hoofing him over ungraciously.

"So what are you, the welcoming committee?" he said, still smiling. He was used to having a certain effect on young women.

"You're needed downstairs," stuttered out Isla, pink to the tips of her ears. "It's time to work."

"Really?" said Konstantin, pouting. "Are you sure you wouldn't rather stay and have a quick . . ."

He had been about to say "cup of coffee," in the hopes of staving off work a little longer, but Isla had been brought up to be very wary of strange men—there weren't many on Mure, which was why they were all so terrifying.

"Get back!" she shouted. *"Get away from me!"*

"No coffee then?" protested Konstantin, as she stared at him menacingly, reversing out back into the corridor. He added impishly, "You know, it was *you* who turned up in *my* bedroom."

Finally, Isla found her voice. "Piss off, you disgusting sex case!" she screamed. Then she turned and bolted back down the hall.

"Wouf!" said Bjårk.

Konstantin frowned, thoroughly awake now. He'd been called a few things in his life, but that seemed rather harsh.

"Sorry!" he hollered down the corridor, but it was too late.

Chapter 13

L isten to me," commanded Gaspard.

Konstantin had made it down ten minutes later. Being unused to a uniform, he was wearing his trousers back to front. Isla moved as far away from where he was standing as she possibly could.

"The next time this happens, you will be doing all the potato peeling, you understand? For one week, two week, four week."

"Yes, all right," said Konstantin, who was confused. Surely they'd been friends yesterday in the bar.

"You do what *I* say in thees keetchen. Then all will be happy. Or you do not do as I say and boo-hoo there is absolute *tristesse,* you understand?"

Nobody did understand, but they could make a stab from his scary tone of voice.

Gaspard had been through a lot of restaurants and found his manner tended to make people scared of him and leave, unless they were good, committed, or—and this was very much what he was counting on at the moment—had absolutely nowhere else to go. He didn't care which.

Modern-day restaurants, with their cost centers and portion control and budgets, didn't suit him. But here . . . he'd sneered at the kitchen, but it wasn't bad, not really—done by someone with money to spend. Here, there was a chance for him. And nobody was going to stand in his way this time, certainly not some posh teenage drunk and a clutch of locals who probably shared one eyebrow between them.

KONSTANTIN HAD ASSUMED Gaspard was kidding about the potatoes. He emphatically was not. The third time he took the skin off his knuckles—he'd never peeled one in his life—Isla finally got tired of listening to his strangled epithets and ransacking of the first aid box. His hands were a riot of blue bandages. Everyone else ignored him. After the potatoes he started washing pots as everyone else got to try out cooking stuff. This was absolutely rubbish and incredibly boring, and it took hours. He tried to catch the eye of the girl who'd been upstairs, but she was resolutely not looking at him. Gaspard just shouted. The blank-faced girl, Kerry, worked like a robot and ignored everybody. His hands were cut, red, and chafing from the hot water. He smelled absolutely terrible; the smells of food got everywhere. How could it be so hard and boring at the same time? He hated his stupid father with an absolute vengeance. He hadn't even been able to tell his friends where he was going. Not only had they stopped his phone, they'd stopped his Wi-Fi. He was completely alone in the universe because of his stupid father, having to grovel and make himself filthy with a bunch of random dicks. It was a joke that had gone too far.

Konstantin had never felt so sorry for himself in his entire life.

Chapter 14

They were doing a test run for Pam's charity dinner. Joel had made a stupid joke about how he would come so he would get a chance to see Flora, which had not gone down well and he'd regretted it almost immediately, especially when she had sat with Douglas all afternoon, showing him seagulls until his little fingers were pink—he hated his mittens and tried to bite them—as he pointed at the waves and she grew increasingly freezing. By the time they got into the Seaside Kitchen for a coffee, Douglas was cross and tired and screamed the entire place down, to the point where even her fondest regulars were finding their smiles growing a little fixed. Why was this so easy for everyone else?

By comparison, she was looking forward to going up to the Rock, testing the kitchen's wings. Iona was coming too to take pictures for the Instagram account.

Fintan was drumming his fingers anxiously on the white table-top alongside Innes and Eilidh, Innes's once-upon-a-time ex-wife, newly reunited and making a great show of being disgustingly lovey-dovey all the time.

They'd tried to leave Agot behind with Eck, who didn't hold

with fancy new food, but she was having none of it and had turned up at the front door of the farmhouse in her ballet skirt, her *Frozen* slippers, and some alarmingly applied lip gloss and with one of her mother's handbags, looking at them with an expression that would have been cute in a five-year-old if it wasn't quite so uncompromising.

"I'll be coming to dinner," she'd enunciated clearly. "I have thought and thought, and now I have decided. *Yes.*"

"Well, I'm not sure that's—"

"Yes, I think so, Daddy. *That baby* is coming."

Innes was a helpless pushover where Agot was concerned, and Eilidh was just so pleased they were back together again—and, frankly, thrilled that boring old Mure island was going to get a fancy hotel, thus not being quite the dead arse end of the world she'd left in a snit two years before—that she wasn't going to halt Agot either, as a result of which Agot marched straight to the Land Rover fully confident.

"Well, it'll be worth it to test how the restaurant deals with really difficult customers," whispered Flora to Fintan, who nodded emphatically in agreement.

There are two ways of getting to the Rock from the south where the village is. On sunny days Bertie Cooper will run you round in the boat to the headland—it's not far, only five minutes or so, and it's delightful on a dusky pink evening to be out on the water. You might see a dolphin and you'll certainly hear the seals barking at you as you land at the jetty with the torches shining up ahead toward the building itself. Fintan had always thought it was one of the most beautiful landings in the world.

This was not one of those times. The wind that had nearly blown

Konstantin and Bjårk Bjårkensson off the roof the previous week was bucking harder. The ferry that day had taken a few tries to get to where it needed to be, and even then the passengers disembarked a trifle green. Gusts were flapping smaller cars out of the way—the farm's and the Rock's Land Rovers could be trusted to take them the few miles up the narrow bumping track that served as the inland road, but you wouldn't want to be in a little tin can, however much Flora might have hankered after a chic little pastel Fiat 500.

Gray clouds dropped out of the sky as night was now falling at four P.M. Sheep huddled close to the mountainside, trying to keep themselves warm, and Flora inhaled the scent of sleepy warm baby beneath her in the car and lightly twirled one of his fine black curls, pressed beneath his best woolly hat with ears—all hats came with ears these days, Joel had observed, puzzled as to why.

"*That baby* is very hairy," observed Agot from the opposite seat, where she was cross because she was in a baby seat "*even though,*" she complained the entire way, "*I am not that baby.*"

"He is." Flora smiled. "Hairy babies are lucky."

"Yes," said Agot. "He is lucky he doesn't have to sit in a *stupid baby's seat* or eat *stupid Dead Uncle Colton's food.*"

"Agot," remonstrated Innes. She had started calling him Dead Uncle Colton after the funeral, and although Flora had furiously tried to get her to stop, Fintan told her he didn't mind it. In fact, it was comforting because she brought him into every conversation, every game she played. She didn't lay a tea table for her dollies (who were usually to be heard getting strict tellings off—who knew where she had even learned them, given that Innes was useless at it and the primary school specialized in encouraging play, not discipline) without including Dead Uncle Colton in the family lineup and was absolutely convinced that he watched every single thing she did. Fintan found it an unending comfort. Flora, watching the little sprite, with her white-blond hair and tiny dancing figure, sometimes wasn't entirely sure she didn't see ghosts.

"That's enough."

Agot lifted her stubborn little chin and stared out the window crossly, pausing briefly en route to shoot Douglas an utterly filthy look. Flora sighed inside. They were meeting Pam and Charlie there too, so they could "discuss menus." *Please, please, let it go well.*

Chapter 15

Meanwhile in the kitchen, all was chaos. Gaspard was shouting, and everyone, it felt like, was crying. The last week had been an absolute trial for everyone, like *Big Brother* without the calm, cooperative atmosphere. The Norwegian guy was absolutely hopeless, so there was never a pot or pan when you needed it. Kerry wouldn't do anything without checking with Gaspard first and would stand around doing nothing except eating crisps, which meant Isla being in charge of cakes and puddings and going nuts. Tam was fine, but his job was bringing in supplies; he wasn't around for long enough to help with anything really useful.

Also, slightly worse, Isla's initial coldness with Konstantin after the way he'd behaved had hardened into an awkward stiffness. He hadn't done anything really awful since, just ignored her, and she didn't know how to talk to him except to tell him how to peel potatoes without skinning himself when he was helping with food prep, or how garlic actually worked, something Gaspard had found so astonishing he'd actually stopped cooking to watch. There was a bad attitude in the kitchen, and they all knew it.

"Okay. Tonight. Try not to be idiots, *non*?" Gaspard was saying, just as Konstantin dropped the most enormous pan on the stone floor. The noise sounded like a bomb going off, and Isla even let out a tiny shriek. There were French expletives, and Konstantin, white as a sheet, looked like he was going to walk out of the kitchen, even as a pot literally boiled over just behind him. Everyone froze as Gaspard marched toward Konstantin.

"You want work in thees kitchen or not?" he snarled.

"*Not*," snarled back Konstantin.

"Well, you can leave."

"Well, I can't," said Konstantin.

It was unbelievable but true. His phone and his debit and credit cards had all been stopped. He'd called the bank to absolutely no avail, because he didn't know any of the passwords. His friends and relations had been warned by his father not to sneak him any dough, and given that most of them were also completely funded by their parents, and were absolutely terrified by the amount of attention their mums and dads were paying toward the elder Konstantin's experiment, meant they were very much toeing the line as well.

He couldn't quite believe it, but he was somehow meant to survive—and feed Bjårk—on the tiny pittance he got, which wouldn't quite cover a single restaurant meal back home but here was supposed to last him a week.

It was a joke. A stupid, ridiculous joke, and he was near constantly tempted to storm off and tell them all where to stick it.

Except he couldn't. He had literally no way of paying his way off the island, and even if he got off, by the time he'd saved up for a plane ticket, what would he do—sit at his father's feet and beg for forgiveness? His pride wouldn't let him do that.

Well, okay. It wasn't so much that, because in fact he'd already tried it. And his father had graciously said, "Thanks for the apology. Now get on with your work and I'll see you in six months."

He was stuck and mutinous, and he stared at the pan on the floor. The room went silent.

"Pick that up or you go now," said Gaspard unwaveringly.

They all glanced at the windows. Hail was hurling itself against the glass. A lovely night to be cozy in front of a roaring fire with a good book and a glass of whisky. A frankly ludicrous night to storm off in a snit. The atmosphere in the room grew as icy as the windows.

MEANWHILE, THE DINING room looked as beautiful as ever, the big wooden fire crackling merrily away, its light gleaming off the tinsel. "Scots Nativity" was playing gently, and the scented air gave everyone a thrill. It didn't matter how old you were: Christmas was coming! And that was always the most exciting feeling. Agot stomped over, irritated that the tree hadn't come yet, but when she realized the highly polished wood was very slippery, she took off her shoes and was soon skidding round the room in her stripy tights. Flora thought, *Health and safety,* and filed it away to mention to Fintan later.

Colton had bought a number of old barrels from a distillery that was closing down, and the wood on the fire had the deep aroma of peat and whisky. It was, as Flora always thought, the most comfortable place you could be, with soft chairs and the anticipation of a good meal ahead. Gala had greeted them happily and brought them drinks, and everyone was stretching out good-naturedly. Agot stopped skating and got happily buried in her sketch pad with her felt-tip pens, as usual drawing everyone in her life including Dead Uncle Colton but missing out Douglas, which was, Flora supposed, something of an improvement from when she'd presented them with a mass family portrait with everyone in it *including* Douglas, but with a huge black scribble across Douglas's face.

Pam, Charlie, and, irritatingly, Malcy, Pam's large father, who'd done very well for himself and liked everyone to know it—and hadn't been scheduled to come—had arrived bang on time, which made Flora anxious. She glanced at Fintan, who patently didn't care. The problem was the Dochertys were big spenders on this island: golf club dinners, big parties, and weddings. They needed to impress these people. She wished Fintan would at least try.

There was no menu, first off, which Flora looked worried about and Innes frowned at. Fintan was drinking and not paying attention, which was almost as worrying to Flora as the lack of menu was. Well, perhaps this was the modern way and it would be something unexpected and magnificent. She ordered some wine off Gala, and they tried to chat even though there wasn't even a piece of bread on the table.

"I'm hungry," came a warning voice from underneath the table, but you couldn't say it wasn't a shared emotion.

INSIDE THE KITCHEN, Gaspard was still holding up a knife as if it were a weapon.

For the first time in his life, Konstantin was on his hands and knees, picking something up. He didn't know what to do with it and was grateful when Tam came and took it from him and put it away in a cupboard.

"*Chop!*" said Gaspard.

And finally, the cold wind still blowing outside, Konstantin decided that for once discretion was the better part of valor and picked up an onion and a knife without the slightest enthusiasm. He stared at it.

Gaspard had already moved on and was shouting about stock. Kerry and Tam were keeping their heads down, waiting for it to pass. Konstantin tried stabbing the onion and let out a heavy sigh. Isla was just next to him.

"Just chop it," she hissed. She couldn't believe they hadn't gotten more prep done this afternoon, but apparently Gaspard had been out and become distracted by a field full of wild garlic he hadn't been expecting, as a result of which she was now chopping up head after head of them to stud the lamb. She smelled pungent, she knew, and it would be seeping through her pores for days.

She snuck a look at Konstantin. He was doing a truly horrible job, hacking away at the defenseless onion like it had insulted him in some way. Isla edged away from him a little. Konstantin noticed and hacked again even more viciously. Great. Here he was locked in a dungeon in a howling storm, and even the kitchen girl didn't want to talk to him. He wanted to tell her that where he came from, the girls who worked in the kitchen *loved* him . . . then he started thinking of what was going on at home right now. The run-up to Christmas in Norway was incredibly beautiful. The Christmas markets went up early, and the delicious scent of glogg filled the air, as the warm, gingery mulled wine was poured over crushed almonds and raisins in the bottom of the glass and topped with a little aquavit that lifted the entire warming scent of Christmas in your two hands, steam curling off the top.

This year they had had early snow; you could see it on the hills, which were thick with it and dark fir trees that seemed to go on for miles.

They'd take the horses out and go steeplechasing even as the snow fell thickly and the night came on early, finishing with drinks before a roaring fire at the lodge his father kept up near Lillehammer. After Christmas, as the weather hardened, there was skating and of course skiing, the toughest courses, the fastest mountains, to build up your appetite for long hearty lunches filled with laughter and bonhomie at the best time of year.

Here the snow was pathetic, wet and bitty, he thought fiercely. It would barely lie at all, totally useless with all this wind.

Up until now he'd felt only cross and annoyed at being, according to him, kidnapped and forced into servitude.

Now it felt worse than that. He felt exiled from everything he loved. He thought of the pretty houses of Trondheim, of heading out into the woods to catch a glimpse of the northern lights, of sitting in the hot tub at his friend's cabin. He was almost unbearably homesick. *And* he'd had to hide Bjårk in his room to keep him out of the kitchen, which wasn't going to work well for very long, judging by the impassioned moaning that had started up as soon as he'd closed the door.

He heaved a great heavy sigh and looked down on his work again, just in time to watch the incredibly sharp knife Gaspard had brought him slice deeply into his thumb.

Once again, the kitchen froze. The blood didn't trickle out: it arced, straight up in the air, right over all the already chopped vegetables, spraying across the brand-new factory-fresh whites.

"*Faen!!*" yelled Konstantin, even though the pain hadn't kicked in yet, just the shock.

"*Merde!*" said Gaspard in disbelief, running his hands—themselves scarred and pitted, like all chefs'—through his thick dark hair.

"Obh, obh," muttered Isla, but mostly to herself.

Then, seeing to her amazement that nobody was doing anything, least of all Konstantin himself, she got up and went to him.

"Come here," she said.

The boy was white; his already pale skin had all the color drained out of it.

"It's just a cut," she said, glancing at it. He looked at her, still shaky, as she led him to the sink and started running the tap. "It looks worse than it is."

Konstantin was still staring at his finger in disbelief.

"I didn't realize we were serving finger food," Isla surprised herself by saying, even as he blinked and put his finger under the running water, wincing as the cold touched the cut.

"That knife was really sharp," he grumbled.

"Yeah," said Isla, looking closely to see if he needed a stitch. "Like some kind of kitchen knife or something."

Everything with blood on it was bundled into the bin just as Gala came in to see if they were ready to start taking food into the dining room. A single glower from Gaspard made it very clear to her that they were not, and she scurried out again, going to find some crisps behind the bar.

Isla examined the wound carefully. Konstantin had very long

fingers on a large, strong hand that didn't look like it had done a day's work in its life, as indeed it had not. She frowned. "I think you'll be okay. I can get Saif to put a stitch in it if you like."

Saif was the local GP, who was just sitting down to dinner with his two sons, Ib and Ash, and wouldn't have been best pleased to hear he was being called out in a howling gale to fix a ridiculous kid, but Gaspard came up and frowned.

"*Non,*" he said. Then he snapped his fingers for the word. "*Gomme . . . glue.* That is it. Glue."

Gala immediately brought some superglue from behind her reception desk.

"*Oui!*" said Gaspard, brandishing it. Konstantin and Isla looked at each other anxiously.

"Let me just google that," said Isla, getting Konstantin to hold his finger up in the air. "Well, the internet says it's fine."

"The internet says the royal family are lizards." Konstantin grimaced.

Nonetheless, he held out his finger and let Gaspard stick the two edges of skin back together. Isla then wrapped it in a blue bandage she'd gotten out of the first aid kit. They were, she noted, running low.

"Do you need to sit down for a bit?" she said, feeling some sympathy for this ridiculous person, so far out of his depth.

"*Non,* there is no time," said Gaspard. "Start again! With the onions! This time, keep all of your fingers, please!"

Chapter 16

Back in the dining room, they were on their third bottle of champagne—Fintan didn't mind depleting the cellars Colton had built up for the two of them. At least it was staying in the family. Flora had a glass. She was barely drinking because she was still feeding Douglas, even though he was sleeping beautifully in his car seat under the table.

Pam, of course, wasn't drinking a drop, as she told everyone who came into earshot at any second of the day, going on to speculate how she'd probably never drink again, she felt so much better than she'd ever felt, and my goodness, didn't Flora's eyes look bloodshot, was she sure she was all right?

Christabel was still strapped to Pam—she was getting very big, it couldn't possibly be comfortable, but it did mean Pam could pull the conversation round to the genius of her child every five seconds. Charlie was sitting looking anxious.

But the boys were getting stuck in, particularly as they appeared to have slightly mistaken the concept of champagne for beer and were more or less drinking it by the pint. Innes kept looking at Hamish as if they might get up and start wrestling in a minute, like the brothers used to when they were children. Agot was banging her knife and fork on the table and singing a song about being hungry and how cruel the world was to five-year-olds. Eilidh was getting a little loose around the eyes, which Flora knew from experience meant she was probably going to start telling the story about how she had started snogging Innes at the table, which he didn't mind in the slightest but the rest of the MacKenzie siblings found a little unnecessary. And when Fintan had more than a certain amount, it was odds to sods he was going to collapse into tears at some point, which was fine but not ideal in front of the staff he was supposedly managing in the business he was supposedly running. They desperately needed some food to mop it up.

She excused herself and crept into the kitchen. What she saw took her rather by surprise.

"I CAN'T EVEN smell cooking," she said, outraged. She looked at Gaspard. "Where is the bread?"

He scowled. "I am not happy with the bread."

He pointed to the fresh loaves that had been made in the bakery that morning.

"Why not?" said Flora.

"Ees local flour?"

"There is no local flour, you dim bulb," said Flora. "It doesn't grow here. This stuff is perfectly good."

Gaspard screwed up his face.

"And the butter is perfectly good, and I know that because it comes from *my farm*."

Isla had rarely seen Flora so cross. She scuttled to the fridge and got out the butter.

"It's fridged," said Gaspard, pouting.

"That's *your* fault," said Flora.

Konstantin quickly looked away. Someone had told him to de-fridge the butter, but he hadn't known what that meant and had therefore completely ignored it.

"Isla, take this out," said Flora. "Before Innes falls off something and Hamish starts making airplane noises."

Isla vanished into the dining room. Through the door came a noise that sounded like Douglas revving up. Pam was enjoying every second of this, Flora could tell.

"What are you making?"

"I 'ave no good stock."

"Well, you're not making it now! What are you making?"

"I am going to make coq au vin."

"That takes *hours*!"

"Ees new kitchen! Ees expected."

"Absolutely bloody not," said Flora, almost trembling. "No way. You can't. Make something—anything—I don't care. But just make it now."

She marched to the big fridge and hauled it open.

"Here," she said. "There's steak."

Gaspard looked at it. "So boring," he said.

Flora was already in the walk-in freezer. She looked up and down all the shelves, shivering in the low temperatures. She was sure she'd seen it in here somewhere . . . somewhere . . . behind the fresh food and the cooking materials . . . *Aha!*

She returned from the cold storage triumphantly, holding her bag high. "Ahem," she said.

Gaspard looked at what she was holding. "Ees *empossible*."

"Uhm," said Isla, coming back into the kitchen. "Uhm, Fintan says if we don't get some food out he's going to sack everyone."

This was a complete lie. Konstantin looked up from where he was trying to make his six-foot frame look completely inconspicuous. He saw a look of complicity shoot between Flora and Isla and was impressed. He didn't think the girl had it in her.

Triumphantly, Flora handed over her freezer find: a large packet of oven chips. Gaspard took it from her as if she were handing him a dead snake to cook.

"*Allez,*" he said, coldly furious, and struck a match as Isla turned on the grill.

BACK IN THE dining room, Pam seemed to have forgotten her pledge to drink absolutely nothing, as she had been sipping small amounts from a glass and was getting rather giggly, a situation that Flora would have dearly loved to have found herself in, instead of pretending everything was fine when she was in fact incredibly worried.

Everyone dived into the bread in starvation, and it disappeared in minutes. Thankfully the butter didn't disappoint: it had a smoked garlic flavor that Fintan had developed to seed through it, and it was so delicious Flora could have licked the bowl even as she noticed with a sinking heart that Agot was actually licking the bowl.

And Fintan was calling for more wine, which almost certainly wasn't going to end well. His eyes had taken on a slightly glassy look, which tended to warn of the arrival of tears. Looking round the room filled with ridiculous, expensive tartan tchotchkes that Colton had insisted on, you felt his presence so strongly and could imagine his loud, cocksure American accent ringing out, his easy laugh, his quick anger and even more surprising kindness. Yes. It was hard.

"Well," Pam was saying, looking pointedly at her watch and getting slightly unsteadily to her feet. "It's nice to know that at least you *tried,* Flora."

"Oh no, I'm sure it won't be long," said Flora in a panic.

"I mean, I thought I'd give you a chance. But this . . . I mean. It's difficult to run a business. My darling Charlie and I have been doing it for years, of course. We know what we're doing, don't we, darling?"

Charlie stared at the floor. Malcy laughed.

"But you can't just walk in out of nowhere and start from scratch—it's just not possible!"

"I don't come from nowhere," said Flora through slightly clenched teeth. "I come from down the road."

"Yes, but all the gadding about? Marrying foreigners and whatnot? You don't really understand what the local community needs now, do you? I mean"—she gave a little laugh—"a bit of dinner at least, don't you think? And how you're going to cope with travelers from farther afield . . . I mean, people do have standards, you know. They'll want a little more than a cheese scone! Which, I notice, we don't even have."

Irritatingly she was right about this; Flora cursed herself for not even having thought to bring up some baking. Mind you, she had felt it would be insulting to Fintan and demoralizing to the kitchen if she'd arrived with backup. Meanwhile, short of being able to Instagram the food, Iona had taken to putting sunglasses on a stag head and photographing it instead.

"Okay, Pam," she said finally as Pam smiled graciously in triumph. "It's all very new . . ."

Suddenly there was a clatter at the swinging doors and Gala appeared, all flustered, but smiling and balancing the first three plates of food.

Chapter 17

It was extraordinary. Wizardry.

It was a simple steak and chips—but what steak and chips. The steak was soft and bloody, with a dark caramel crispy outside and a melting inside. There were crispy fried onions (courtesy of Konstantin) on the side, perfectly salted, like the best seaside treats; the chips were triple fried in goose fat and satisfyingly crunchy; the salad was tart and green; and next to it all was the most wobbly, mustardy, perfectly set hollandaise sauce Flora had ever tasted.

It was an absolute rave, completely and utterly delicious.

Without saying another word, Pam simply sat back down. Flora half smiled. Obviously there was wanting to walk out—and then there was how insanely hungry you got as a feeding mother.

Gala poured the wine, a particularly beautiful private bottle of Colton's, and brought cola for Agot, which she wasn't actually allowed, but nobody could stop eating for long enough to explain this. The room fell into a reverent silence, punctuated occasionally by people saying, "Oh my God," and "Bloody hell," and Iona trying to photograph plates before they got emptied. Even as she was eating it, Flora felt sure and slightly sad that every single steak and chip she ate in her life after this would be a completely pale imitation of it, a true disappointment. She felt like Edmund in Narnia looking at the empty box of Turkish delight when she'd finished, staring regretfully at the empty plate.

There was a little scraping of knives and forks and then everyone sat back, Innes letting out a contented sigh.

"Well," said Pam eventually. "Well. I suppose that might just . . . I mean, it's a little plain."

"It was magnificent," said Fintan crossly. "Gala, could you get the chef out?"

Gaspard came out, looking mutinous. "And what?" he said.

"That was amazing," said Flora, meaning it, and everyone else added in to a round of applause.

Gaspard tried to look like he was still cross with them but couldn't quite manage it. A tiny twitch appeared on his thin lips. "I have no time! No food! And my team are *tellement* cretins."

"But it was still magnificent," said Flora.

Gaspard sniffed. "*Bah oui.*"

Chapter 18

Konstantin, exhausted from all the new experiences, was absolutely ready to retire to bed. Working past nine o'clock was, he mused, hardly a practice for gentlemen. He wondered too: he had never once given a thought, in his life, to all the serving staff, the waiters, the barkeeps, the servants at the palace, who stayed up as long as he wanted them to stay up. His feet hurt and his back was sore from bending over to chop, and his hand was throbbing from the cut, even though the bleeding had stopped. How did people do this every day? And how long was he going to have to do it before he either collapsed or got to go home? His father could not be serious about six months.

He heaved a sigh and turned toward the door. A small cough met him as he left, and then a slightly louder one. He turned back. The little scullery maid Isla was standing there, blushing as usual and looking apologetic. Tiresome. He wanted to go to bed.

"What is it?"

She gestured to the kitchen, which was covered in grease and spattered remains of chip fat and onions.

"What?" he said again, but with a steady sinking feeling in his stomach. They couldn't be serious.

"Uhm, we kind of need to clean up," she said, so quietly he could barely hear her, and that accent was totally ridiculous.

He held up his bandaged finger. "Uh, I know, but I'm in terrible agony."

"*Lazy boy!*" came a voice from the other side of the kitchen. "*Work!!* I make deener for you."

Konstantin noticed that Gaspard had fired up the grill again and appeared to be about to make them all the rest of the steaks. He also noticed that he himself was completely and utterly starving; he had been too worked up to realize just how hungry he was. He hadn't eaten all day and the steaks smelled absolutely unbelievable. Gaspard was smearing them with garlic butter, and the pan was sizzling with lightly popping fat.

"But do eet properly!"

"I do it properly!"

There was massed laughter from everyone in the kitchen. "No, you don't!"

Konstantin was annoyed. He'd been slogging his guts out, for God's sake.

"Okay," he said crossly to Isla. "Show me. How to do precious washing up your proper way."

She looked at him. "It's like you've never done the washing up before?" she said in incredulous disbelief. He didn't like that one bit; she sounded like she was looking down on him. And also it was true.

Isla took the spray faucet and the scourer in disbelief and

showed him how to wash out the pots before you put them in the dishwasher, which ran fast and hot, and left him to it.

It took him ages, particularly with Gaspard jeering that he had no idea what it was going to be like when they got a *real* kitchen going and how he was going to have to get ten times faster than that, and his finger really was hurting now and he was having, in fact, a very, very bad night indeed, which got even worse when they handed him a mop and bucket.

He could only imagine the laughter of his friends if they could see him now. They certainly wouldn't believe it. *Well done, Daddy,* he thought sullenly. *You wanted to bring me down a peg or two and you've certainly done it now.*

At last, having done a frankly terrible job of mopping, he sat down at the staff table and Gaspard *finally* handed him a plateful of food. The combination of tiredness, his finger, his predicament, and the amazing scent and taste of the food was so overwhelming that for the tiniest split second, Konstantin thought he might cry.

Isla, sitting opposite him, noticed this with some surprise. It made absolutely no sense to take a job and then hate it so much. He was such an odd person.

"Go to bed," she said, when they'd finished and there was just the staff meal to clean up. "I've got this."

Konstantin was instantly taken aback by the kindness and, annoyingly, the very obvious fact that he was absolutely shattered. But he couldn't think about that now; he had half a steak wrapped in a napkin that he needed to get upstairs, so he simply nodded and scuttled upstairs without a backward glance, fed Bjårk, took him out on the roof again, and fell into bed, absolutely out for the count.

Chapter 19

Stupid Bugglas was in the way again. If there was one thing Agot really hated, it was how distracted her beloved uncle Joel had gotten ever since the baby had arrived. Even when Joel had been on the outs with various other members of her family, Agot had adored him from the get-go, which Joel found slightly alarming. He didn't really know how to talk to children. This was 100 percent what Agot liked about him. He treated her entirely like the small adult she fully believed herself to be.

This was one of the long number of things Douglas had completely ruined, in Agot's eyes. Uncle Joel was always staring at the stupid baby, or picking up the stupid baby, or asking her if she'd seen what the stupid baby could do now. The things the baby couldn't do—dance, play shinny, sit up for a tea party, look at pictures of ice-skaters, watch ice-skating on television, talk about ice-skating, and pester her father to watch old Torvill and Dean videos and skate about the kitchen floor on clean dishcloths, pretending to be an ice-skater, much to the annoyance of anyone else trying to get anything done or anyone who didn't want *Boléro* in their heads for the next six months—were huge. Agot was trying to shout louder to get them to pay her some attention, but it didn't seem to be working.

Seeing him cooing over the stupid baby the next day in the kitchen gave her an idea. She went through to where Flora was squinting at her phone. Everyone looked all day at their phones, then if she wanted to do it they said, "No, no phones for you, Agot," even though if it was bad, why did they do it all day, and then they would say, "Agot, you are being too noisy," and she would absolutely not be noisy if she had a phone. Why was everyone so *stupid*? And why was Christmas *so far away*? When you are five, four weeks is forever.

"Auntie Flora," she said conversationally.

"Darling," said Flora, who had been looking at flour sourcing and wondering why the hell Fintan wasn't.

"I think," said Agot seriously, "I think Uncle Joel does not love us anymore."

"Do you?" said Flora.

She glanced above Agot's head and saw Joel dancing with the baby in the kitchen, little Douglas giggling and reaching up his little fingers. It was a pretty sight.

"What makes you think that?"

"Because it is true." Agot sighed in a world-weary fashion. "He loves *that baby* now."

"I think it's possible to love more than one person at once," said Flora.

Agot frowned. "One time," she said, "I dropped Big Fox and Daisy Duck and Jamford into a puddle at the *same time*, because it was a wet, wet, *wet* day."

Jamford was a small stuffed cow she dragged along, the origin of whose name was lost in the mists of time.

"And," she said darkly, "I picked up Jamford first."

Flora thought about that. "Well, yes, I can see that," she said. "But you picked up Big Fox and Daisy Duck next, right?"

Agot shook her head solemnly. "No," she said. "Jamford was very muddy, so I had to fix him."

"And you left Big Fox and Daisy Duck in the mud?"

She shrugged. "Oh, maybe Daddy got them."

Flora looked at her. "I don't think Uncle Joel would leave you in the mud," she said.

"Not *me*, silly," said Agot. "You!"

Then she clambered up in Flora's lap.

"Hmm hmm hmm, oh, look, a phone," she said, repeating herself and getting gradually louder until Flora handed it over. Agot sat back with a contented sigh, while Flora glanced over at Joel, who had to be in London that night and was patently unhappy about it.

BACK AT THE Seaside Kitchen, Iona had filled her Instagram feed with beautiful shots of the previous night to go with all the lovely pics she already had of the café. She wasn't getting much traction, and everyone else was getting annoyed with her, as she insisted on lining up every single thing perfectly, buying so many fairy lights their electricity bill was going up, and using a ruler to straighten the edges of her Battenberg cake to make sure it looked absolutely perfect in the photographs.

She had lobbied Flora to buy new artsy-looking cake stands,

which Flora was dead set against—it was hard enough to keep the lights on through the winter as it was. And now old Mrs. Mc-Clocherty was waiting to get served at the till, and Mrs. Barr behind her, who was having to deal with the wait for cake by listening to an exhaustive list of Mrs. McClocherty's latest medical symptoms.

Iona reflected that she needed something better than this.

Chapter 20

The success of the dinner somehow softened the atmosphere in the kitchen. And Gaspard was softening too to what was available on the island. He pulled in a huge side of locally smoked salmon one afternoon to experiment with canapés and insisted they all try a bit.

"You have to learn," said Gaspard. "Only have what is good."

"Won't that make you very expensive?" asked Isla shyly.

He glanced at her. "Yes," he said. "You pay sheet you get sheet, okay? We must get out and see the terroir."

"I don't know what that is," said Isla. "But the Seaside Kitchen has millionaire's shortbread."

Gaspard snorted loudly.

"Can I come?" Konstantin asked.

"You are pot boy. Is not necessary for you. Scrub pot cupboard, please."

But Konstantin had looked so pained and sad that Gaspard relented, and he'd practically bounded upstairs to grab an extremely expensive-looking coat and scarf and his ridiculous dog.

They strode down the long road to the village. It was snowing, the sky gray and low and the fresh flakes bouncing into their faces. Bjårk was happily stamping his massive paws in and out of frozen puddles that cracked every time and surprised him anew every time. Konstantin was like a teenager, his long legs stretching out the journey, as the snow finally fell away and the breeze dropped and a watery winter sunlight appeared. He cracked as many puddles as Bjårk did, covering a lot of ground as if just delighted to be out in the open air, as indeed he was.

Isla was snuggled in her new teddy bear coat. Konstantin had frowned when he'd run into her at the kitchen door.

"You look like a bear," he'd said.

"So?" said Isla, who was nervous and not paying attention and not really in the mood to go out in the freezing cold with a temperamental chef and a spoiled man-boy. Kerry and Tam were getting to stay in and do prep in the nice warm kitchen, and she'd much rather be with them, however many dirty looks Kerry shot her.

"So you are buyer for the Seaside Kitchen," said Gaspard.

"I don't need to be the buyer," said Isla. "I know exactly where to get everything from. Bread from Mrs. Laird, dairy from Fintan and Innes, smoked fish from Linhorn, and fresh fish from right outside my front door."

"Well, then you must show me, and we can make sure together. It is important for a kitchen to understand provenance."

Near the entrance to the farm, they were stopped in their tracks by a loud voice.

"*You are a bad dog!*"

"Hé hé," said Konstantin. "I don't think he is a bad dog."

Agot came up to his knees. "He broke my skating rink!"

Everyone looked at the muddy, icy puddle in which Bjårk was standing.

"I am going to the 'limpics and now I cannot practice."

"You're going to the Olympics to ice-skate?"

"*Yes!*"

"This is Fintan's niece, Agot," said Isla. "Agot, this is Konstantin. He works at Colton's hotel and this is his dog, Bjårk Bjårkensson."

Agot looked at Bjårk with undisguised dislike. "I don't like his dog."

Konstantin looked at her, insulted. "That's a puddle, not an ice rink."

There was a pause. Then Agot turned tail and rushed back to the farmhouse, bawling her eyes out.

"Well done," said Isla crossly. "She's five. And your boss's niece."

"Well, she should have better manners," said Konstantin, going slightly pink.

"So should you! She's a child!"

"I am now concerned we will be banned from their dairy," said Gaspard. "You—keep your mouth shut."

Flora came down to meet them, holding hands with a howling Agot. Konstantin immediately went forward to meet them.

"I am very sorry," he said, crouching down in front of the child, although he still sounded sullen. "My dog should not have broken your ice rink."

"That's because he's a very bad dog," said Agot, and Konstantin bit his lip to stop himself saying any more and straightened up again.

"Okay," said Flora. "Is that it?"

"I am not sure," said Isla to Flora quietly, as they headed up toward the dairy, "which one of them is more spoiled."

And Flora would normally have leaped to defend her family. But today, with Douglas being fretful because his dad was away, she just laughed. It had been a challenging day. The baby had grizzled and growled, and she had found herself jealous of Joel sitting on a plane, both hands free, drinking a cup of coffee, reading the paper, even though she knew he didn't want to go and sit in meetings, didn't want to leave them. But the day stretched ahead, and she'd been up three times in the night and her brain was a fog, and there was so much laundry to be done but she couldn't put the baby down. Sharing a laugh with Isla was definitely an improvement.

Chapter 21

Flora brought everyone into the kitchen, where she had made Fintan lay out a selection of everything, so Gaspard could choose what he wanted and how much he was going to use. The idea of using another supplier was not on the table, and Fintan hadn't wanted to do it at all, but Flora had talked him round by stressing how important it was and how the more their produce could be used, the better it would be for everyone.

So there were plates laid out with butter: salted, unsalted, garlic smoked, and olive, plus an exquisite fleur de sel, which had large salt crystals in it and, when spread cold on fresh warm bread with a cracked exterior and a yeasty crumb, could make grown men weep.

It was warm in the farmhouse. Bramble got up from his normal spot lying practically in the fire to say hello to Bjårk, who returned the bum sniff then, both of them satisfied neither was interested in fighting or shagging the other, casually followed him back to the fire and lay down with him back to back. Bjårk had been walking for approximately twenty minutes; the lazy creature now required approximately forty-eight hours of recovery rest.

Agot, performing skating moves by herself in the corner, gave him the occasional dirty look.

"So what ees this," said Gaspard, indicating the first butter, and Fintan took him through their processes: the difficulties of getting certified organic; how their cows were smaller, given the grass was not lush this far north but hardy and sweet; and how highland cows were some of the best out there. Gaspard mentioned something about how Brittany cows could almost certainly beat his in a fight, but Fintan didn't really notice and, after the first bite, neither did anyone else.

Konstantin had originally been slightly taken aback by the shabbiness of the vast old farmhouse kitchen, with its range, piles of papers, back copies of *Farmers Weekly*, old horse brasses on the walls, a clutch of Agot's plastic toys in the corner, and old boots lined up by the fire to dry. It wasn't shabby chic; it was just actually shabby. The plates were mismatched, half from Eck's old wedding service, with delicate tulips painted on them and scalloped edges, and half modern pastels Flora had ordered from the mainland for the Seaside Kitchen, with the farmhouse benefiting from the overspill and the chipped. There weren't quite enough chairs, and even the few available were mismatched and a little wobbly on the flagstones, with the rugs here and there.

But it was filled with the scent of the coffee brewing in the little pot on the stove top, as well as the fragrance of warm bread rising in the air, and the sounds of the crackle of the fireplace, the comforting *swish swish swish* of the dogs' tails, the ticktock of the ancient grandfather clock in the corner, the gentle twitter of BBC Radio nan Gàidheal in the corner, the pouring of tea into cups, and the clatter and chatter of old conversations steeped into the walls: the daily chat about the weather forecast, the grain price, the good health of sheep.

Sitting down on the least comfortable chair—he had somehow been last to choose; having been used to being offered the best of everything, it was very confusing—Konstantin found his eyes heavy, practically drifting off, as people ate and talked and the clock ticked in his ear. It had been a very stressful time.

"Konstantin? Konstantin?"

There was a voice that sounded like it was coming from far away. He was sure, suddenly, that he was, once again, in trouble for something—knocking off the bursar's hat or spilling champagne down the exiled princess of Romania again. When he opened his eyes, though, instead he saw a group of people smiling at him. He blinked.

"What do you think of the cheese?"

"I haven't had any cheese."

"Your plate is empty."

Everyone looked at Bjårk, who was licking the inside of his mouth reflectively.

"He likes it," said Konstantin, blinking.

Gaspard's face was grave. "You know," he said, "of course, the only cheese I would really wish to sell is French."

"We do know," said Flora brightly. "But you're not going to!"

"But if I have to—if I absolutely have to serve something else . . ."

"Which you do."

"Then this is . . . *pas mal.*"

And Flora beamed at Fintan.

Chapter 22

The snow had swept away by the time Pam's grand charity dinner came round in early December. Joel was back home, having mentioned the new hotel to everyone of course. Flora wasn't crazy about this: Would there be lots of his gorgeous, skinny blond exes showing up? Joel was not remotely worried about this; instead he was pondering on what to do about these Christmas lights. He had contacted a few firms in London, all of whom had given him the traditional London shrug-off, laughing at him, saying, "You wot, mate?" and suggesting that only an absolute idiot wouldn't have started planning this eleven months ago. Whatever Flora thought, Joel didn't actually miss London in the slightest.

He looked good in his suit. Flora was having trouble zipping up her old black velvet dress, which was extremely annoying. Unbelievably annoying, in fact. Pam kept wanging on about how she'd accidentally lost all her baby weight so quickly after Christabel, it was amazing, really—baby weight was a myth held on to by lazy people. This was obviously nonsense, but still, thought Flora, knowing she had a healthy and beautiful baby wasn't really helping with the fact that she also had a horrible and unrelenting zip.

"Let me breathe in really hard and you zip it," she said to Joel, who made a face.

"Just wear something else," he said, kissing her shoulder. "You'll feel bad all night if you're uncomfortable."

"Are you calling me fat?"

"No! You look amazing!"

"Well, if I'm not fat, I'll still fit in this dress," said Flora crossly, sucking herself in as Joel tried not to catch her with the zip by mistake.

"Right," she said. "Let's go. If Gaspard can pull this out of the bag again and Iona gets enough photos for Instagram, I think this might be a bit of a success."

She desperately hoped so. Fintan had done basically nothing, and she didn't really have the marketing skills to open a hotel. If they had some lovely pictures, they could get some brochures done and hopefully all would go well for the launch.

But this was Fintan's problem, obviously. She should, Joel kept pointing out, just relax and enjoy it.

It seemed like the entire island was there, mostly because it was. Pam and Charlie were from two very old Mure families, and there were few people who weren't connected with them somehow. And everyone supported their work; they brought impoverished young people from built-up cities on the mainland to Mure, taught them how to camp and look after themselves, gave them outward bound experiences, but more than that: fresh air, self-reliance, and a break from whatever might be going on at home. They were, undeniably, a force for good. Most of the money to fund this came from the lawyers and office johnnies they charged vast amounts to sit in a freezing tent and eat beans and tell each other it was a bonding experience (it was: they all tended to bond very tightly indeed as to how much they hated Charlie and Pam for putting them through such a miserable experience).

The building looked ravishing as usual, and Flora had booked the lovestruck ferryman Bertie Cooper, who had never gotten over his teenage crush on Flora, even though she now had an actual baby of her own. He was an optimistic sort.

"Quite the night," he observed, rowing her and Joel round in choppy waters. Joel was looking at the island behind him, frowning. "Wouldn't want anyone to accidentally tip over the edge, leaving baby without a daddy," said Bertie quietly.

"Well, no," said Flora, puzzled, then went over to Joel.

"What are you thinking?"

"I was thinking," said Joel, who had barely celebrated Christmas as a child and had felt the lack very keenly, "that when you look at it from out here, there's barely any lights on the island at all."

"Yes, well," said Flora, "that's because we're out at sea on a boat, and people very rarely decorate for people passing by for two minutes on a boat. The next nearest people who could see it are in Norway."

"Hmm," said Joel. "Only I was thinking . . . it is Douglas's first Christmas . . . I really need to get on it."

"I'm aware of that, thank you," said Flora, smiling to herself at the sheer amount of extraordinary woolen garments that had already come her way from her older customers, with more to come, she knew. That poor child would get eczema before he was two.

"I haven't managed to allocate Colton's lights provision yet."

They looked at the dull island.

There was a council ruling every year that the money that other places set aside to use for their Christmas decorations actually went toward extra street lighting.

School finished in the dark in the winter months, and the school itself was at the very top of the hill above the village. Extra lighting and handrails on the hill meant more children could walk to and fro on their own, without parents having to drive up and get them, increasing danger to the other, still-walking children. It was a sensible arrangement. But it left the island rather devoid of decorations elsewhere. Joel hadn't noticed it last year. This year, of course, everything was completely different.

"Cool," said Flora, whose mind was on other things as they completed the short journey and Bertie held out his hand to lift her off.

"You're looking lovely," he said, lightly depositing her on the quayside.

"Thank you!" said Flora, genuinely grateful as it helped cheer her up quite a lot about the zip situation. Bertie was happy. He'd made her beam. There was always hope.

Chapter 23

One, thought Lorna MacDonald. She was getting dressed for the dinner in her flat near the tiny school where she was headmistress and thinking about Saif, the island's doctor, who had come as a refugee from Syria and with whom she was passionately in love, even though he had no idea if his wife was still alive. Oh, and she taught his children.

It was, frankly, an incredible mess, and now the end of the year was nearly upon them, and she was doing a mental tally and not liking in the slightest what it showed.

One night at the beginning of the year, snuck under the cover of darkness.

One night in the springtime, when the boys went camping with the Scouts.

Three nights: they had managed a long weekend in Edinburgh, when Pam and Charlie had taken the boys on an Outward Bound course they had had free places for.

Saif had been bowled over by the city's dark, extravagant beauty, its glorious, brimming-over atmosphere, the tiny closes and cobbled steps, the hidden-away bars and vast vistas.

They had stayed in a turret of a hotel they could barely afford, climbed Calton Hill in the rain, eaten every type of food they couldn't find on Mure, which was, frankly, pretty much all of them. They'd even found, on the corner of an ancient square, a Middle Eastern restaurant, which he pronounced "not bad," even as Lorna laughed her head off at the sight of him absolutely stuffing his face with baba ghanoush.

She had a couple of photos of the two of them. The sun had shone down and they had grabbed an extraordinary amount of unlikely food from Valvona & Crolla and sauntered to Princes Street Gardens, and they sat out and had an actual picnic in the shadow of the castle, and she had taken a selfie of them both, his head next to hers, laughing and slightly embarrassed at the same time; guilty seeming, always.

But she took it anyway, even though she knew, a million times over, that she couldn't post it anywhere, couldn't put it on her social media. She sent it to Flora, who was half dead from breastfeeding and couldn't do much more than send a weak thumbs-up. But Lorna looked at it all the time. They could be any couple in that photo. They could be normal. If they weren't in secret. If she wasn't his children's teacher. If his wife wasn't missing. If they could go public . . .

Well, there was no point in thinking about that. They couldn't go public, they just couldn't. Little stolen moments, occasionally when he was on call. She hated them being furtive—they both did—it felt grubby and tawdry.

It also felt wonderful, which was very much a part of the problem.

Oh, and Halloween, which really oughtn't to have happened

at all. She blushed slightly. Well, it had been very dark. There had been a lot of parties and a lot of people in and out of houses, and the boys had been away with all their school friends for hours—children could always roam freely on Mure, it was safe as houses.

Six, she counted. Six nights in a year. This couldn't go on. She brushed out her lovely thick red hair crossly.

THE LITTLE JETTY, in contrast to the rest of the island, was absolutely festooned with lights twinkling in large jars, leading the way to where a red carpet was laid up the steps to the Rock's front door and a piper greeted them with a lamenting air.

It was beautiful, and the people disgorging behind Joel and Flora oohed and aahed their way appreciatively up the steps, even though the cold wind was blowing straight off the sea. At either side of the door was a gas brazier jetting fire into the air, which looked incredibly impressive too, and inside all the windows glowed an inviting yellow and orange, temptingly warm and cozy, and the scents of champagne, ladies' perfume, and woodsmoke filled the air, along with, of course, the great heavy Christmas wreaths everywhere.

Flora felt a flush of pride. It was going to be okay. The Rock was going to be fine. Several of the guests from the mainland were staying over tonight, some in the main house, others in the guest cottages dotted around the grounds, which came with underfloor heating and all the mod cons. Joel had lived in one of the cottages when they'd first began working on Mure. Even thinking about those days now gave her a little frisson. She looked at Joel to see if he was thinking the same thing, but he appeared to be texting Eck, who was babysitting and who didn't pay any attention to his phone or know how to text, so she wasn't sure how useful that was going to be.

Inside, Gala was standing with flutes of champagne and sparkling juice for the guests, and waitstaff recruited from the village were already circulating with canapés. The fires were burning high, and everywhere were groups of well-dressed, happy-looking people, many local but incredibly unrecognizable out of their tweeds and fleeces. Mrs. Docherty sparkled in a glittering diamanté shirt and bright fuchsia lipstick that Flora would wager (correctly) was the only lipstick she had ever owned; the farmers scrubbed up well in ancient handed-down kilts, patched and mended. Pam was wearing a bright purple satin dress with puffed sleeves. Flora thought she looked like a Quality Street candy tin, but kept it to herself as Pam swept in to see Joel.

"Come on, darling, I have to rush you away," she said. "You don't mind, do you, Flora? He has to meet the sponsors."

Flora did mind, very much. This was the first night they'd had out, just the two of them, since Douglas had been born. She was hoping to say a quick hello to everyone, then grab a bottle of champagne and retire to one of the as-yet-uninhabited suites. She had been hoping for that very much. Perhaps a bit of dancing first (Joel did *not* dance, but he liked watching her at it), followed by an amazing dinner, then . . . well, she had quite a lot of plans for Joel Booker that evening, as it happened.

But here he was, allowing himself to be impounded by Pam. Charlie came up, smiled at her apologetically, and kissed her on both cheeks. Pam turned round and gave him a stony stare, which meant that the nice little chitchat Charlie had been very much looking forward to with Flora about baby sick—he couldn't discuss anything tough about child-rearing with Pam, as she insisted it was all brilliant and everything was perfect at all times—was not going to be in the cards at all. So he smiled apologetically again and backed out of the entry hall. Flora eyed the big stag head over the door.

"Just you and me, kid," she muttered, handing in her coat.

IN THE KITCHEN, Konstantin was once again despairing. He'd been supposed to practice chopping vegetables all weekend. Instead he'd spent the time hiding in the airing cupboard, the warmest place in the building when there were no guests, reading *Ivanhoe* and composing desperate missives to his friends back home to launch a rescue mission. He needed to buy a phone and considered stealing one.

"Can I borrow your phone?" he asked Isla brusquely.

"Please?" she suggested mildly.

He grimaced. "Please," he said, feeling like an idiot.

She handed it over and he took it then stared at it, frowning.

"I can't remember anyone's number," he said.

"I know," said Isla. "Where's your phone?"

He shrugged. "It doesn't work anymore."

"You can get credit at the shop," said Isla, "when we get paid."

"Credit?"

"Phone credit."

"Will that make my phone work?"

Isla wondered if Konstantin was, in fact, educationally subnormal. "Uh, duh?"

Konstantin looked so upset she nearly laughed.

"You can log in to Facebook if you like," said Isla finally, when he showed no sign of handing the device back.

"I'm not on *Facebook*," he scoffed.

"Fine," said Isla. "Give it back then."

"No, no, hang on. I can sign in to Snapchat and DM."

He fiddled with some buttons.

"Sure, use my data, you're welcome," said Isla, but it fell on deaf ears.

Konstantin had never paid a phone bill in his life. He tapped a few buttons. Then a few more. Then he really did swear.

"What now?" said Isla.

"I can't remember the password."

"Well, ask them for a new one."

"I have," said Konstantin. "They've texted it. To my phone."

Isla couldn't suppress a grin, which he noticed.

"It's not funny," he said, roughly handing back the phone.

"Noo," said Isla. "But can I ask . . . why are you here? Without a phone or any money?"

Konstantin sighed. He was always too embarrassed to say he'd been banished. So he shrugged. "I'm meant to be learning things."

"Well, you can start back at those potatoes."

So Konstantin was in a filthy mood, because he was falling behind, and Gaspard was in a filthy mood with him, because, as he, Gaspard, never ceased to tell him, when he was seventeen years old he had learned to chop for six hours a day in order to save up for his very first set of knives, the knives he still carried today, because if you wanted to excel at something you had to practice it. Which was exactly what Konstantin had heard from his music teacher, sailing teacher, math teachers, English teachers, science teachers, and art teachers his entire life. He felt about three feet tall.

"Faster! Faster!!"

The menu was simple: pâté, followed by red wine–braised venison with Hasselback potatoes, roasted carrot and turnip, and a beautiful vegetarian haggis dish for the non–meat eaters, but the timing was crucial. There were sixty people out there, all of whom needed feeding at the same time, and if half the room had nothing and half the room had rapidly cooling plates, you could be assured that absolutely nobody would be happy.

But things, Isla was starting to notice, were coming along well. The ovens worked brilliantly and fired the potatoes in record time; the whisky sauce was smelling absolutely delicious. The starter was a selection of local pâtés, which had been made in advance and stored in the huge fridges; the mushroom, white pepper, and brandy was so very delicious Isla simply couldn't imagine it was made from things you could find on the island, but Gaspard assured her both that this was the case and that he absolutely 100 percent wasn't going to poison anyone this time, and Isla had stared at him for a long time and he had said, "Ees joke," but she wasn't 100 percent convinced.

Outside, she could hear the happy din of pleased donors, as the champagne kept coming and people readied themselves to open their checkbooks. It was nice to have something like this on the island, when everyone could get together and complain about the people who visited the island. And because it was getting into

Christmas party season, there was a nice feeling of kicking everything off in style. She wished her mother would have come. She'd have got her a ticket, got her out of the house for once. Her mother had harrumphed and told her it was a completely stupid waste of time and the MacKenzies were going to ruin themselves up at that big house, everybody knew it, and Isla would be out of a job, and they'd hardly want her back at the café—it had been running much better since she left.

Iona slipped into the kitchen.

"You're not supposed to be back here."

"I know!" said Iona. "Hee hee. I came to laugh at you because I don't have to work nights. Oh, and take reportage photographs."

Isla didn't know what those were but decided it was best to keep quiet.

"Hey, who's that?" said Iona in, as usual, a voice that wasn't nearly quiet enough. She meant Konstantin, who was dolefully chopping the slices in the potatoes, wearing an oven glove because Gaspard didn't trust him enough not to cut off his own hand again. It didn't matter that Iona was being loud, though, because Gaspard had the food processor blaring away, drowning out all sound.

"Ugh, he's a drip," said Isla. "Some dropout. He's absolutely useless."

Which would have more or less been fine, had Gaspard not chosen that exact instant to mute the food processor.

Silence fell in the kitchen apart from the radio burbling away in the background. Konstantin's pale skin suddenly flushed bright pink, right to the tips of his ears. He concentrated on chopping, the knife sounding clumsy and unruly on the board, and very loud in the quiet kitchen. Isla went bright red too, not helped by Iona bursting out laughing.

There was no time to dwell, however, as Gaspard batted his hands at Iona to get her to leave his kitchen, then rallied them to go faster and faster. The potatoes were beautifully crispy, like tiny toast racks, roasted in local duck fat and sprinkled with rosemary and crystals of sea salt—he used, Isla noticed, quite an alarming amount of salt in almost everything. Perhaps that was a chef secret she was previously unaware of.

"Okay!" shouted Gaspard. "Are we ready? To go? Thees is our first big night of service, so we are ready, table one, you go, table eight!"

The young waiters nodded, looking serious. Isla and Konstantin were plating up together. She sidled up, face flaming.

"Uh, sorry about . . ."

He gave her an extremely imperious look. "What would I care what you think?" he said, blinking.

Stung, Isla went bright red once more, hating him, and back to plating up. The waiters moved at lightning speed as Gaspard looked at the big clock on the kitchen wall and shouted, "Three, two, one, *let's go!*"

Chapter 24

In the dining room there was a pleasant hum of conversation. The pâté had been cleared away, and people were spreading napkins and refilling glasses, ready for the new course. There was a pleasant clink of conversation, dominated by Pam, who was also going to be starting the speeches afterward, as she kept telling everyone, and about how this was about the children really, which Flora knew already, and how amazing it was that Christabel was sleeping through the night so they could easily leave her with a sitter. Flora narrowed her eyes at this last bit. It couldn't be true, could it? Well, maybe it was true, she thought, but Pam was following one of those evil regimented baby care techniques that involved them being left to cry themselves exhausted for hours on end. Flora decided this absolutely had to be it.

"Yes, they're just so much happier in a lovely structure," said Pam.

"I thought you never put the baby down," said Flora, in a voice that came out much more accusatory than she'd intended. Pam blinked at her.

"Well, yes," she said. "For the first few months. It made her happy and secure enough to be left whenever and however."

She smiled beatifically as Flora ignored her phone, which was bleeping, almost certainly a message complaining that Douglas was yelling blue murder and Agot was joining in.

Flora headed over to speak to her friend Lorna, who was looking beautiful in a new green dress, earrings sparkling.

"Wow, look at you," she said.

"I know," said Lorna. "Too much?"

"Mrs. Docherty is wearing a diamanté fascinator *and* a jeweled comb."

"Okay, compare me to somebody else."

Flora gave her a hug. Lorna didn't even pretend to hide what she was feeling; Flora was her only confidante.

"So he's not coming."

"I'm not sure he's really a posh dinner kind of a person."

"You don't know what kind of a person he is," said Lorna, too quickly, then bit her tongue. "Sorry."

"Don't be," said Flora. "Don't think I'm not sympathetic, because I am. Do you want me to fake a medical emergency so we can call him? Nothing disgusting, just a fainting fit or something?"

"No, don't," said Lorna, pointing at Mrs. Laird, Saif's babysitter, who was wearing a gold dress with batwing sleeves from the 1980s and cackling wholeheartedly with her mates over a gin. "If we ruin Mrs. Laird's night, she'll start spitting in the flour."

"I'm sure she wouldn't," said Flora, watching Mrs. Laird cackle once again. "But yeah, let's not take the risk."

"I wish . . ." said Lorna. "I wish I could give him up."

"There are men here," said Flora.

"There are men everywhere," said Lorna. "Have you seen the Highlands Tinder?"

Flora allowed that she had not.

"Loggers. Fishermen. Farmers. Renewable power analysts. Rig workers. Ferrymen. The Highlands has about ninety percent of Britain's available men *and* a lot of them are fit."

"But . . ." said Flora softly.

"But none of them are him."

"You do look beautiful," said Flora again.

"Thanks," said Lorna, reminding herself not to drink too much. The temptation to go over to his house would be huge, and the repercussions potentially disastrous. The idea of waking the boys was so unutterably traumatic and disgusting she couldn't bear it.

"More fizz?" said Flora eagerly.

"No," said Lorna regretfully, covering the top of her glass with her freshly manicured hand. "No, thank you."

The doors to the kitchen were suddenly flung open, and Flora turned her head interestedly to watch the food come out. Instead, she was greeted with absolute mayhem.

IN BJÅRK'S DEFENSE, he had been cooped up in Konstantin's bedroom a lot, and even when he was taken out, it was for gloomy walks around the small headland north of the hotel, as Konstantin looked out at the wind farms across the water and felt terribly sorry for himself.

It wasn't entirely his fault that he needed some exercise, plus he was desperate for company. Back at the palace it was considered perfectly normal for Bjårk to wander the hallways, almost always ending up in the kitchen, where the staff spoiled Bjårk as much as they spoiled Konstantin; there was always a tidbit or two for them, as he obligingly accepted treats, hugs, and confidences.

"Let's go!" a voice shouted loudly, which sounded very much like what they called out—*"La oss gå!"*—in Norway when they were chasing stags through the woods, or racing their horses across a crisp snowy field, just for the fun of it, as the low winter sun made everything sparkle like diamonds. "Let's go" was a call to arms, a call to run.

And Bjårk, lonely, bored, on his way to the kitchen to see what smelled so absolutely wonderful, couldn't help but respond to it.

Like a big furry bullet, he shot straight through the kitchen and through the door, *bang,* straight into one of the waitresses, who shrieked and toppled the artful collection of plates on the wide tin tray. The noise it made was unbelievable. Someone in the room screamed as well, so surprised by the sudden cacophony. This startled Bjårk so badly he plowed headlong into the nearest table, knocking it straight over, drenching several white shirts with bright red wine. Someone else started yelling. Now there was a rampage.

Gaspard appeared at the door.

"*Mon dieu!* The dog! The dog!! Breeng heem to me! I shall keel him and serve him as delicious next course!!"

Konstantin appeared next, white-faced. "Bjårk! Bjårk! Heel! Come here! Heel!!"

But Bjårk was cavorting now, having discovered some cracker bits he'd upturned on the floor, and was eating and dashing about, unable to see beyond the tables and badly confused.

He was so big and hairy—and an unknown—that people were unwilling to lay a hand on him in case he bit it off. Some old farmers made a grab for him, but he was still bucking about, tail waving madly now, having a fabulous time as he caused absolute havoc. It didn't help that at that point the piper thought it was his cue to come in from the outside (where his fingers were freezing off), immediately starting up a noise incredibly loud even in the big room, startling the most hardened bagpipe listeners, never mind poor old Bjårk, who immediately leaped even harder and started barking, trying to join in.

"Bjårk!! Kom hit!"

"I will keel your dog and then you! It shall be a bouillabaisse and you may both float!" said Gaspard, waving a meat mallet—the closest object he had to hand—in the air and going straight after Konstantin, who ducked straight under him to get on his way. The entire room was havoc and chaos, between people genuinely upset at losing their dinner in this way and everyone else, who were doubled up in helpless laughter as the entire kitchen staff chased a bouncing dog round and round the tables.

"Och, everyone, be quiet!" shouted Flora finally, and grabbed a piece of the venison off the nearest broken plate. This was all so awful, but she couldn't let herself think like that right now. Instead she knelt down and opened her hand to the dog. "Come here, sweetie." She spoke in the soft voice that worked incredibly well with Bramble, Douglas, and, as it happened, Joel.

She held her hand out steadily as Bjårk paused in his bounding for a second.

"There we are, come and try this," she said softly and soothingly. The dog paused and she didn't move, so he stealthily made his way toward her.

Just as he opened his mouth to take the meat, Konstantin pounced on him from behind with a makeshift lead made from two tea towels hastily tied together and managed to restrain him for long enough to pick him up, whereupon Bjårk immediately wrestled his way out of Konstantin's arms and knocked over another table. As if as a final word, the table hit the wall, hard, and the huge stag head that was hanging on a nail fell off, striking the ground with a clang. Bjårk, confronted with what he thought was a stag, instantly went absolutely berserk and started growling and advancing on the stag in a menacing fashion, belly to the floor. Konstantin clapped his hand over his eyes, then threw himself on the floor behind Bjårk and dragged himself along on his own belly until he got close enough to grab the dog's back legs. Front paws struggling mercilessly, Bjårk complained vociferously all the way backward through the swinging kitchen doors as they slammed behind them.

Iona put her phone down. She might, she thought, finally have her Instagram story.

There was a moment's stunned silence. Then Hector McLinn, who ran the large, unrewarding farm that covered the western side of the hill range, grinned with his big ruddy face and started clapping. Flabbergasted, Flora turned toward him, already wishing the floor would swallow her up. But the whole thing had been such a disaster, so very awful, that there was really, in the end, nothing to do but laugh about it. Pam looked like she was about to go ballistic, but just as she did so, the waiters quietly opened the kitchen doors again and started beavering away, serving people food, and Flora ordered free wine from the cellar, which put everyone in an absolutely tremendous mood, and by the time everyone was seated again, there was the sense—particularly as it had been so very dreadful, as Fintan carefully picked up the stag head, and Hector, who was six foot four in his stockinged feet, went over to help him rehang it—that actually it had been quite the adventure.

INSIDE THE KITCHEN, however, it was a different matter. Bjårk had been sent outside the kitchen door—"He can jump in the sea, I do not care"—and was trying to keep out of the cold and howling wind and whining and yipping loudly, occasionally scratching dolefully at the door, adding a strange punctuation to the righteous bollocking they were getting from Gaspard, who was managing to simultaneously scream his head off at Konstantin—and Isla for not helping, which Isla felt was extremely unfair—while also finishing off the dishes that were now going out like clockwork from the kitchen and, very shortly afterward, coming back scraped clean, so delicious was the food. Every time the kitchen doors swung open, they could hear the noise of happy diners rising, the conversation and laughter becoming more pronounced, even as Gaspard continued to hector them with how utterly useless they all were.

Finally, furious, spent, he turned round to finish the preparations on the marmalade tart pudding—being French, Gaspard thought marmalade was an incredibly exotic and rare ingredient and used it in everything—and Isla and Konstantin were left together alone in the middle of the kitchen. Isla risked a glance at Konstantin, who was staring at the floor.

A second later, Konstantin risked a glance at her. This time, she was looking up and caught his eye. And the oddest thing happened. They both smiled; they couldn't help it.

"Get on! Clean!" spat Gaspard from the other side of the kitchen, and they hurried back to their roles immediately. But neither of them felt quite so bad.

Chapter 25

It is a truth universally acknowledged that the more freely flowing the booze at a charity dinner, the more money stands to be raised, and even though it involved the sacrifice of some of Colton's wine collection, it turned out to be quite an incredibly lucrative night for Pam and Charlie's charity, and Pam, who had been rather looking forward to dispensing "What a shame they can't handle that big place on their own. It's just such a pity, isn't it?" stories all over town, was reduced to admitting that in fact everyone had had a brilliant time and that the stag head was fine, although the heads of many people waking up in the morning were not.

The more obvious effects over the next couple of weeks were found in the kitchen. It had been, it turned out, surprisingly galvanizing. Konstantin realized that if he was sacked, everything was going to get massively worse for him and Bjårk massively quickly, and he set about trying—just a tiny bit, and he wasn't very good at it (it would still never have occurred to him, for example, to make his own bed in the morning)—to try harder.

He practiced his chopping till he found, after many bloodied fingers and a lot of strangulated swearing, that he could chop everything quickly and efficiently—if not up to Gaspard's standards, certainly a step up from his own.

IONA GOT ON it the day after the dinner. This was exactly what they needed, she figured. She'd tag it a million times. She remembered that viral video that was just a dog running around a park. This would be *much* better. And it would show off the beautifully curated shots of the island and the hotel itself. She was looking forward to this.

She posted it at nine P.M., the time statistically most people were scrolling lazily through their feeds, looking for something to distract them. And she ran it all in capitals. OMMMGGGGGG FUNNIEST VIDEO EVER! YOU HAVE TO WATCH THIS!!!!!! she typed, hashtagging it a million times with #funnyvideo #funnydogvideo #dogvideo #restaurantfail #hilariousvideo #manfallingover and literally everything else she had ever heard of, posting it simultaneously to her Facebook and her mum's Facebook. Her mum was amazing at sharing all sorts of crap and had about nine thousand old lady friends around the world who also loved sharing absolute crap, so even though there was absolutely nobody Iona's age on Facebook anymore, she expected it to get good currency nonetheless. And she sent it to the Twitter accounts of all the newspapers she could think of. Sometimes they had more space to fill than people realized. Iona liked Mure, in a faintly haughty fashion, but she knew she was destined for greater things. This was just the start she needed.

Nothing. After an hour she crossly shut down her phone and went to bed.

Chapter 26

The snow lying was such a surprise. It was usually cold enough—that was rarely a problem on Mure. It was instead whether the wind would cease for long enough for snow to fall and lie on the roads, across the fields, gently papering everything in its soft and lovely gentleness.

Bramble had barely seen snow, and being particularly old, and also a dog, he couldn't remember if he had or not and charged out into the lower field, rolling on his back and tossing himself around, paws in the air, like a much younger dog. Then it soaked in and he stopped liking it so much and slinked back in to dry himself off in front of the fire. It did not smell good.

THE CHILDREN WERE having such a good time up at the school that Lorna, the headmistress, gave up on trying to get anything done and took the two classes outside for a healthy snowball fight—no hitting in the face and no rocks in the snowballs and no putting down necks were the rules, but there were still a few tears here and there. Mrs. Cook, the only other teacher at the school, already had the urn on for hot chocolate, so tears were assuaged and little pink hands and noses warmed after the laughter and exercise of the morning, and Lorna resumed reading *The Dark Is Rising,* their Christmas book, although as the room warmed up and the hot chocolate took effect, more than a few of the little heads began to nod. It had been a long term, after all; everyone was more than ready for the two-week Christmas break. And she still hadn't heard from Saif.

SAIF, FOR ONCE, wasn't thinking about Lorna. Instead he was staring, for the umpteenth time, at his most recent letter from the Home Office, asking him to come in for a visit. It wasn't for him—he had his indefinite right to stay. It wasn't about the boys. Which left . . . what? Was it his wife?

A scientist by bent, a doctor by profession, he had been rigorously trained not to speculate but to deduce, carefully; never to jump to wild conclusions.

It was proving extraordinarily difficult.

UP AT THE hotel, it was quiet—Gaspard was talking to suppliers, and there was no dummy lunch service that day. And Isla knew today was the day the Christmas trees arrived—everyone on Mure knew, it was quite the excitement—so was happy to be heading down to the port to see everyone.

She pulled on her old gray coat, which looked jollier when she added her tam-o'-shanter and a red scarf. It had been a present from Flora the year before, and she thought it was a little showy—red was such a big color—but it suited her dark hair and pink skin, and it was made of very good lambswool.

Just as she left the Rock she happened upon Konstantin, who

was out throwing a stick across the wide white lawn for Bjårk, who was gamboling toward it in a leisurely fashion. He was rather overweight for a dog, but Konstantin tossed the stick over and over again regardless, his long arm stretching up into the air of the now bright blue sky, sending the stick far and true.

He looked boyish and, for the first time, truly carefree, not shackled to a kitchen he despised, in a world he didn't understand. The hangdog look was almost completely gone.

She found herself watching him for a while; there was nobody in the hotel on this side, he obviously didn't realize he was observed.

"*Sing med myg!*" he shouted. "*Mitt hjerte alltid vanker . . .*"

He sang loudly and quite well. To Isla's amazement, Bjårk immediately sat his capacious bottom down on the snow, pushed back his head, and howled loudly along to the sky.

"*I Jesus føderom . . .*"

"Aooo!"

Isla couldn't help it, she giggled aloud, and Konstantin whirled round, his cheeks bright red, his white teeth showing.

He stopped as soon as he saw her and his face immediately took on that closed look again, and she remembered once more with horror how he had overheard her talking to Iona.

In fact, for an instant, Konstantin hadn't recognized the shy little scullery maid who hated him in this pink-cheeked laughing girl in the beautiful red scarf, her long dark hair streaming underneath it down the back of her coat. His first instinct was to smile, then he'd realized awkwardly who it actually was and set his face.

Bjårk had no such compunction and bounded up to her happily. You couldn't really ever say a Mure person was frightened of dogs; there were so many dogs it would be ridiculous, like saying you were frightened of sand, but nonetheless Isla remained a timid sort and her mother had always warned her away from them. Gingerly, she put her hand out a little. Bjårk sniffed it, disappointed as soon as he worked out there was no treat in it, but nonetheless wormed his way under her hand and pushed his ears in her direction so she could scratch underneath them, which, slightly tentatively, she did.

"You're a very bad singer," she whispered to the dog, who minded not in the slightest. "Uh," she said, as Konstantin still stood there. "Sorry to interrupt. I was just heading down to the village."

"Oh," said Konstantin, who had a whole day free and not a clue what to do with it without friends or money. At the spur of the moment he said, "Well, so am I."

Isla didn't look pleased, he noticed. For goodness' sake.

"Or maybe not," he added pointedly.

"No, no, come with me," said Isla immediately, feeling miserably aware of having fallen short with her manners. It had just flashed through her mind that if she said he couldn't come, he'd just end up walking about three paces behind her, given that there was only one road down into town anyway. But what would he think of everyone being so excited to see a few trees? She told herself she didn't care and carried on.

The island looked so pretty, though, if you were wrapped up, the fresh snow scrunching cheerfully beneath your soles, the clear imprints of paws and birds' feet that had gone before you, including the lovely squishy shape of the ducks' footprints, plopping along on duck business.

Conversation was sporadic as they neared the little port, where quite the crowd was forming.

"What's the crush?" said Konstantin. "Has someone got the island's first computer? Be careful nobody panics when they see a moving train."

Isla looked at him crossly, but her expression was hidden underneath her hat and he didn't notice in the slightest.

"*Hello!*" shouted a small voice. It was Ash, the younger of Saif's two sons, who had spent many a day while Saif was handling an emergency more or less being babysat at the café, so he knew Isla well.

It was hard not to have a soft spot for Ash, who still had a limp from a badly set leg in Syria and a desperate, confused desire never to have to go through his bad experiences again. In Ib, his older brother, this manifested in a certain wariness and sullenness. In Ash, an openness to the world that made him friendly as a Labrador. On the tiny island of Mure, this was always happily reciprocated in a way that made Saif alternately happy and then worried all over again for when his darling boy had to face the real world and found out everyone wasn't quite so friendly.

"Hello, Ash," said Isla, tousling the boy's too-long dark hair.

"The trees are coming!"

He turned to Konstantin.

"Trees are big things that grow in the ground," he began confidently. There were, of course, no trees on Mure; it was simply too windy. "You put them up at Christmastime. They're for hanging lights on," he continued.

Isla expected Konstantin to be wearing his usual annoyed

frown, but to her surprise he had an interested, engaged look on his face. Ash stretched out his arm as the ferry got closer.

"*All the trees are coming!*" He lowered his voice. "I is going to be at the front for the biggest one."

Konstantin looked at him. "How are you going to carry that?"

"My daddy will. He's '*normous,*" said Ash of his pleasantly tall but in no way enormous father. "I will sit on it till he is here."

"That's a brilliant plan," said Konstantin.

Ash narrowed his eyes as the ferry started to chug in reverse. "Don't take the biggest one."

"I won't take the biggest one," said Konstantin. Ash held his gaze meaningfully as Konstantin turned back to Isla, smiling.

"Do you normally take the biggest one?" said Isla.

He smiled ruefully. Konstantin always took the biggest one. "Well . . ."

More and more people gathered as a huge pile of Christmas trees started to be unloaded onto the dock. People were trying to look unconcerned about it, and not be casting too beady an eye, while all mentally planning exactly which one they wanted. There was a beauty at the top.

"Where are these from?" said Konstantin to the cargo loader who was ticking things off his inventory.

"Came out of Bergen last night, ken," said the man, and Konstantin briefly wondered why the man thought his name was Ken, but still, there was something about seeing the beautiful trees, their dark green needles already tumbling out onto the dock, that made him even more homesick than usual.

"Okay," he said, staring sadly.

Flora had arrived—Fintan was still in bed—and made straight for the dispatcher. "I'm going to need the ten-footer for the Rock."

"I wanted that!" said old Mrs. MacGregor, who didn't see quite as well as she once did.

"But you live in the mill cottage," said Flora as gently as she was able. "There isn't space."

"I can chop it up and have it twice," said the old lady mutinously.

"I have a lovely five-foot tree for you," said the dispatcher smoothly. "Don't worry about it."

More and more people were arriving on the docks now, picking up their beautiful trees with cries and shouts; a tractor was called into service by Hamish, who loaded up the farmhouse's six-footer with a huge grin all over his face. Flora had harbored hopes of decorating it before Agot got home from school and put her special stamp on it, but didn't hold out much hope for that happening.

KONSTANTIN WATCHED SADLY.

The palace at Christmastime was ridiculously overdone. Partly it was because they had so many visitors, some paying, some local schoolchildren. Grand companies held their Christmas parties there, so his father pointed out it made sense economically. But deep down Konstantin knew it was because he loved it, because his mother had loved it so much.

Trees four meters high lined the huge, ornate staircase at the main entrance to the palace, with heavy green ivy wreaths wound up the delicate filigree banisters on both sides. Similar heavy wreaths were pinned perfectly along the walls, and the trees were lined with both artificial lights and real candles, lit up only on Christmas Eve eve, when just the family gathered round to exchange early gifts and eat lutefisk in preparation for Christmas Day itself, the main event.

His mother had loved the traditional songs and booked the local choir repeatedly to come and sing *julesanger*. She had said it was for the visitors, who filed through the public rooms to see the palace come to life throughout December, but Konstantin had always known on some level that it was for her; she hummed the songs wherever she was in the house.

It had been so much . . . Well, he was a kid. He hadn't known anything.

It was special to live in a palace, he knew that. People mentioned it all the time. But actually, the really special thing had been having a mother who loved and adored him. He'd taken that completely for granted, not given it a second thought.

It occurred to him to tell everyone where he was from, get them to stop treating him like an idiot. But would they, though? The horror of it, thought Konstantin, if they didn't believe him or, worse, thought it was funny. Laughed at him. He couldn't bear it. Better they thought he was a drifter than an absolute loser who'd been banished by his own father. He bit his lip, hard.

"Uhm, are you okay?" said Isla eventually, realizing how quiet he'd been. Even Bjårk wasn't gamboling anymore. She thought Mure looked beautiful—always did this time of year, when the lights were slung up along the lampposts on the quay. It was just the one string, and usually something was wonky, but it was like a fairyland to Isla. It always cheered her up.

"I miss home," he said simply. Then he looked around the docks. "Are these all the lights there are? Is this it?"

"I like it," said Isla.

He fell silent.

"What's home like?"

"It's amazing," he said suddenly. "Where I'm from, up near Bergen . . . there are thick pine forests everywhere, up the mountains. You can smell the fir trees too. Everything smells of pine and fresh white snow. It's dark like here but not so windy, and you can ski every day. It's not flat like this place."

Isla frowned. "Well, we've got the ben," she said, referring to the hill behind the MacGregor farm, which was misleadingly treacherous to climb, and led to the spine up the northwest side of the island of craggy hills that bristled with heather in the spring but now were dull and bare. Konstantin looked at them like they were puddles.

But the dock grew busier and happier. Enterprisingly, Iona had set up a table with mulled wine and hot chocolate for sale while people waited to bid on the tree they wanted. Few were the children who, on seeing another child with a cup filled with marshmallows, cream, and cinnamon, didn't immediately pester their parents for one. Although more than one parent pointed out that it was absolute highway robbery, most gave in with good grace. It was a part of it, and ritual was important at Christmastime.

"Okay, six-footer, would suit a flat or lovely front room," bellowed the dispatcher again.

Several people stepped forward; some held back in case there was a fatter, greener tree beneath. Isla waved at Lorna, who was buying two: one for her lovely little flat to sit on the table, and one, out of her own pocket, for the school. She and Mrs. Cook, the other teacher, came in on the second Sunday of advent and decorated it in secret, partly to give the children a wonderful surprise on Monday morning, as if it had happened by magic, and partly because if you invite thirty-five children to help decorate a Christmas tree, nothing good happens, and there's a lot of needles involved.

Inge-Britt sidled down lazily from the Harbour's Rest hotel. It needed a big tree, and she would only bother to decorate one side of it, because really, who would see the other side? And she'd have to make two trips up to the attic, which would seriously impinge on her afternoon nap. Inge-Britt was a brilliant person but temperamentally highly unsuited to running a clean hostelry—something Flora was very much hoping to capitalize on with the Rock.

The women clustered together, as both Lorna and Inge-Britt put their hands up for a big tree.

Lorna, however, was momentarily distracted; if little Ash was by the quayside, it meant his father, Dr. Hussein—oh, who was she kidding—Saif, the man she was desperately in love with, couldn't be far behind.

"Hey, Lorna," shouted Inge-Britt, holding up a hand to indicate that they would share catching the big tree as the dispatcher moved over the ten-footer, expecting her friend to catch it . . . but Lorna's head was turned in a dream and she wasn't there to catch the tree as it fell.

Chapter 27

It happened very quickly. Lorna turned on hearing her name, but it wasn't—was never, it seemed—the voice she wanted to hear her name from at all, and she was scanning the crowd even as Inge-Britt was asking her to help.

Ten-foot Christmas trees, even wrapped in netting, are heavy, unwieldy things, hard to get a grasp on, even if you are a tall, glamorous Icelandic girl.

"Lorna!" Inge-Britt yelled, but Lorna was still searching the mass of faces, looking for the one pair of dark eyes she could drown in, looking for that shaggy black hair, always in need of a haircut, that rangy frame, the golden skin ...

The tree fell straight over, heading directly for little Ash, whose damaged leg (and wide-eyed demeanor) meant he wasn't always as quick off the mark as he could have been.

It happened as if in slow motion: Isla looking on in concern as the tree toppled out of Inge-Britt's arms toward the little boy, until, like a flash, the tall blond man beside her dived underneath it and pushed the boy out of the way and crashed onto the cold port tarmac, with a tree crashing down on his broad back.

"OH MY GOD." Lorna dashed down at once. "I wasn't . . ."

"I thought you'd heard me," said Inge-Britt, as they both knelt down in front of the stunned Konstantin. Inge-Britt shot Lorna a look.

"Are you all right?" said Isla softly, sitting down on his other side.

Konstantin blinked at her. "This is cold and wet," he said. "Even more than everything is here already."

Ash was looking at the man astounded, as Saif rushed forward to pick him up. Lorna couldn't look him in the eye in case she found him blaming her for nearly whacking Ash on the head with a Christmas tree.

"Ash, I told you to stay out of the way," he said gently into the boy's ear, but making sure he didn't raise his voice or sound cross. How Lorna loved his voice.

"Do you want to get up?" said Isla to Konstantin. "Or are you quite comfortable?"

"It's all relative," said Konstantin, as Saif rushed over to him to make sure he was all right, which, apart from some gravel in his hands and some tears to his surprisingly expensive raincoat, he was.

"Thank you," muttered Saif gravely. "Thank you for saving my boy."

Konstantin looked up at the tree, as if surprised at himself. "You're welcome. I didn't even realize I'd done it until I had."

"Well, you are brave," said Saif, cleaning off Konstantin's hand with an antiseptic wipe.

"Ouch, that stings," said Konstantin. "So now I think that I am not."

"Is this a cut filled with superglue?"

"Can we talk about that later?"

"Here," said Flora. "Have some free hot chocolate for being heroic."

"Can I have some free hot chocolate?" said Ash.

"You were antiheroic!" protested Flora. "You got in the way of the trees!"

"Oh," said Ash, crestfallen.

"Of course you can," said Flora, feeling guilty.

"I'm sorry," said Lorna, as Saif carried her two trees up the hill, with Ash helping from the back. He didn't say anything. It was very difficult when the boys were with them.

"You didn't do anything," he said in his usual calm way, but his mind was far away. There was a reason he had been avoiding Lorna—deliberately avoiding her. For months. He knew it was cruel and unfair, but he didn't know how to tell her, because he didn't know *what* to tell her.

After querying the letter, he had received word through a back channel in the Home Office that there was some chatter and to stand by, and he could think of little else. His wife had now been missing for nearly three years. It was impossible to focus on the situation with his wife *and* Lorna, as well as a highly demanding job as the island's only doctor and being a single father to his two sons. And all the time having to stand by. He couldn't give heart space to Lorna, because he knew if he did, she would consume him utterly, and he couldn't—he couldn't let that happen. He could barely even look at her.

He can barely even look at me, thought Lorna, her heart aching.

Chapter 28

A whole group headed off to the Harbour's Rest for lunch, and Konstantin amazed himself that he noticed all the things Gaspard would not have stood for in his kitchen, how far below the standards of the Rock it fell. He genuinely was surprised at himself.

Isla had slipped away to take her mother a tree: a little sweet three-footer that could sit on top of the nest of tables in the good room.

Her mother sniffed. "Well, that's just going to shed, isn't it?"

"But it looks so pretty," said Isla. "And it smells good too."

"I don't know why I bother," said Vera, smiling sadly. "Are you really working Christmas Day?"

Isla owned that she was, if they got the bookings.

"Well, Flora's got you run ragged, I see," said Vera. "I never saw you as a kitchen maid, Isla."

"I'm not!" said Isla, stung. "Gaspard is teaching me loads."

"That Frenchman! I saw him in the Harbour's Rest. He looks filthy."

Isla bit her lip.

"And those tattoos! I don't like the look of him."

Vera didn't like the look of many people, though.

"You'll come, though," said Isla, trying to build bridges. "Can't you bring a friend? I can book you in. It can be my Christmas present to you."

"Sitting in a strange hotel eating Christmas lunch on my own? No thank you," said Vera, who had fallen out with her two sisters for reasons that were misty in the memory, possibly even in Vera's memory too, but it meant Isla hadn't even seen her cousins for six years.

"Well, maybe you'll change your mind," said Isla. "I'm heading back up."

"Again?"

"We're doing a dinner service. It's going to the old folks' home. You could go and help serve it if you like. We're doing something new, I think it's like a kind of French cake. You'd like it."

Vera sniffed again. "I doubt it," she said. "And it's *Escape to the Sun* tonight on channel four."

And for a rebellious second, Isla really, really wished she would.

Chapter 29

Back at the Rock, Gaspard appeared in the kitchen, looking furious as always, a cigarette being thrown out behind him. Flora had left a huge fire bucket there to try to catch them all, but it didn't always succeed.

"Today!" he said. "Tarte tatin with leeks from the kitchen garden. No messing. We have a million winter leeks. This rock is a good place for growing leeks. Aha, *bien,* ah *oui,* who knew. *Alors:* everyone learn. I will need your help to make starters."

And they spent all afternoon learning how to perfectly roast the leeks in purest butter, made pastry again and again under his disappointed eye, rolled and blind baked and wasted butter, and marveled at Bjårk's frankly extraordinary ability to eat remnants of pastry while carefully separating out any hint of greenery and daintily spitting it out of the corner of his mouth. By the evening, all of them had more or less presentable—and undeniably delicious—leek tatins sitting in tiny ramekins.

Konstantin stared at his in something like awe.

"Is that, like, the first time you've ever made something?" teased Isla quietly.

"Yes," he said simply, still looking at it in amazement.

They sat at the kitchen table and he took a bite. Gaspard had whipped up a hollandaise sauce to eat with it too, and it was absolutely sensational, but to Konstantin it was something new altogether.

He was even more surprised when Isla, who had been looking at it all afternoon and getting annoyed by it, scooted over when they'd finished eating and lifted his coat down from the stand.

"What are you doing?"

She frowned and showed him one of the small sewing kits the hotel was full of. "Do you want to do it?"

He blinked. "You're going to sew up my coat?"

Isla went bright red. She had genuinely barely given it a second thought; she had darned for her father and was always proud of her neat stitching, and couldn't bear looking at the beautiful expensive coat with the tears in the fine material. It was mostly habit.

And partly gratitude; he had, undeniably, despite his bad attitude, saved Ash from at the very least a nasty hit to the head. His hands were still red and cut.

"You don't have to do that," he said, which made her feel even worse, like a servant he was being kind to.

"Well, you helped my friend," she said, her voice timid and shy.

Konstantin blinked.

"You can do it if you want," she said again.

"I don't know how."

"You can't *sew*?"

He laughed. "Of course I can't sew! Who can sew?"

"I can sew!" said Kerry.

"*Moi aussi,*" said Gaspard. "Of course. We are not animals."

"So, everyone can sew," said Konstantin suspiciously. If he ever ripped anything, he tended to throw it away; he thought everyone did.

The kitchen staff looked back at him.

Isla would have put money on him saying something snotty and cutting, or just leaving them to get on with it on his behalf. Instead, he sat back in his chair.

"Okay," he said. "Teach me to sew."

THEY HAD A little time before the cleanup and dinner service. Gaspard went off for his daily *sieste.* Kerry and Tam went out to collect eggs, a job Isla was absolutely terrified of but they both seemed to quite like. It depended very much where you stood on chickens. Isla was scared of their beady little eyes, but she was a little scared of a lot of things. Konstantin hadn't been drafted yet in case Bjårk ate all the eggs. Bjårk tried to go help, but they were having none of it.

Isla retuned the radio from the shocking French pop music Gaspard liked (Flora had commented dryly that his good taste in food obviously had to be evened out somewhere else by his frankly horrible taste in music) to BBC Radio nan Gàidheal and let its gentle music run through the big kitchen.

The low winter sun briefly showed its face, illuminating the clean white tiles on the walls, the shiny metal implements, the good wooden table. She bent her dark head to his blond one and, with some swearing and a couple of pricks to the fingers (his hands, he pointed out, had never been in such a state, and she was tempted to say his hands were so soft he should be ashamed), she showed him a simple running stitch, then a cross-stitch. She made him practice on the tea towels, though; she wouldn't let him loose on his good coat.

"You'll ruin it."

He looked uncharacteristically thoughtful. "I ruin a lot of things," he said suddenly.

She looked up at him then, and the sun caught her dark hair and made her huge dark eyes shine very brightly. "Well," she said. "You didn't ruin the Christmas trees."

"True."

"And you didn't ruin the leek tatin."

"Mine was by far the worst."

"Well, everyone else is a chef and I'm a baker."

"It did taste good, though," he added almost to himself.

"And now you can do a running stitch!" she said, and he glanced down at his handiwork.

"Oh," he said.

"What?" said Isla, even as she noticed him smiling.

He held up his hands. "I've sewn the tea towel to my shirt."

Isla burst out laughing as he stood up, the towel flapping off him. He tugged at it.

"Don't pull it! You'll rip another hole in your clothes! Stay still!"

And she carefully approached him, the low sun streaming in through the windows, and was suddenly very conscious of him and his long, hard body through his expensive twill shirt. She realized the kitchen scissors were in the dishwasher. There was no help for it. Carefully and deftly, as he lifted his arms, she bent toward him and neatly bit through the loop of the thread, then pulled it out, leaving no trace.

She caught a faint scent of his aftershave too, something oddly like leather or tobacco or something . . . Where on earth did a kitchen boy get all these expensive tastes? It made no sense at all.

She was blushing harder than ever as she straightened up. He was looking a bit startled too; he hadn't realized she was going to bite it. Her face was so close to his, as the sun shone down on her shiny dark hair, that he felt . . . well. It had been a while. He felt a jolt, then stopped himself for being ridiculous. It had taken him a little bit by surprise, that was all.

"I could have got Bjårk to do that," he said, checking the shirt again, hiding his slightly pink face just in case she could read his thoughts from it.

"Next time," said Isla, scuttling off. "We'd better get cleaned up."

And in a second she had her unflattering kitchen cap on again and was elbow-deep in hot soapy water with the ramekins, and everything was back to normal.

Chapter 30

So Isla didn't get to see Iona till later that night, and then she pointed out that Iona, despite being the supposedly great social media maven, had turned her Instagram to private after she'd flirted rather disastrously with a celebrity and forgotten to turn it back on again, and Iona reposted the entire video from the dinner again.

At first, Facebook take-up was slow, but Instagram was quick.

And then one of the Scottish papers retweeted it, then the radio stations started to pick up on it—and then it really started to move. By the time the numbers were clicking up exponentially and her phone had started to glow hot with the notifications, the girls were staring at each other, half in delight, half in horror.

Iona plugged her phone into the wall to stop it from dying and texted Flora.

Go take a look at my insta!!!!!!!!! but unfortunately by then it was after nine o'clock at night, which meant Flora was lying spread-eagle on her bed in the mansion, fast asleep, a television show playing on her computer screen to which she was completely oblivious. She was oblivious too to Joel giving Douglas his night bottle, half smiling, half wincing at the noisy snoring noises coming from the master bedroom.

Flora was taking too much on, and he probably should be doing more, he thought. She was the one who was meant to be on leave. Except . . . he wasn't entirely sure that actually going to the hotel wasn't good for her. She was made to be busy, Flora. He wondered, mildly, if she hadn't overestimated how much she would enjoy sitting in a rocking chair.

He looked down at Douglas, who was sucking his bottle with an expression of exceptional happiness on his face. Douglas drank deeply, smacked his lips in contentment, and allowed himself a long, luxuriant fart.

"If you had told me," said Joel softly to the little one, "how much I would be perfectly fine with another human being taking a massive fart in my hands, I think I'd have found it quite difficult to believe you. In the past."

Douglas smiled dreamily, as he had taken to doing at the sound of his father's voice, and, as usual, Joel felt the familiar catch at the heart, laced once more with sadness that his own parents hadn't felt the same way, or if they had, they—teenagers as they had been—still hadn't been able to look after him, protect him. Whereas now, looking down at this little face, he couldn't think of a single thing he wouldn't do to protect Douglas, to keep him safe, nor a single place on earth—he peered out into the dark night— that would be better for him to do it in. Yes, he should get back to work. Those damn lights, he was running out of time. But oh, it was better right here, right now.

Under the great cold stars of the North Atlantic, all was well.

The following morning, all hell broke loose.

Chapter 31

The phone at the Rock, explained Gala, looking absolutely mortified, had been ringing off the hook since five A.M. that morning.

Nobody had gotten any sleep until Gaspard had stormed down in a rage of swearing and unplugged it. When it had finally gotten plugged back in, every time they went to pick it up, it was a journalist called Candace from the *Daily Post,* wanting to know how things were at "Britain's Worst Hotel!"

The papers didn't arrive in Mure until the day after publication, it taking that long to get them up there, but Flora, completely confused, opened them up online and was absolutely astounded by what she saw.

"McFAWLTY TOWERS!" screamed the headline, with a freeze-frame of Gaspard tripping over a dog and a plate in the air.

"Scotland's wackiest hotel," the story went on, "left by eccentric, flamboyant billionaire . . ."

"Flamboyant!"

Fintan marched into the Rock, his face absolutely puce. *"Flamboyant!! Flamboyant!* You know what that means."

Flora patted him on the shoulder.

"They mean gay! They're calling him a laughingstock! And me! We're laughingstocks to them! Those . . . those utter bastards!!"

"I know," said Flora. "I don't suppose . . . it *might* be good publicity for us."

"Britain's worst hotel?" said Fintan. "Run by fairies. How's that going to work? Oh, screw it. I'm going to shut it down."

"But Colton wanted you to run it."

"I don't care what he wanted," said Fintan, his face white with fury. "I don't care! I hate this and I hate them and I don't want pricks coming up to look at our 'eccentric' hotel and I am going back to the farm and I am going to make cheese and be miserable and everyone else can just *fuck off.*"

Flora gazed after him in despair, then quickly noticed the anxious faces of Isla and Gala peering out at her from reception.

"Does this mean we're going to lose our jobs?" Isla asked tentatively.

"I don't know," said Flora miserably. "I'm sure he'll calm down. It'll be fine."

She was too cross to go and find Iona, who was hiding out in her bedroom and refusing to come out from underneath the blankets. She had let her phone die because she couldn't bear the constant *beep beep beep* of more and more and more incoming messages, and she knew she had to turn it back on, that she would just be scaring her friends and then they'd start coming round and then things really would get bad. It was meant to be funny and make them popular! It wasn't meant to be "THE WORST HOTEL ON EARTH."

She plugged it in but still left it on the other side of the room, too afraid to touch it, like a spider or a red-hot poker.

FLORA STALKED INTO the Seaside Kitchen looking for Iona. She did not get angry very often; it wasn't really in her makeup. But she was unutterably furious. Every single table in the café fell silent as she entered, which gave her a pretty good idea what they'd all been talking about.

"Where is she?" she hissed to Malik, who glanced up at her, startled.

"She hasn't come in," muttered Malik.

"Hasn't she," said Flora. "Well, I can't say I'm surprised."

"She texted me to say sorry to you."

Flora looked squarely at Malik. "Do you think that's how apologies work?"

"No."

"Neither do I. Tell her to get down here."

TWENTY MINUTES LATER, a bedraggled Iona in a holey pair of jeans and a farm jumper so threadbare that it absolutely begged for sympathy emerged through the side fire-door entrance into the kitchen, where Flora was making angry scones with chili and Szechuan pepper.

"I'm not sure those will sell," said Iona softly.

"Oh well, obviously you're the marketing guru," said Flora.

Iona's eyes were red. The girl was so young. Flora almost softened.

"What were you *thinking*?"

"You said get on the Instagram!"

"To make us look beautiful and wonderful. Which we are!"

"I posted loads of those too!" said Iona, pulling out her phone and showing Flora the many lovely shots: the Endless Beach in a ravishing pink sunset, the bobbing red and blue fishing boats, a heavily filtered shot of the Harbour's Rest hotel, which made it look bleached out and charming rather than dilapidated.

"And did people share those?"

"Uhm, not so much . . ." Iona's voice trailed off.

"Why didn't you ask me if you could post it?"

"You said post stuff!"

"Iona! I have had twenty-five journalists on the phone this morning, every single last one of them asking to be comped for bloody Christmas week!"

"Well, that could be good," said Iona. "Maybe?"

"They want to make us a laughingstock," said Flora. Her heart dropped. Everything they had worked for. Everything that was Colton's legacy. "We already are."

Her phone rang and she picked it up, listened for a second, then cursed roundly.

"And now our chef's disappeared," she said.

"I'm sorry," said Iona, cringing.

Flora took a deep breath. "It's not your fault," she allowed, finally. "But, Christ. What a mess."

Chapter 32

Back at the hotel, Konstantin had wandered down into the lobby to see what was up. Phoneless, he knew nothing about what had happened. But he was still amazed. For starters, nobody had knocked at his door that morning and it wasn't a Sunday, so he had absolutely no clue why he wasn't in the kitchen peeling potatoes and the skin off his knuckles while also getting yelled at.

Down in the lobby, Gala was still desperately trying to answer the telephones while Isla was standing, looking concerned.

He frowned. "There has been a nuclear attack," he said. "Everyone is dead from all the zombies. We are the only people left on earth."

She looked at him.

"What?" he said. "Come on, it would be cool."

"Zombies would be cool?"

"Sorry, it's just most Scottish people . . . Maybe it's the lack of sunlight."

"Stop it! You're being so rude!"

He liked seeing the dimples come out on her face, though. It felt as if . . . well. To make her smile when at first she would barely look at him. Without impressing her or showing off. Goodness, he'd been in this awful uniform the entire time. It was, undeniably, a nice feeling.

Even so, there was no doubt the hotel was very eerie without the usual clatter from the kitchen. Now Gala had unplugged the phone to stop newspapers getting on to them, so there wasn't even a ring or a conversation to be had. Gala headed out, muttering mutinously about this not being what Uncle Mark had signed her up for.

Isla tried to explain the situation to Konstantin after she'd gone, but he wasn't really listening. Instead he looked at her slyly.

"What?" she said.

"There's nobody here."

"So?"

In response, he ran to the large brass baggage cart and jumped on it, then pushed himself off and glided across the wooden foyer floor.

"I've always wanted to do this!" he said, beaming. "Come on, jump on!"

"Oh no, I couldn't," said Isla.

"Of course you could! You're far too well behaved! I bet you never got into trouble at school or anything."

Isla blushed. He was absolutely correct.

Konstantin came to a stop, whizzing the baggage holder halfway round right in front of her, then jumped off.

"Come on! Your carriage, m'lady."

"You are being ridiculous!"

"Quick! Quick! I can't hold the horses."

Giggling helplessly, Isla accepted his outstretched hand up onto the cart.

"Hold on tight!"

And he rushed her across the smooth floor at high speed, then twirled her around just as she was about to hit the wall, as she shrieked with laughter, her face pink, and he reflected briefly how pretty she looked when she smiled. Her curly hair flew out behind her in a sheet as he made giddy-up noises and started galloping for the door . . . which was where they came face-to-face with a very stony-looking Fintan, who had been shaken out of his dolor following his fight with Flora by the horrific amount of social media abuse that morning. It didn't help either that he had barely slept, was now in an absolutely filthy mood about it, and woe betide anyone who got in his way.

Chapter 33

"What the *hell* are you two doing?" he screamed, as Konstantin, surprised, pulled the baggage cart to a halt, causing Isla to stumble backward.

Instinctively, he caught her, and she found herself equally surprised to be in his arms. He held her tight, just for an instant, and she felt her face grow even hotter, if that were possible. He was tall and lean; not skinny, just slender. *They are all like that, those Scandis, aren't they?* she found herself thinking, then blushed even harder as his long hand brushed her waist as they both squirmed to stand upright in front of Fintan's undeniable fury.

"What the fuck is this supposed to be? A crèche? *Toytown*?!"

Both of them stared at the floor.

"You know we're an international laughingstock?"

"Oh, it can't be that bad, man," said Konstantin.

Konstantin still didn't have a phone. Even though he'd been there a month and had earned enough to get one sent from the mainland, now something strange had happened: he'd found himself not actively minding too much.

Funnily enough, even though he thought of himself as some-one who could take or leave social media, he realized just how much he'd used it, been on it. And, conversely, how relaxing it was not to be on it. He was, he'd noticed, sleeping better since he'd come here. Something to do with hard work, he supposed, and getting up early, and no booze (unless Gaspard was feeling generous), and somehow being away from everything, including the fun, also kept him away from the other things too: the empty echoing corridors of the palace, the constant sense of someone missing, the wasted mornings and pointless days, the bored in-dulgences, the rooms where his mother had used to walk.

It was the first time, truly, that he had distance from every-thing and he had a little time and space to himself. Not to be on-line, not to be playing with his friends or tearing things up. Just a little time to contemplate the world and a little discipline. He had found an old book in the library about wintering in the South Pole and was engrossed in it, feeling, sometimes, that the person's experience wasn't massively different from his own. Peace, quiet, dark, and contemplation.

So he wasn't really taking in what Fintan was saying.

Meanwhile Isla—how pretty she had looked, he thought again, when she laughed. How soft she had felt in his arms. Isla was look-ing absolutely terrified at the prospect of getting into trouble. It made her seem very young.

Fintan pulled out his iPad and set it up on reception, then showed them the news headlines.

Isla's knees trembled. This was awful.

Konstantin threw back his head and burst out laughing. She looked at him.

"Oh, come on," he said. "This will be great for business."

"Being the worst hotel in Britain?"

"Having a very handsome dog!" He frowned suddenly.

"What?"

"How many shares?"

It was, he had just realized, not impossible that someone he knew had seen it. Seen him. Oh well. That wouldn't mean anything, would it? Would it?

"Forty thousand," said Isla in awe. "Oh my God."

"Don't plug the phone back in," said Fintan. "But bloody well start behaving like professionals."

"We're pot washers," said Konstantin.

"I'm junior kitchen manager!" gasped Isla, suddenly aware she sounded exactly like her mother.

Fintan ignored her. "Well, professional pot washers then, for Christ's sake. It's not difficult. Where's Gaspard?"

It was the first time Konstantin realized there was no telltale smell of something delicious—slowly caramelizing onions, fresh roasted garlic—emanating from the kitchen.

"Did you even think to look for him?" stormed Fintan. If he had been disenchanted and sad and fed up with the hotel before all this, well, now he outright hated the entire enterprise.

As the two of them shrugged sheepishly, he ordered them into the kitchen to clean up and stormed off in search of his chef.

Chapter 34

Gaspard wasn't in his room or the library or any of the rooms of the hotel at all. Fintan sighed. Oh God, he couldn't lose his temperamental chef. Not with the grand opening coming up and, now, with the eyes of the world on them. He couldn't get over what a stupid idea the Instagram post was and couldn't believe anyone had signed off on it.

He pulled on his hat and headed out into a wild, windy day, utterly despondent. All of Colton's dreams, all of everything he'd invested in this land he loved so much. He'd entrusted it to Fintan and he'd mooched around being depressed and ignoring the business, and now it was all going to be ruined because he'd just been too damn sad to do it properly.

Which made him feel even worse than he did before.

Outside, he was fully at the mercy of the elements, and the weather reflected his mood. There was absolutely no difference between sky and sea at all; everything was a tempest in gray and steely blue, the line in the horizon merely a suggestion. No ships were to be seen, just a simple single spiraling world of ferocious North Atlantic fury, the hills and the crags equally gray as the spray hitting them. Gulls and terns huddled together against the tempestuous fury. As Fintan walked over to the tiny pier, seals splashed around in the shallow water, barking like dogs and looking excited at the influx of new creatures and fish the storm would land them.

Fintan ignored them. Where would Gaspard be? Propping up a corner of the Harbour's Rest bar was entirely possible, if Inge-Britt was even awake.

Burying his hands in his arctic overcoat, Fintan headed slowly against the wind in the direction of the Endless Beach. Nobody would be crazy enough to go out on a day like this, surely. But then who could predict Gaspard's mood? Fintan decided to take the long way round, try to work out a little of his panic and bad temper, and hopefully by the time he reached the Harbour's Rest he would have calmed down sufficiently not to carry on yelling at everyone: he was so tired—so very, very, very tired—of being so angry, of being so sad, of being so lonely.

FINTAN MADE OUT the figure from afar; it was the only black shape on the white sand, the gray sky and sea, the heavy hail and rain, swirling around it—it was as filthy a day as could be imagined. He stepped forward a little, then a little more. The figure was trying to light a cigarette, an absurdly futile task on a day like this, or in fact on quite a lot of days on the Endless Beach. He was cowering behind a sandy dune, but it didn't seem to be doing much good. Fintan watched him. He was absolutely furious—it was clear, even from a distance—flicking angrily at his Zippo and kicking the sand in dismay.

He moved forward. As soon as Gaspard spotted him he started

screaming at him, first in French, then, as he grew closer, in English.

"What the hell have you done? What is this nonsense! You breeng me here, you breeng me to this place in the meedle of nowhere, and I cook for you and want to make things nice for you, and you make me look eediot, eediot in front of whole world. Thees is funny for you? Thees is a joke with all your friends, watch Gaspard, he fall over now, ees this funny? Ees it?"

"It's not at all funny!" shouted Fintan back, cross with himself. *"You think I wanted this shit to happen?"* He kicked furiously at the dancing sand around his shoes. *"You think I wanted any of this shit to happen? None of this! I didn't want any of this! I don't want any of this."*

Both of them at this time were panting from the exertion of shouting over the pouring rain and howling gale and crashing waves on the shore of the Endless Beach.

"I don't want any of this."

"Any of this?" echoed Gaspard suddenly, a taut, strained look on his face, his wiry body long and braced against the wind.

And the next second they were kissing fiercely, passionately, the turmoil of the storm's hysteria reflecting their own.

Chapter 35

Saif Hussein was hurriedly eating a sandwich in his office. It was a miserable day, and he'd promised to make house calls rather than risk his older patients catching pneumonia marching over the ben to his surgery. Nevertheless, he checked his Facebook, as usual. He was not a social media user. He did not post pictures or forward inspirational memes or like other people's pictures of their dogs. He was simply there in case.

It was ritualistic now, just going through the motions. He had his old Syrian mobile number, still paid up and available, connected to his dusty, ridiculous, old, outdated BlackBerry. It never rang. And he still had his Facebook account, with a picture of him and Amena on their wedding day as his profile pic and nothing else. He had absolutely no idea how to source the information as to how many times his profile had been viewed, which was lucky, as Lorna had clicked on and stared at that photo more times than she would ever have admitted to anyone under torture.

Today, there was something. From someone he did not know. In Arabic. That was nothing particularly unusual.

Of course it could be anything. A scam. Someone trying to rip him off, either personally or automatically: there were people who targeted clearly Arabic names in Western countries, making promises about finding relatives or tracking down bank accounts or moving money or all sorts of nefarious things. It could be any of those.

But there was something about this one, though.

Or it could be something else. The avatar of the sender was the little Saudi Arabian *Temsa7LY* puppet crocodile. Well, he was quite a famous crocodile. Anyone could have one of those.

But also: the favorite video of the boys when they were little. Their very favorite thing.

With shaking hands, Saif clicked on the message. His heart fell. Yup, just more spam, like it always was. **GET BEST PRICE!** it said. **EVERYTHING HEART DESIRE PAGE! FOR NOTHING! NIZ!!! 43!!!!!**

That was all. Saif looked at it. Just flotsam, floating through the internet, looking to snag the unwary—nothing out of order. The same as any other day.

But it felt different. It felt different.

Niz, he thought suddenly, rubbing his beard. That didn't mean "nothing." Not in any language. And why would you put "43" next to it?

Something stirred. He remembered the book of Qabbani poetry they had had in their little apartment in Damascus. Of course he did not have it now, but the internet could be a wonderful thing. He downloaded the first edition he could find, stumbled to the page he thought would be nearest to page 43 in the original text.

And, suddenly, there it was. One stanza, all alone:

لأن حبي لك أعلى من الكلمات ، فقد قررت الصمت.

Because my love for you is higher than words, I have decided
   to fall silent.

He started. And stared. For a long time.

He wrote a note asking if it was her and sent it.

Nothing.

The next day, he tried something else and sent a poem. Then a
code.

Still, he received no reply.

Finally, in absolute desperation, he wrote to her straight out,
begging and asking her when she could come and what she
would do.

The next time he opened his computer, with trembling fingers,
the account had gone, vanished forever, and it didn't matter how
many times he logged on, how long he lay awake torturing himself, wondering if perhaps it had indeed been a mistake—that he
had been replying to spam, to some bot; that it was all a coincidence and nothing more.

Chapter 36

The papers were still bad; their social media was still a mess and everyone was looking at them suspiciously. But to the kitchen's surprise, the following day the storm had broken, and Gaspard turned up in a ridiculously mellow mood that nobody understood in the slightest (although no one was complaining).

It was as if the previous day hadn't happened. The phone was still off the hook, but the fight had gone out of Gaspard completely, and there was music playing (back to terrible pop rock) once again in the kitchen. The clouds had abated, and the sun peeked through the back windows, as Bjårk happily bounced around the lawn.

Gaspard had decided to line everyone up and teach them how to make poached eggs, due to a surfeit in the coop.

"And *queek* and smash and in and whoop with the wrist!" Gaspard was hollering.

Isla had absolutely no trouble poaching an egg. Konstantin, on the other hand, was having a terrible time, as his big pan of water bubbled up and over. He hadn't, as it turned out, ever even cracked an egg in his life, something else—there seemed to be a lot of things—that completely horrified the people around him.

Well, in his world he was completely horrified that they'd never attended a state banquet, so there, but it wasn't the kind of thing he felt like bringing up.

Even as Gaspard called him a left-handed moron who couldn't kiss a pig, or rolled his eyes again at his ineptitude as he wasted yet another egg, there was a distinct and definite fact: since Konstantin had arrived, he'd actually learned quite a lot. Not just chopping and pot washing, although both of which were new skills. But he'd had to launder his own clothes, keep his room tidy, and look after Bjårk, who normally got taken out by the palace staff once or twice a day so Konstantin didn't have to do all the more tedious bits of dog ownership like picking up poo. Now everything was on him.

But Konstantin, for all his faults, was merry at heart; it was hard for him to be down for long periods of time without his natural buoyancy reasserting itself. Although the worst realization, which made him slightly coil up in agony, was that all the time he thought he was surrounded by friends and employees who thought he was simply charming, it became increasingly obvious that that, in fact, was not the case at all, and if people weren't actually being paid by his father, or enjoying the fruits of the family's largesse, then some people liked him and some, notably Isla, very much didn't and, what was almost worse, lots of people, the entire population of the island really, were almost entirely indifferent to him. Back home everyone knew who he was. Here everyone knew who everyone else was, but nobody gave two shits. It was something of a head-scratcher.

So. He still had absolutely no intention of letting anyone know his background, even if his first inclination had been to shout and scream about it and make a fuss till everyone let him get out of this hellhole. Now . . . he didn't mind it so much. And he was quite excited about learning how to poach an egg.

More than that: Isla taught him—or at least let him watch—how to make pastry, keeping her hands cool and precise as she baked amazing spiced mince pies, orange cinnamon Christmas buns, and warm gingerbread, and they replicated their menu day after day just to be sure, before sending many of the results down to be sold at the Seaside Kitchen and the rest to the school and the old people's community center, where they were fallen upon with gusto (and some complaining about modern newfangled ingredients from people who thought putting anything other than salt on porridge was a spoiled affectation).

He learned how to make a proper sauce, watched in awe as Gaspard made liters and liters of stock from bones for the freezer; Isla even let him ice a cake one day, which he made a fantastic hash of. Bjårk was happy getting lengthy walks along the bracing front of the incredibly long beach, which Konstantin had found completely by accident, and it was really hard not to start saying hello to the same people and dogs he saw every day. He could see, somehow, how this place could get under your skin. I mean, it wasn't Norway, but it was beautiful in its own way.

To EVERYONE'S SURPRISE, their supposed boss, Fintan, put his head round the kitchen door. Everyone braced themselves, but in fact, he was almost smiling.

"*Come, come,*" Gaspard was saying.

"What have you done to Colton's kitchen?" said Fintan in dismay. "It looks like a chicken holocaust."

"We are making the *perfect* poached egg," said Gaspard. "You will practice too! It needs practice! And a wrist! And vinegar! Proper vinegar! Not vinegar of Scotland. Vinegar of Scotland is for removing of the wallpaper! Here!"

He brought out an elegant glass bottle marked VINAIGRE, picked up a fine muslin, and grabbed an egg.

"Okay, begin!" he said.

"What, me?" said Fintan.

"*Pourquoi pas?* Kerry, make space."

The woman obediently did so, and Fintan, unsure how to get out of it, washed his hands and stood in line.

"Crack the egg! Now, put it in the muslin cloth!"

Fintan cracked an egg and made a horrid mess of it all over the bowl. Gaspard sighed heavily. Everyone else in the kitchen came over to watch, as the deep pan on the stove bubbled.

"You are almost as bad as Konstantin."

"Nobody is as bad as Konstantin," said Konstantin.

Gaspard handed over another egg; Isla retrieved an apron to protect Fintan's lovely cashmere jumper.

This time he managed to crack the whole thing without getting it full of shell; he then strained it through the muslin and popped it into a ramekin.

"Okay, what now?"

"Stir the pot!" said Gaspard excitedly, handing him the big wooden spoon. Fintan looked suspiciously at everyone watching him, wondering if this was a joke.

"Faster!" said Konstantin, watching him as it went.

"Oh yes, you're the expert." Isla laughed and he laughed back.

Fintan stirred.

"Faster! Make a vortex! Make a hole in the water," said Gaspard, finally, in frustration, grabbing Fintan's arm and making the water whizz round the deep pan.

Fintan breathed deeply and wondered if anybody noticed. Last night had been so strange, such a shock.

He had expected to be full of guilt at sleeping with another man, full of remorse. But it was the oddest thing. Instead he'd felt better. Just . . . alive. He told Gaspard he hadn't known he was gay, and Gaspard had snorted and said, "How ees these people make a choice *comme ça,* huh? I never understand. Boy, girl, *pfuh*—I like, I like, you see?"

And Fintan did see and tried to say "pfuh" with the same amount of emphasis, which didn't come out quite right and had started them laughing, and yes, it was quite something to be having sex again.

But it was *really* something to be laughing again.

BACK IN THE kitchen, the feel of a pair of strong tattooed arms around him was like an electric shock once more, another physical defibrillation to a system that had all but shut down. He froze, deliciously, could barely move his hand at all, even as Gaspard clasped his arm, moved it round and round until there was indeed a hole, or vortex, in the water.

Gaspard appeared happily oblivious to the tumult he was causing in Fintan—or at least cheerfully unconcerned, lifting up one hand to drop a tiny tear of vinegar into the pan and the smallest hint of salt. Then, as Fintan started to stir furiously, he gently plopped the egg in and they all watched, fascinated, as the white knitted itself strongly around the yolk.

"That is not fair," said Konstantin, whose first six attempts had gone horribly wispy with bits of unpleasantly snotty white albumen everywhere. "Gaspard is helping him too much."

"Yes, but he's not professionally working in the kitchen," pointed out Isla.

"Neither am . . . Oh yeah," said Konstantin, briefly forgetting himself.

Gaspard made Fintan repeat the process, Isla quick-wittedly stuck in some of the good sourdough bread to toast, and within five minutes, Fintan was sitting, somewhat surprised, in front of a huge plate of poached eggs on sourdough, accompanied by an enormous mug of tea.

It was the best meal he'd had in months. He realized yet again how often he forgot to eat. He was starving, ravenous. Gaspard watched him eat with a look so direct it was astonishing to Fintan that everyone else didn't catch on instantly.

"I don't know what I'd do without you," he said to Gaspard.

"Good," snapped Gaspard with a smile. "I should like a raise."

Behind the two of them, Kerry noisily dropped a ton of china into Konstantin's sink, and the day went on.

Chapter 37

Yes, yes, he'd gone off his usual standards since Douglas was born. He got that. Why wouldn't a beautiful, delightful baby be more interesting than his actual job? Joel was feeling guilty in front of the computer, trying to catch up as Douglas napped in his crib in the corner of the room.

And now he was staring at his computer in consternation. How could this be so *damn hard*?! It was a few Christmas lights. But he couldn't find a damn thing anywhere.

Every year from time immemorial, the town council had voted that money that would otherwise be spent on Christmas lights would be diverted to provide a lighted path for the children down from school, which was at the very top of the hill, the old redbrick building a happy sight, normally overrun with boys and girls even after the school day was over; the gates were never locked, and in the light summer evenings there would be a game of football or hopscotch, and anyone who wanted to could join in, pretty much.

From the back of the school there was the cobbled road downward. There were few cars on the island, and they mostly knew to go painfully slowly, not just for the children but for the occasional sheep or cow who wandered into the road at will.

But in front of the school was a grassy hill with a winding path, and this was always a much more attractive prospect. You could roll, tumble, or simply tear down the gradient, or if you had a scooter, you could attempt to steer it round the worst of the mud on the path. It was a universal option, and for years the council had lit it up—it was private land, but almost nobody could remember who on earth it belonged to; it was certainly too steep to build on—so that when it got dark at 3:00 or 3:30, there was still a way to get down, although it guaranteed you would be covered in mud and anything covering your knees would probably have a hole in it. The rule about wearing shorts to school (for the boys) had once been abolished some time before, but the mothers of the town, weary from darning the knees of trousers ruined on the wee brae, had revolted and insisted it be brought back for boys and girls. So now the only casualties were a few skinned knees, and the people of Mure were very much of the unfashionable opinion that you couldn't be a kid without a few skinned knees.

Colton, however, was from California, where you'd sue someone for letting a kid skin their knee, and he found the entire thing incomprehensible. He'd also grown up in Texas, where people started putting lights on their roofs and huge inflatable Santas on their lawns and vast displays in every single window straight after Thanksgiving, and felt it was a basic human right to have a bit of the same in Scotland, particularly when it was so goddamn dark all the time.

So he'd left a provision in his will for a set of lights to be lit up at Christmas—and Joel had overlooked it completely. Joel had known only miserable Christmases in and out of foster homes as a child. Decorating and doing something up would simply never have occurred to him.

Flora, on the other hand, adored Christmas: had her cake all ready, had the gifts ordered—or she normally did. Even with her being busy up at the Rock, they still had the tree up, hung with carefully wrapped ornaments from years gone by, every year supplemented with something new—this year, from Mark and Marsha, a large "D" for Douglas, beautifully carved out of a dark hard wood, covered in leaves that reflected the firelight and gleamed. Dougie put out a pudgy little hand and tried to stick it in his mouth and nearly brought the entire tree down, but it had been saved, and its dark green fragrance lit up the entire room. Underneath it parcels had started to appear, which were being feverishly policed by Agot, who had to be regularly warned off them, as well as to stop pressing the buttons that made the lights on the tree flicker on and off as she was giving everyone a migraine.

But there it was in black and white: a large, very generous budget to decorate the town. What did he mean by "decorate"? How did that even work? Would it need planning? Would it have to pass the council? This was, frankly, a ballache he could absolutely do without. He was a lawyer, not a bitching . . . well, whatever this job was.

He sighed and picked up the phone. Perhaps if he called Malcy, who ran the local council, he would list a stream of objections and there wouldn't be a meeting before Christmas and it absolutely couldn't be done in time, and Joel would have to mentally apologize to Colton but it would have to be done next year.

Unfortunately Malcy was on the golf course, teeing off with some equally fat-bottomed friend, and passed the call on to his deputy, Mrs. McGlone, who never got anything fun to do and thought Joel was incredibly handsome.

"Oh, that's *marvelous!*" came the tremulous voice on the other end of the telephone. "We always loved Colton."

This was a big fat lie. They'd tried to block his hotel about four times and dumped a wind farm in the full sight line of his house just because they found him American and annoying. Who Mrs. McGlone *did* like was Joel.

"Well, I'm guessing it's too late for planning," said Joel reluctantly.

"Oh no, there's retroactive planning for the lights! We just diverted the money instead, but it's all totally allowed. Oh, this is so wonderful! When are they going up?" Mrs. McGlone cleared her throat. "Will you be needing . . . someone important to turn them on?"

"Oh God, I suppose I'd better book someone," said Joel.

"Oh," came the voice. "I see."

"Or perhaps . . . I don't know . . . maybe you could do it?"

"Oh, do you really think so?" came the voice in full gush again. "Well, I must say it would be an absolute honor! Let me clear my diary! This is wonderful."

And she hung up, leaving Joel staring at the computer, fervently pissed off. This was all he needed.

Fortunately for Joel, every company in the world, it seemed, that did lights on the mainland was already booked up and booked out. Except, unfortunately, Mrs. McGlone had rushed straight to the Seaside Kitchen, and the island's equivalent of Instagram had now announced to absolutely everybody that they were going to get proper Christmas lights! On the promenade! In memory of Colton, and *she* was going to do the switching on, wasn't that wonderful? "I know, I can't believe they asked me, you'd think they'd want a celebrity!!"

Then she would give a little pause so the person would say, "Oh, you are basically a celebrity," which, to give her credit, most of the time they kindly did, and very soon Joel couldn't leave the house without Jonny from the fiddle band coming up and offering to play for him, or one of the kids from the school running up wide-eyed and saying, "When are the lights coming? Are the lights coming today? *Is it today?*"

THE NEXT DAY Joel headed up to the Rock with Flora to grab some paperwork, dodging the Murians who came their way to express gratitude and thanks for something that hadn't even happened yet.

Flora had contrived to find herself there as usual—this was not surprising, but seeing Fintan there too was—and she beamed with delight when she saw him. "Come eat!" she said, smiling. "There is some good stuff going on here. We're going to show all those bastards."

Indeed there was. Instead of the usual shouting and screaming, there was an atmosphere of quiet reverence.

"What's going on?" whispered Joel.

"Disgusting things," snapped Gaspard, who was unwrapping something white from a pot with the steamer on.

"It's lutefisk," whispered Isla. "He likes it."

Konstantin was standing there shrugging. "What? It was just a suggestion."

"Ten days! The fish has been there for *ten days*," said Gaspard crossly.

"I didn't make you make it!"

"You said, 'Gaspard, you couldn't make lutefisk,'" growled Gaspard.

"Exactly!" said Konstantin, frustrated. "So, that is the end of it."

"That is the *challenge!*" said Gaspard.

"French people," said Konstantin crossly.

"*Exactement,*" said Gaspard. "French people will not eat fish that is *ten hours old*. Thees ees *ten days old*."

Joel stared at it.

"This is going to be disgusting," said Flora. "It was just we had some spare."

"Oh, it's nice," said Joel, completely surprising her.

"What?"

"Oh, I was out in the Midwest for a while. They eat it there."

"Yes!" said Gaspard. "They eat fish in America when they are thousands of kilometers from any sea. Here, we have the problem. Norwegians and *Americans*."

They all looked at it. With a furious snort, Gaspard covered the white inflated fishlike substance in a thick layer of salt, twisted it in paper, and threw it in the steamer.

"Thees ees a *bad experiment*," he said grumpily.

Konstantin, on the other hand, was rather excitedly going through drawers and cupboards.

"What are you doing?" asked Isla suspiciously. She was always trying to get him to make less mess, not more.

"We need bacon and peas," said Konstantin. "And look! I have boiled the potatoes."

Isla blinked and looked into a pot. He had boiled potatoes—not new potatoes, just ordinary potatoes—with their skins on. There were bits of dirt floating in the water.

"I'm not sure I've ever met anyone as useless as you," she said, shaking her head.

Konstantin was crushed. He'd felt he was doing well. She caught his expression.

"Oh, don't worry, it's solvable. Quick, set the big pot on, there are some local potatoes somewhere and they boil fast. And there are some fresh lardons in the larder."

Konstantin jumped to what she was saying, and Flora gave Joel a look, as if to say, *Look how much better we're all doing*, and found it slightly amusing how excited Joel was suddenly looking about lunch.

Twenty-five minutes later and, amazingly, there were mashed peas, fresh tiny boiled new potatoes covered in butter and salt, some little bits of crisped-up bacon, and some sour cream on the side of the old washed table, as Gaspard crossly slung down the pan of lutefisk without even putting it on a plate.

"Okay," he said. "I am finished with thees experiment. I am going to look for snails. Fintan, you come weeth me."

The others laughed and beckoned him back and made him sit down, as Konstantin divided the fish and Joel smiled cheerfully as the familiar salty scent reached his nostrils.

"This was about the only happy Christmas I ever had," he said quietly to Flora. "In Minnesota. I had to go out of state; they couldn't manage to keep us all on. It wasn't for long. They were good people."

Flora laid a hand on his arm. "I think that's the only nice memory I've ever heard you mention from your childhood."

"Meanwhile Douglas already has a model railway set."

Flora smiled. "It's okay, isn't it?"

Joel tucked in. "Oh, it's better than that."

Against all odds—and Gaspard refused to touch it, like a grumpy toddler—the lutefisk was a great hit, and Flora immediately made a mental note to put it on the menu. It was complicated to make, but not difficult, and the ingredients were cheap and local and authentic.

"But eet betrays all my culinary principles," said Gaspard.

"I thought rules were made to be broken," said Konstantin slyly.

"*Oui,* yes, *your* rules! Not my rules!!"

Over lunch, Joel found himself explaining the lights situation to the newcomers who couldn't help, but it felt good to talk to them regardless.

Konstantin thought about it. "Oh well, of course you could find someone."

"There are no lights to be had in the whole of Scottish mainland," said Joel crossly. "Or London either. They only keep enough for themselves. I cannot even begin to tell you how inefficient it was for Colton's trust to pay me to ring up all these people."

Konstantin shrugged. "Oh well, in Norway—"

"Oh yes, in *Norway,* in *Norway* you eat things that are rotting and you screw reindeer," said Gaspard, who had at least managed to drink the eau-de-vie Konstantin had found in the dusty back of the bar and insisted lutefisk could not be enjoyed without a tiny shot of.

"Well, anyway, there are always a lot of lights up north because, you know, twenty-four-hour darkness. They keep a lot of spares. We're nearer there than London."

"But I don't speak any . . . Oh." Joel took off his glasses. "Seriously, you'd help?"

Nobody had ever asked Konstantin for his help before. It was a strange situation. Konstantin considered it. "Would it get me out of scrubbing lutefisk off the metal tins?"

"*Non,*" said Gaspard.

But Konstantin offered to help anyway, something of a new sensation, but a pleasing one.

OF COURSE HE'D theoretically done good things. Normally, it had been Konstantin's job to turn up and stand at his father's side for anything important and ceremonial. He had absolutely hated it; it had been the most boring thing ever. Endless speeches and people thanking people for other things and congratulating them and wah wah wah, it just went on and on. Normally standing outside in the freezing cold.

Now, as he made the calls to his homeland, he realized why people got thanked for doing this kind of thing for absolutely no money.

Because it was, frankly, a total pain in the arse. Still better than scrubbing—lutefisk, it turned out, was an absolute bastard to get off a pan—but still a massive time suck nonetheless, particularly when trying to get manpower and goods to a remote island nobody had heard of or could pronounce or spell.

Again and again he tried different companies and got the same results. Too late, already booked. On the hotel computer he did, just once, quickly google himself in Norwegian. A picture came up of him looking absurdly drunk with two models draped over him and a gossipy headline in *Se og Hør* saying "No Sightings of the Playboy Prince . . . Is He in Rehab?" and he winced and turned round quickly in case anyone at the hotel had seen it. Thank God they didn't read the Norwegian papers. He had been briefly outraged, wanted to say of course he wasn't in rehab—but the real story, of course, was worse, and oh my goodness, the last thing he needed was everyone to know he'd actually been banished. He'd shut the web page and decided to block everything out from the outside world. It was actually rather easier to do that on Mure than he'd realized.

Finally, at last, he found an old artist who said he could maybe do it. He lived in the north and worked with light and was willing to come in—at great expense, but Konstantin never noticed expense, and fortunately Joel's budget was generous—and "see if the space worked for him."

Konstantin had asked if the space often worked for him and didn't receive much of an answer, but it was the best he could do. The artist insisted on flying in for a morning and out again, by which time apparently his artistic sensibilities would have taken in all they needed to know.

"I need to charm him," Konstantin announced to the kitchen. "He needs to want to make one of his creations here."

"I thought it was just hanging lights on a lamppost," said Isla.

"Me too," said Konstantin.

Konstantin was much more crestfallen than he would admit. He was used to impressing people fairly easily, something about himself that had somewhat evaporated in the last month. Still, either the artist wouldn't care or he'd tell the papers, neither of which was ideal.

"I don't know how to impress him. And he's only here for breakfast."

"You could make croissants," said Isla. She meant it as a joke, but Gaspard came skidding across the kitchen like he was on roller skates.

"You make croissant?" he said, his lip curling.

Isla couldn't help it, by habit she trembled slightly under his gaze. "Uhm . . . Flora showed me once."

"You do it?"

"Well, I—"

"*Aha!* I knew it. Do not lie of croissants!" He turned to stalk away.

"I am not lying of . . . about croissants."

The only reply was a contemptuous sniff.

"Okay then! We'll do it!" said Isla, surprised at herself.

"You cannot pronounce the word, how you do it?"

Isla couldn't believe where she found the courage. "You'll see," she said.

"I will see," said Gaspard, but there was hope as well as disdain in his voice. "Pot boy, he help you."

"I'm sure I can do it by myself."

"No. You watch and learn." He pointed at Konstantin. "Or if ees rubbish, you can forget."

Which was how they found themselves, the night before the artist, Gunnar, arrived, up at four o'clock in the bloody morning—Isla resigned, Konstantin astounded—Isla having to come in the freezing dark to the warm, still kitchen in the middle of the night.

Gaspard had refused to let her use Flora's recipe and left his own instead. She didn't really remember much of Flora's methods anyway. Spread chilled butter. Then roll it into the dough she'd started the night before. Then fold over the dough. Then chill. Then do it again. And again.

"This is ridiculous," she said, looking at the enormous mound of butter. "How does anyone ever have the patience to do this? I forgot it was such a pain."

"No, is croissant," said Konstantin, trying to figure out the coffee machine and hoping if he did it badly enough that Isla would just take over and do it for him. She didn't get his joke either. He straightened up. "Don't people make croissants every day?"

"Yes," said Isla. "Insane people."

Outside an owl hooted. It was so late and dark and odd to be in the kitchen, they both half smiled, Isla immediately stopping herself in case it looked like she was smiling at him on purpose.

They parceled out the dough between them and tried to smear the cold butter over.

"If anything gets warm it is . . . '*poubelle,*'" said Isla, reading carefully off the instructions. "What does that mean?"

"It means you put it in the bin," said Konstantin without thinking.

Isla glanced at him. "You speak French?"

Konstantin shrugged, annoyed he had given himself away. "Ah, hardly any."

He certainly didn't mention he also spoke Swedish and German.

"I mean, why are you working here?" said Isla. "You obviously hate it."

"Well, seeing as you know everything about me, I don't think I have to answer that question," he said as they each carried on with the butter, then put the layer to chill for twenty minutes in the fridge. A silence descended.

Isla got up and made coffee. Konstantin was delighted.

"So, tell me what's great about Mure then," said Konstantin, sipping the coffee, which was in fact excellent, surprisingly enough.

"You really want to know?"

"No, but I've got to wait twenty minutes and I don't have any credit on my phone."

Isla sniffed. "Well, you obviously just haven't been paying attention."

"I have," said Konstantin. "But the wind keeps blowing my hat over my eyes."

Isla almost smiled. "Well. It's got the most beautiful views everywhere you go. It's just a wee island, but when you stand on the ben, it feels huge. You feel like you're nowhere near anybody, but if you want company, then everyone is pleased to see you, or at least will be happy to have a chat. You're safe wherever you go. Nothing bad is going to happen to you as long as you don't fall in the harbor."

"Does that happen often?"

"When I was wee," said Isla, smiling despite herself, "I heard that someone had fallen off the gangway to the ferry and the selkies took them, and I was *so terrified*."

"Did you know them?"

She shook her head. "It was always someone's friend's cousin who was visiting from the mainland. Then my mum said she'd been told that when she was small, and her mother too back when it was the old boats. I think it's just something they tell children to keep them away from the water."

Konstantin smiled. "What's a selkie? A drowned person?"

"Not quite. A seal person would take you to play with you. And sometimes they send a seal back in your place who would be good-looking but weird."

"We have something like that too! The King of Ekeberg. He hated his own children, so he would swap his for yours. So if you woke up and your child was different . . ."

"That's strange," said Isla. "That there's different stories about changeling children."

Konstantin shook his head. "I don't think so. Most cultures have them. I think it's how they explained autistic children before science."

Isla hadn't thought of that before. "Goodness," she said, thinking of the legends of the children, so beautiful but so strange behind their seal eyes. "That's so sad."

"Well, it comes on at about that age . . ." He stopped himself. "It's not always sad, though, is it? Just different."

Isla thought of Flora's train-obsessed big brother Hamish, who had never been able to leave home or really be trusted walking down to the shops by himself, but was adored by everyone.

"I suppose you're right," said Isla. "They must have been so frightened, though."

"Oh, I think people are very frightened now," said Konstantin. "They think it's an evil doctor with an injection."

"They do," said Isla, pondering. "Gosh."

The ding on the timer slightly startled them both, speaking about changeling children under a dark and freezing moon.

Together they jumped up and rebuttered and folded their dough companionably, chopped it up into twelve crescents each, then popped the trays in the hot oven and refilled the coffee machine.

"This can't be good for you," complained Konstantin. "This is a heart attack amount of butter. Why aren't the French all dead?"

"Because it's good butter," said Isla soothingly. "That's the other great thing about Mure. Everything we make here is pure and local. There's a cow, there's some rain—"

"Quite a lot of rain," added Konstantin.

"And some grass, and salt from the salt pans, and there you are."

"Okay," said Konstantin, breathing in the warming scented air. "If that tastes as good as it smells, you'll absolutely have convinced me."

This time he brought Isla a coffee, and they sat together, and he let her tell him all about the myths of the land—the princess who stepped onto the iceberg to escape the Vikings, the witches who ran ships aground—and he told her about the trolls of the great dark forests and the elves who came to give strange gifts in his northern homeland. And then finally the croissants rose up, warm and steaming and light as a feather and absolute miracles, and they added, to their giggling shame, even *more* butter, and ate one, which was too hot, and then another, frankly, because they couldn't help themselves, they were so airy, crunchy on the outside and yielding and miraculously light underneath, the most ambrosial things Isla thought she'd ever tasted, and the smell even drew Gaspard down from upstairs, who entered the kitchen with his eyes closed, saying, "*Vraiment?* It cannot be true. I am in Lyon, no?" which was as high a compliment as he could possibly give, and then they had to hide them to keep them for the artist, and Gaspard suggested they both get up and make croissants at four A.M. every day, and of course they chorused, "Noooooo," but they were both a little disappointed nonetheless that he didn't insist.

IT WAS FAIRLY obvious who the artist was as he stepped off the tiny plane into a howling snowstorm. He was wearing pink-and-purple trousers, for starters, and very in-your-face glasses. He scowled, even as they led him to a cozy corner of the lounge and plied him with coffee and croissants, which he declined.

"I need to see," he said, just as they were hoping the warm setting and lovely food would be enough to convince him. "Show me! Let me walk."

Konstantin put the croissants back in the kitchen with stern instructions to people not to eat them, whereupon Gaspard picked up one in each hand and defiantly took a bite out of both. Konstantin rolled his eyes and walked out with the artist, who spoke little English.

They stomped off down the road together. Gunnar didn't ask Konstantin anything about himself, which was something of a relief, but instead pointed out various things Konstantin hadn't noticed at all before: the contrasting colors of the little buildings along the harbor, the way the sun moved across the water, the speed of the shadows. He obviously saw the world in a different way from most; he took his time, ambled, glanced around at everything. Finally they made it to the little hill outside the school and he stood and hummed.

"No," he said finally. "My work has drama. Scope. This is too limited. People will not like it. This place, you know. It is *cozy.*"

He said this as if it were the biggest insult he could think of.

"Well, it's nice," said Konstantin, feeling suddenly defensive about the island.

"Exactly. *Nice*," Gunnar growled, pushing up his trendy spectacles.

Konstantin's heart sank. He'd been sure if he could get him here the deal would be done. And he'd promised Joel, who rather impressed him—he thought Joel was quite a grown-up person. And the kitchen. And now he'd just look like a stupid idiot who couldn't handle anything. He sighed. "Well, you could make it amazing."

The artist shrugged. "Why?"

"*Excuse me*," came a small voice on its way to school. Agot came deliberately early to find the best iced puddle, and these two were right in the way.

"*This is my puddle.*"

Konstantin eyed the child, who eyed him straight back. He had the uncomfortable feeling she had the measure of him.

"I think it's everyone's puddle," he said.

"No," said Agot. She took off her little fur-lined boots and proceeded to scoot across the thin ice in her socks.

"You can't skate in your socks."

"*You* can't."

She proceeded to hum *Boléro* very loudly to drown them out, doing her best to pirouette around the ice, with varied results.

"You have wet socks," said the artist in thickly accented English.

"Your glasses are stupid," said Agot without pausing.

"Sorry, she's a very rude island girl," said Konstantin in Norwegian. Agot fixed him with such a look then that he was almost sure she'd understood him.

Gunnar ignored him. "What would you build," he asked Agot, "if you were making something for Christmas?"

Agot looked at him like he was an idiot. "An ice rink."

"I do not do ice rinks."

Agot sniffed as if to say, *So much for you then.*

The artist smiled. Then he stood back. He looked at the little girl, then up at the top of the hill and back down.

Agot's friends (and/or terrified acolytes) had come running up behind her, and the artist walked left and right, looking at them and the hill and back again. Agot put her soggy feet back in her boots and marched off without giving either of them a backward glance.

"I suppose they're pretty tough up here," said the artist, almost to himself.

They watched the little crowd weave its way to school, kicking, shouting, laughing, throwing snowballs, tumbling down, scrambling back up again. Parents didn't need to walk their children to school on Mure, although some did of course. It was safe and close by for almost everybody. They made a merry sight in their red sweatshirts and hats.

"Hmm," said the artist. "Okay. Okay. I can do it."

Konstantin felt himself break into a huge grin. "Really?"

"Yes. For the children. Yes."

Gunnar took out his phone and started taking lots of pictures of the site from all different angles. Konstantin could have skipped.

"Would you like a croissant before you go catch your plane?"

"Christ, no."

Chapter 38

So, just to get this straight," said Joel, who felt a headache coming on. "You don't actually know what's turning up?"

They were down at the docks, two weeks later, to pick up the light installation. Gunnar had worked quickly but hadn't answered any of Konstantin's emails about what he was actually doing or how big it would be. They needed a power source on the hill, that's all he knew. Joel was trying to pacify Mrs. McGlone, who was getting slightly worried about what Malcy would say.

"He's an artist," said Konstantin, in the hopes that this would prove enough. Innes was standing by with his truck, as was Ed the policeman, and they watched the ferry dock in some nervous anticipation.

It hadn't occurred to any of them that he couldn't possibly have such a group of people together loitering on the wharf on a workday without arousing frantic amounts of chitchat and suspicion, and indeed, a lot of people gathered in the Seaside Kitchen to keep an eye on them.

"Who is that new chap anyway?" said Mrs. Brodie suspiciously. "I'm just saying. He's a bit of a ride and no mistake."

"Elspeth!" said Flora reprovingly. She glanced out the window. Nobody, she thought, was ever handsomer than Joel, ever. His curly hair, his horn-rimmed spectacles, his long, muscular body . . . She sighed happily. But yes, sure, the blond stranger was cool too, if you liked that lanky Scandi look.

"He's a ride," said Mrs. Brodie again, and the Fair Isle knitting group looked up to see whom she was talking about, then vehemently nodded as one before going back to their intricately patterned wool.

"He hasn't been in here?" said Flora, confused. Most people popped in sooner or later. It wasn't as if Mure was falling over itself with different places to go.

"He's a pot boy," said Mrs. Brodie. "He must be skint."

"Working his way round the world maybe? Student?"

"That's an expensive coat he's got on. And shoes."

"Doesn't stop people wanting to work."

"Well, maybe scouring out all those pots will give him some proper muscles," said Mrs. Brodie, all but licking her lips.

"Mrs. Brodie! That's quite enough."

Lorna came in for a coffee.

"We're talking about who's a ride," said Mrs. Brodie, and Lorna looked at her without quite taking it in. Flora pulled her aside.

"Are you okay?"

"He's been called in," said Lorna in a low voice. They both knew what that meant. "Home Office."

"Oh shit. What now?" said Flora, genuinely worried. Not just for Lorna, her best friend, or Saif, whom she liked very much. But she was slightly scared that he would leave the island and they'd be without the best doctor they'd ever had. It was a helicopter ride to get to the hospital; she was much happier with a baby and her father getting ever older knowing she had Saif to call on.

Lorna shrugged. "They won't ever tell you. He has to go in."

"Are you talking?"

She nodded. "Yes. But he doesn't know any more than me. But he's terrified."

Flora patted her shoulder. "Are you?"

"Yes."

FLORA BUNDLED UP the largest piece of gingerbread she could find, added an extra shot to Lorna's coffee, and sent her on her way. Meanwhile the rest of the Seaside Kitchen patrons were trying desperately to pretend they weren't still spying on what the men were doing.

"Maybe they're landing a new car!" said one. "Maybe it's a Christmas present for someone!"

"Who for?"

"Maybe it's you, Flora. That rich lawyer of yours."

Flora snorted. They absolutely did not feel rich. Joel had given up all of his lucrative practice to work for Colton's charities and was paid to reflect that, and there had been no money to spare for maternity leave.

"It's the lights," she said, and everyone nodded happily.

"Already?" said Mrs. Brodie. "That's efficient."

"The children are going to love it," said Mrs. MacPherson.

"And I'm going to love watching the men put them up," said the inexhaustible Mrs. Brodie. "Oh, and that reminds me! Pay up for the Loony Dook!"

There was a lot of good-natured grumbling at that. The Loony Dook happened every Boxing Day. Two pounds to charity, then you had to run in the sea in your swimming trunks. It had become bizarrely popular, even though everyone dreaded it and there were numerous rumors of pneumonia. The Loony Dook was a tradition, and that was that.

IT WAS BOX after box, all enormous. Everyone looked at each other anxiously. There was at least a collection of typed A4 instructions as to how to put it together. Unfortunately they were all in Norwegian.

"Uhm," said Konstantin. "Okay."

"Can you put this stuff together?" said Innes.

"I can read the instructions," said Konstantin. He looked really worried. "Oh God. I'm sorry. I might have completely messed up."

He stared at his shoes and looked very young all of a sudden.

Innes shrugged. "Ach, you read 'em out, we'll build it," said Innes. "I'll text Hamish."

Konstantin's face snapped up, amazed. "Really?"

"Have you never built anything?" said Innes.

Konstantin had had more than enough of "have you never" questions, so he got stuck into helping the others lift the incredibly heavy cases into the truck—the last few all hung over the back— and they headed up to the Rock, waving merrily at the ladies of the Seaside Kitchen as they passed by.

The men all met again after work, at nine when much of Mure was already asleep. They had decided to keep it a surprise, because, indeed, what was in the boxes was a genuine surprise to them, and it was becoming quite a major operation.

Charlie was joining them too, and Hamish, who was getting very excited about the welding equipment.

They started setting up in one of the Rock's old garages, which was fully equipped with brand-new tools that had mostly never been used. Konstantin read out instructions and watched in some awe as the practical men of Mure started welding and bolting everything together, except for Joel, who was practically useless—his eyesight was horrendous—but good at holding things still.

They had to throw open the big doors of the garage as the object started to take shape. It grew bigger and bigger, but everyone was getting so excited they barely cared, even as the cold wind blew straight in off the sea. Everyone had gloves and hats on and was toiling away with stiff old-fashioned metal bolts and tiny Allen keys. It was like a vast Lego kit, and they were secretly all having a brilliant time, even as they complained about the crappy freezing weather and the bloody buggering metal bolts.

Finally, just before midnight, the team stood back. It was done. The lights from the garage didn't show much. It was completely blocked out by the towering edifice.

"Bloody hell," said Innes, whistling through his teeth.

"Is this really going to work?" said practical Charlie.

"It certainly cost enough," said Joel, studying the diagrams in the instructions with some care.

"*C'est énorme!*" said Gaspard, coming out to have a cigarette. It was indeed, and was going to have to be held in a dug-down hole and secured with concrete, yet another thing that was news to Konstantin.

But through all the hard work he had translated, explained, made tea, even learned how to use a spanner and a wrench. The others laughed at his uselessness, but to Konstantin, learning something else new—something useful and practical—was miraculous, even if Hamish had to do everything again after he'd finished, just in case something fell off and killed someone.

Gunnar's work was four meters tall—about thirteen feet—and when they stood back, they gasped.

What they had was a huge, beautiful, smooth-faced contemporary angel, designed in a gorgeous shiny steel. When you turned the central crank, a vast pair of wings, too wide for the garage, came out and spread for what seemed like miles. They hadn't even plugged it in yet. It was, Konstantin couldn't help thinking with a smile, going to blow everyone's tiny minds.

"I'm not sure these are the fairy lights people were expecting," said Charlie.

"Good," said Joel, who thought it was rather fine.

"Shall we give it a shot then?" said Konstantin, pink-faced with excitement.

Joel carefully moved toward the plug socket and put in the European pin adapter. "Okay!" he said, and pressed down.

Every light went out for four square miles.

Chapter 39

Meanwhile, back on the south side of the island, where the lights were still on, in the old rectory, Saif Hussein was staring at his computer and wondering how on earth he had ever believed that he had come to Mure for a quiet life.

There was no doubt that his children were thriving here, even though that sometimes made him a little sad, that they could be Scottish now, British if they wanted, but their Syrian culture was falling away, day by day, however much he tried to interest them in their own background and keep up their Arabic. Frankly, he was working too hard and was often too tired to remember; he spoke to them in English more often than not.

And Lorna. He hadn't expected to fall in love. The idea of it was so far beyond his concept of what life would be like. Just surviving had been the priority for so long: making it into Europe, claiming asylum, resitting for his exams, being sent to the end of the world. Then when the boys came home, dealing with that: trying to heal their trauma, even as it meant that their memories of their homeland were dropping behind them like a scene glanced from a passing train.

And now he was staring at something on his computer, shaking, trembling. Because everything was about to get a lot worse.

By the following afternoon, he was in Glasgow, back at the same horrible, horrible Home Office police building he'd been to the last time, when they thought they had found his wife, and it had turned out to be somebody else.

He had told Lorna he'd been summoned but that he didn't know why, and she had longed more than anything to go with him, although they both knew that that was impossible. So he had gotten on the plane, and she had gone to school, as always.

ONE OF THE good things about being a primary school teacher, Lorna had always thought, and was more grateful than ever for today, was that it left simply no time or mental space for pondering or mulling over things. Children didn't care what was going on in your private life. Children had absolutely no idea that you actually had a private life in fact. Even though they lived in a small community, the little ones still gawked when they saw her out and about at the post office or the grocery store, as if she lived in the school stationery cupboard.

No matter how upset or worried you were, you had to come in, smile, and you would instantly be distracted by Hamish McGill's underpants mysteriously appearing on the outside of his trousers after PE, or Robbie's poster paint incident, or getting everyone to put their hands on their heads, or correcting math while simultaneously preventing a muddy scuffle over the toy elephant, so big you could ride it, that Fintan and Colton had kindly donated the Christmas before last, which unfortunately was so much better than all their other handed-down toys and games that it caused World War III at least twice a week.

So she threw herself into school life as usual, trying not to think about what was going on in Glasgow, two hundred miles to the south.

Except of course Ash was in her class, and every so often she'd look up and he'd be eyeing her anxiously. He sidled up after break.

"My daddy is away."

"I know," she said.

She was concerned, always, about giving Saif's boys special treatment. The problem was, what if, as in Ash's case, they patently needed special treatment? And it was wrong not to give him a bit of extra fuss, even if she was absolutely terrified of giving herself away or stepping out of line. Why, why, why was it all so complicated?

"But he's coming back soon?"

Ash nodded. "Soon," he said. "I don't like it when he's away."

"I know," said Lorna. "But you like Mrs. Laird, don't you?"

"I like sausage rolls," said Ash. Mrs. Laird, their babysitter, was one of the great bakers of the island, and she did indeed make a mean sausage roll.

"Well then," said Lorna. "It won't be for long."

"It will," said Ash gloomily. "I'll be sleeping. *But.* I won't really be sleeping!"

"I am sure," said Lorna, putting out the rubber cement, at which Ash's expression perked up a bit. When you were six and rubber cement was coming out, you knew it wasn't extra math. Even a downhearted child could be perked up momentarily by some rubber cement.

"I was thinking," said Lorna, pragmatically changing the subject, "would you like to help me hand out the glitter?"

"*Glitter!*" Ash almost forgot himself. "*Yes, I would.*"

"Okay then," said Lorna, as the bell went for the end of break. "And, Ash," she said, as he took the little plastic canisters containing the tantalizing shiny dots of silver and gold, red and green, which were going to decorate their Christmas pictures, which in turn would wallpaper the entire entrance of the school.

"Uh-huh?" he said, turning the glitter containers upside down and back again, enthralled.

"Your dad isn't going to mind you waiting up for him. Not at all."

"*Look! Agot! I has glitter!*" Ash was already shouting as his partner in crime came charging in, pink-faced, from outside. Immediately she pulled up, furious.

"*I do glitter. I help.*"

"Just let Ash do it, Agot, please," said Lorna, who was so fond of lovely laid-back Innes and didn't know quite how to break it to him that his beautiful daughter—and her best friend Flora's beloved niece—was a stealth hellion.

"*No, I help!*"

She made a grab for the red container, and Ash instinctively jerked his hand back, which meant he shook the lid off the container and the glitter went in the air. A huge "Ohhhhhh" went up from the other children streaming back into the classroom, in awe and excitement, sensing a row in the offing.

"*I did not do that,*" yelled Agot immediately. "*That was Ash!*"

And Ash's face screwed up, ready to cry, and Lorna had to dash forward to sort it out, and, well, it was an effective distraction. She supposed.

Chapter 40

It was the same wet day in Glasgow—did it ever stop raining here? Seriously? In Mure, high up and east, the rain blew in and it blew out again. Glasgow was undeniably beautiful and vibrant and noisy and fun. But it felt like it was in a sunken valley forever under a gray cloud. He suspected if you ever asked a Glaswegian, they would defiantly declare that they liked it that way.

But also he had never been there for anything other than fairly rotten news. So that probably colored things too.

"How is it going?" said Neda in her usual no-nonsense way. She had a heavy caseload—well, who didn't in social care. But Saif was a bit of a special case. She'd managed to place many refugees with other Syrians or people who spoke Arabic at least. Saif had had to manage entirely on his own, at first without even knowing whether his children were alive. The fact that he had not only done so but was patently thriving (even if he would not call it that, his patients adored him and he was a more treasured member of the community than he knew) made him one of her successes and she was proud of him. Therefore this was harder than ever.

"You need a haircut," she added.

"I know, I know," said Saif. There was a female hairdresser, not a barber, in the village, and Saif had been somewhat reluctant. It was just habit, he knew, but even so. Neda had a neat flattop that always looked tidy.

"There's a Turkish barber just down the road," she said. "You could pop in afterward."

Saif nodded numbly. *After what?* he wanted to ask, but he knew Neda couldn't tell him, even if she knew herself. It had to be done under the proper circumstances.

IT WAS THE same secure, dull, ugly low building, the same signing in and military personnel. The same grave expressions and long corridors and bad coffee, and the same tedious administration of the state, of inconvenient persons and complicated caseloads and tired human beings trying to work out a way to be fair to one another, to live with one another, when they weren't given enough money or political support always to be kind.

Saif knew he should be grateful to his adoptive country—and he was, he absolutely was, of course; he and his children could be in a horrible refugee camp, or conscripted, or dead by now. But the very act of having to feel constantly grateful could also feel like a burden, and he wasn't sure how he could express that. A rich country trying to be parsimonious and magnanimous at the same time was a painful thing to witness.

He was led into a small room, and a man who looked like he

didn't normally wear a suit cleared his throat. Without preamble, he opened a plain brown file and took out three large photographs. He turned them round to show Saif, and time slowed down.

In many ways Saif told himself he'd been waiting for this, or something like this.

But, he discovered, he had not. For this was beyond imagining.

Chapter 41

Colton having the best of everything had more or less panned out for them, and they lit up the second generator until Hamish, a handier electrician than his huge meaty fingers would suggest, managed to change out the plug. But there was no doubt. The sculpture was going to have to get wired into the council main if they weren't to blow the fuse for the entire island.

"What's it going to look like?" said Innes. "A disco?"

"How much wattage does it suck up?" said Charlie.

Konstantin looked absolutely blank. He had totally no clue what they were talking about.

So the next day, while Saif was heading to Glasgow, Innes had gone down and had a word with Bert the Councilman, or, to be more specific, took a couple of very good fat hens down to Bert the Councilman, which isn't to say Bert wouldn't have been immediately amenable but is to say it might have cut through a bit of the red tape involved in waiting for the next council meeting, and a debate, and having to deal with Malcy, which nobody liked if they didn't have to, and sure enough, Bert lent them the skeleton key to open the supply on the promise that they'd do it carefully in the dark and not tell anyone, and that only Hamish would do it, and that if they all killed themselves they weren't to come running to him, and Flora was furious because Innes had nicked two of the best layers and the demand for eggs in the Seaside Kitchen and the Rock combined was absolutely massive—didn't he ever think?—and Innes looked defiant and very like Agot, whereas Hamish hung his head, but it didn't matter, it was too late now, and this Big Special Project better be very worth it, said Flora.

The boys could hardly wait until dark, though. They even (and Flora rolled her eyes like you wouldn't believe) got all togged up in balaclavas and scarves over their faces. She pealed with laughter when she saw Joel with his best Burberry cashmere pulled up.

"You are kidding. This isn't a heist."

"Legally," said Joel in his studied way, "it absolutely is a heist. We're hacking into the council electricity supply."

Flora frowned. "If you get killed, I will absolutely kill you."

"Roger that," said Joel, looking at her, and she laughed again and kissed him full-on.

"What was that for?" said Joel, confused.

"Joel Booker, since I have known you, I have loved everything about you. But I don't think I've ever seen you have much fun."

Joel frowned. "Except . . ."

"Yes, except for that," said Flora. "But there is more than one type of fun."

"It's freezing out there and I might get electrocuted," said Joel.

"Yeah," said Flora. "But you're still having fun."

Chapter 42

Saif had stared at the pictures for a long time. He hadn't been able to believe what he was seeing. It didn't make any sense at all; he felt like his brain was broken. A part of him thought if he could shut his eyes, if he could close everything off, then this would go away. He could unravel everything, travel backward in time, leave this country, go home, start over. A cold sweat crept over him as he remembered Amena suddenly, caught a glimpse, could almost smell the familiar scent of bougainvillea, traffic fumes in the warm night, cooking from the other apartments across the courtyard where they lived, the air heavy and orange; remembered her walking Ibrahim up and down, singing Arabic lullabies to his baby.

The person in this picture . . . He stared and stared.

It was Amena, yes. It was her. He couldn't deny it. But it couldn't be. The picture was of her looking straight ahead, staring into the camera. She looked older, but her beautiful eyes were still just like Ash's, the long eyelashes flicking off toward the sides; mother and son were so very similar.

But this woman . . . who was and was not Amena. She had her

arm through another man's. On her left hand glinted a wedding ring, and it was not the ring of coiled silver that Saif had given her, had brought from Beirut, bought on a medical student's meager salary. This was a thick dull band that could have been gold or could have been a brass curtain ring for all he could tell.

And underneath her long traditional robes, far more conservative than anything she had ever worn when they had been together, was the round swell of a pregnant belly.

He pushed the photograph away.

"No," he said. "It's not her."

"Are you sure?" said the commander persistently. "Take another look. It's not like last time, when we simply didn't know. We have good intelligence that this is who she is."

Saif could barely lift his shaggy head, couldn't let his tear-filled eyes even focus on the picture.

"I do not understand what this means," he croaked.

Quietly, the man placed another picture on the table. She was there again, but this time standing next to someone: a man with a large mustache and a small beard. He was dressed plainly in a thobe but he had a large gun and a sword hanging from his belt.

"This is from a little earlier," said the man. "We believe . . . We think that it's a wedding photo."

Saif stared at her face.

"But she is already married," he said numbly. Neda put a comforting hand on his shoulder.

"There are forced marriages," she said. "You understand this?"

But Saif was staring at the wedding photo. The woman in the picture was smiling.

TEA WAS BROUGHT and the situation outlined, although he could hardly take it in, none of it. It appeared that Amena Hussein, née Abboud, had remarried a Syrian freedom fighter two years after the disappearance of her husband and sons.

Which led to many problems. Not least of which whom the freedom fighter was believed to be fighting for.

"We cannot . . . In the situation it would be extremely difficult to extricate her to the UK. In the current political climate . . . I'm afraid it could get extremely awkward."

Saif looked up and stared straight into the officer's eyes. The man was not unkind, he knew. This was a profoundly bitter truth.

"She. Is. Not. A Daesh. Bride," he said, as carefully and calmly as he could manage.

The man merely nodded.

"And her two sons are here. You would deny her her sons?"

Again the man did not speak. Then: "If you can make a positive identification—"

"*What?*"

Saif's eyes were brimming over with misery. His first thought was could he go back, find her? But what was there to go back to? The war wasn't over. Who knew what kind of hellscape was happening in Damascus. Who knew what effect it would have on his children, his entire world. How could he pull them out of their wonderful environment, their fabulous school, and, most important of all, most important, more important than anything in the world, their safety?

Mure might be small, chilly, out of the way.

But oh my goodness, it was so safe. Nobody would be harmed.

Nobody would be pulled out of bed by soldiers; there weren't any, unless you counted the occasional Russian nuclear submariners who secretly resurfaced from time to time and emptied the grocers of vodka, but Saif didn't, seeing as they weren't meant to be there at all, and when they were there, all they wanted to do was drink vodka and chat up the café girls.

His children were safe. What could be more important than that?

Well. Their mother. Seeing their mother. What child would not brave the whole world to be in his mother's arms?

But what if there was another baby already in her arms?

Chapter 43

It didn't take long, this time of year, to wait for dark, but they had decided, through some unspoken agreement, that they really needed to wait until everyone had gone to bed, and the men all skulked about, Hamish unable to stifle his giggles. A farmer through and through, it was extremely unusual for him to be up and about after nine o'clock at night.

The great metal sculpture was hollow, otherwise it would have been completely unliftable—but they were still going to have to get it to the hill and set it in concrete.

"You realize," said Joel, "that this means it'll be here forever?"

"I hope that councilwoman fancies you as much as Flora says she does," said Innes, confusing Joel, who didn't have a clue.

Nonetheless it weighed an absolute ton, and they sweated and panted loading it onto the island's only flatbed truck, which belonged to Anndra the builder, who fortunately had four stout children, so hadn't needed much persuading; it was a dang sight easier than having to fly them all to Inbhir Nis to see the Christmas lights. Now all they needed was a Santa. Politely, nobody mentioned to Anndra that with his rotund belly and fine beard, he was almost certainly the best specimen they had.

Isla came out with hot toddies for everyone, partly because it was freezing, partly because everyone else was insane with curiosity as to what they were up to and it had fallen to her to try to wheedle it out of them.

"No chance," said Konstantin, rushing up to her. "Stay there!" he commanded, then came up behind her and put his hands over her eyes. "Don't look! Hold the tray still! You can't see!!"

"Don't be ridiculous," said Isla, but she stood stock-still nonetheless. It was the oddest sensation, feeling his long smooth hands in front of her eyes, sensing his tall presence behind her. She found herself trembling slightly. It was the cold, had to be.

Of course he wouldn't be thinking anything of it—he was only playing. On the other hand, he stiffened too, she was sure of it; for just a second, she thought she felt him quiver, and in an uncharacteristically tremulous voice he said, "Come on, everyone, take your drinks! But don't let her see it!"

"I want to see it!"

"You can see it when it's ready."

"That's very unfair when I've made all the hot toddies!"

"I don't care! Turn around."

Reluctantly, she turned around, his arms making sure she didn't stumble, and looked up at him. Her tray was empty now; he held the last two glasses and handed one back to her.

"Can you come and find me when I can see it?" she found herself asking him.

"Immediately," he said, without hesitation.

And just for a second, under the freezing dark starlight and the moon halfway through its travels to the east, they looked at each other, her small head tilted upward toward him. And Konstantin felt something quite unusual; it was, he thought, not unlike the feeling you got when you saw a little bird or a kitten—something very fragile, very innocent, that you had to be very careful not to touch or disturb.

It was the oddest thing; he'd barely given his sink mate a second thought. But now he saw her eyes wide open, looking up at him, a frightfully appealing look around her face.

"Oi!" shouted Hamish, and she broke free.

He watched her, thoughtfully, as she took the tray back up to the hotel. She kept her promise not to turn around.

THEY HAD TAKEN the wings off the sculpture, but it was still a monster as they strapped it down with guy ropes, and finally, Innes started very carefully backing out of the driveway of the Rock, the others jumping around the outside, making sure it didn't wobble too much, then, very carefully, Innes did a four-hundred-point turn and headed off, trundling down the headland away from the lit-up hotel and on toward the village.

Sure enough, they didn't meet another car on the way down the road. One day, Joel thought, he'd like to think that there would be many people coming up here, coming to stay at the Rock, enjoying its beautiful surroundings and peace and quiet—with only twelve rooms, they would never get crowded.

There would always be all the space, fresh air, peace, and quiet that anyone required there, the kind of peace of mind he himself had found. Well. Who knew? And this ridiculous project of Konstantin's might even help. He eyed the young blond man. For a spoiled rich kid, he was doing surprisingly well. His father would hopefully be pleased.

As he watched, Konstantin finally figured the statue was safe enough on the flatbed and, with a giddy run, threw himself and his long legs onto the bed of the truck, beckoning Bjårk up behind him.

"So long, suckers!" he yelled cheerily, looking very young all of a sudden. "Enjoy your walk!"

Innes suddenly turned the wheel briskly and he nearly fell off (Bjårk, with his low and hairy center of gravity, was completely fine), and a long leg went up in the air. Normally this would have peeved him; he hated to look foolish in front of people, most of whom were always telling him how cool he was. But here it didn't matter. Hamish was laughing so much it looked like he was going to fall over himself, skidding on the icy ground. Somehow, half of them walking, half riding, they made it down, although they made such a commotion they frightened the cows in the field.

At the foot of the hill that led up to the school, they stopped. The spot they'd chosen was as well positioned as they could make it, their most important thing being not to beam the installation's lights in anybody's window all night and send them completely insane.

The buried connection was about halfway up the hill, round the back of an old barn, so they weren't in much danger of bothering anyone. Innes had already had the hole dug, causing much interest among the children, including many who wanted to bring spades of their own and *do digging*, which was hard enough in the frozen ground, but he told them it was farm business and to be on their way. It being after school, when most children are in absolutely dire need of a large snack and a sit-down before going out to play again, this more or less did the trick, except for Agot, of course, who stayed *doing helping* and shooing off any other children who came by, saying only she was allowed to help as it was farm business, which was actually quite helpful.

Now, the concrete mixer was churning away, and everyone was incredibly excited. As well as the headlamps from the flatbed, they had some storm lanterns to light everything and made sure the angel was straight as they carefully winched it down, hand over hand, into the hole. Then, when everything was as plumb as it could be and the wires were fixed, they got out of the way and let the concrete cascade down into the hole.

They stood back to admire their handiwork. There was no doubt about it, the thing was huge. It had changed the face of Mure forever; you'd have to saw it apart to take it down.

"Oh my God," said Innes.

"Marsali does know it's four meters high?" said Konstantin, finally feeling a bit worried, though of course it was far too late.

"No," said Joel. "Because you wouldn't tell me what was happening."

"Yes, but did you tell her today?"

"I told her it was four . . ." Joel let his voice trail off.

"I'm not sure," observed Innes finally, "that she ever got metric."

There was a pause.

"You mean she thinks it's four *feet*?" Konstantin hooted.

"That," said Innes slowly, "is a distinct possibility."

They all looked at the concrete, now rapidly hardening.

"Oh, come on," said Konstantin finally, mischief creasing his features. "Let's just set it up."

Chapter 44

"Bloody hell" is rarely something you want to hear your pilot say. Fortunately it was rather muffled, even in the tiny space of the minuscule prop plane that acted as a rural bus between the far northern islands, with its eight seats and rather rudimentary noise insulation.

Saif didn't need to hear it, partly because he'd been entirely sunken in a misery so deep and vast the black endless sea and sky outside did nothing but mirror his mood.

In fact, before he realized what had just been said and snapped to attention, a tiny bit of him considered that if the pilot was saying the plane was about to plunge into the sea, well, that wouldn't necessarily be the worst thing in the world, it would at least bring an end to the maelstrom of thoughts tearing up his head, which was an idea so horrifying and upsetting he banished it from his mind immediately, astounded.

But he had thought it nonetheless.

He wrenched his mind away from everything, all the dark thoughts swirling there, and blinked several times.

They were descending, so they were nearly at the tiny airstrip in Mure, manned by a husband-and-wife team who also ran the post office, so there was absolutely nothing they didn't know about every single soul on the island.

Normally from the left-hand set of portholes you saw exactly what you'd expect to see: a tiny mound, like an extended comma in shape, with lighthouses dotted all round it to protect passing shipping and lights clustered on the whole of the southeast corner, where the village was, tiny pinpricks of warmth in a vast dark ocean; homey, and comforting, and somehow a tiny bit awe-inspiring, the way human beings could thrive and prosper so far away on such a tiny spot of land, so far out at sea.

But tonight it wasn't like that. It wasn't like that at all. Just behind the main streets, on the hill that led to the school was . . . Well, what the hell was that?

Saif and the other travelers—a bird-watching couple from Nova Scotia who had excitedly tried to engage him in Gaelic and a young, smartly dressed woman on her own—all peered out the left-hand side until the copilot came back and told them to balance up the plane and stop craning on one side.

"Obh, obh," said the older woman, and Saif could kind of see her point; it looked like the island was on fire. A great big shaft of light was beaming straight up in the air, leading down to a vast white shape below.

"Is that hazardous?" he asked the copilot, who frowned.

"Well . . . it's *vulgar.*"

Saif stared at it. He had been lost in contemplation, remembering and trying to remember every single word of every bit of the conversation from that afternoon.

"Why hasn't she been in touch?" he had choked out. "I still have the same number. I'm on Facebook. I'm on Red Cross and Red Crescent."

The man had looked strained. "There might be a few reasons," he said awkwardly. "If she's in a refugee camp she may not have access."

"Anyone can borrow a phone."

"She may . . . Her husband may not allow her access."

Saif's eyes squeezed together. "Who would not let her contact her own children?"

"Someone who did not want her to have had another family," said the man, kindly but plainly.

Saif shook his head.

"Or," said the man, "she understands the situation all too well and doesn't want to make life difficult for you."

Saif frowned. "What do you mean?" He looked up. "I got a strange message that didn't . . . I thought it might just be coincidence."

He explained and the man shrugged.

"Well, she knows the status of jihadi brides in the West. She knows that it would be nothing other than disruptive to you. That the British government would be unhappy, would not let her enter the country. May not even let you stay. It is possible she is counting on her silence . . . keeping you safe."

And Saif had been quiet for a long time after that.

He leaned his head on the plane window again.

It was—it couldn't be—but it seemed to be a large angel, built of light. He couldn't help but stare at it. An angel of light. Mikael, the archangel of mercy.

He squeezed his eyes shut. He was a doctor, a man of science. He was not the kind of person who believed that angels would suddenly appear, would suddenly manifest, just to help him, personally, out of a predicament. That made absolutely no sense at all. Of course not.

Nonetheless, he had left Mure that morning. He had dropped the children at school. He knew beyond a shadow of a doubt that there had been absolutely nothing on the hill in front of the school, except for the little tree lanterns that were slung there every Christmas. And now . . .

Saif stared on, absolutely hypnotized. It grew bigger and brighter as they drew closer to it. It was completely otherworldly.

"Bloody hell," said the pilot again. "Ladies and gentlemen, I'm just going to . . ."

There wasn't another plane for hundreds of miles. He took a little detour. Just to take a look. The copilot took a photo, but it only showed itself to look like a mad, massive UFO, which was even worse. They flew low to see it, but it made no more sense close up than it did from the air.

Except it was beautiful.

It was visible from the airfield, right across the other side of the island. It was almost certainly visible from everywhere, possibly including space.

Billy and Effie McGlone, who ran the airfield, rushed out to meet them as the plane taxied to a standstill.

"We've had everyone on the line!" they exclaimed breathlessly. "Pilots and everyone on the radio are going absolutely ballistic."

"What on earth is it?" asked the bird-watchers.

"Apparently," said Mrs. McGlone. "Apparently it's our Christmas decorations."

THE YOUNG WOMAN who was disembarking started taking loads of photographs. She'd taken a few out of the side of the plane, but they bounced back off the thick glass and didn't show anything except a blur. She did, though, have a sense that there might be more to this story—her editor wanted more on the "Worst Hotel in Britain," and in these days of reduced budgets and strained newsrooms, it was normally pretty difficult to find enough money to send a reporter out. But she'd convinced him that it would be worthwhile, and here she was, a zillion miles from God knows where, with one mission in mind—find the worst hotel in Britain.

Chapter 45

There was absolutely no chance Mrs. Laird could have gotten Ash and Ib to bed even if there wasn't a large commotion about the town and various people walking the streets at unfortunate hours to see what on earth was going on up the hill.

Even without that, they weren't so relaxed they could deal with their father going off the island, particularly as he only ever did so if it absolutely couldn't be helped.

Ash's eyes were looking particularly wide as he ran into his dad's arms. It hurt Saif to look at him. So like her. So like Amena. Ib too. And as if being away for just a day had made him see them anew, he noticed once again how much they had both filled out. Ib had taken a stretch; he was going to be tall like him. Ash, possibly not. Saif knew infant malnutrition could lead to growth issues. But Ib was looking tall and strong. Amena would never see him look like this, never see him so big.

How could she bear it? How could she not be desperate to see them? Or perhaps she was. But there she was, married to another man. Pregnant. His head told him of course that she might clearly have no choice.

But . . . the smile.

Of course smiles could be forced. Of course.

And then again, what if she truly believed they were dead? What if she had spent two years as wretched as he had? What if she'd known the boys were lost, assumed the worst? What if she had grabbed at any brass ring of happiness, at any morsel?

After all, wasn't that exactly what he'd done with Lorna?

But he had his children; and if he had not, he wouldn't have been able to . . .

Well. Would he?

But it wasn't the same.

Wasn't it?

He buried his tortured face in the hair of his youngest boy.

"Abba! Abba! There is a spaceship and we *must go see it*," Ash said with some urgency. Agot was—madly, in Saif's opinion— allowed to use her father' s mobile phone and had apparently woken the entire house, ordering them all down there even though it was 9:30 on a school night and 5 degrees below zero.

Ash was already pulling on his fur-lined boots.

"Off we go to see the spaceship," he said, in a way that showed he was pretending to be very confident about something happening in the hope that that would help it happen.

"It won't be a spaceship, stupid," said Ib, who absolutely had to be contrary, but it was a weak effort on his part; he was obviously as desperate to see it as Ash was, not least so he didn't miss out on the playground conversation the next day.

Mrs. Laird rolled her eyes. "I think quite a lot of people are going out to see it," she said.

Saif sighed. On the other hand, what was the alternative? Going to bed to lie for hours and hours absolutely fiercely awake, thinking of Amena every second of the night, letting every possibility, terrible and worse, run through his brain? Explain to the children that their mummy was alive, but she had another family now?

It hurt like a physical pain. He might as well walk it out.

IT WAS FREEZING outside, a windy night with snow bouncing around lazily and more—much more—on the forecast for coming in.

The boys were beside themselves at getting up in nighttime, long past bedtime, as if the normal rules were forgotten. And how exciting too, once they'd gotten jumpers and padded jackets and hats and scarves and socks and Wellingtons on over their pajamas, to leave the house, each with a hand in their father's— normally Ib didn't like being seen out and about holding hands with his dad, it absolutely wasn't cool in primary seven, but he was making an exception for tonight and Saif was deeply and profoundly grateful for it.

Everywhere doors were opening as they walked down the street to the village from the rectory, and excited chattering— and some very disapproving chattering—could be heard here and there. There was loads of noise as overexcited child shouted to overexcited child and more and more joined the parade. Agot came charging up to Ash, and they did their usual bouncing-up-and-down dance they did when they saw each other outside of school—they were truly the best of friends.

"*It me!*" shouted Agot. "It an angel. Like me!"

Agot was playing the angel in the nativity play. Lorna would like to have said there was no nepotism in it, and in a way that was true. Agot was so unbelievably irritating about how much she wanted to play the angel Gabriel that it was easier just to let her—it wasn't a big part like Mary—rather than deal with the aggro everyone would put up with if she was denied. On a very deep level Lorna knew this was a bad lesson for Agot to learn, that by being a monstrous pain in the arse she'd get whatever she wanted. On the other hand, Lorna had a full class, a mountain of paperwork, a school to run, an unhappy love affair to obsess over, and plenty of other children, as well as, it appeared, a space rocket materializing just in front of the school building, and Agot wouldn't be her problem forever, so this one she was just letting fly.

"They built a statue of you?" said Ash wonderingly. He thought everything Agot did was marvelous.

"I *think so*."

"I don't think that's you, *mo graidh*," said Innes fondly.

"*Yes, it is me*," said Agot with a happy sigh. Then she frowned. "*I needs my angel costume.*"

Innes rushed on ahead when he spied Flora to avoid having to get into that precise conversation.

"What the hell is it?" someone asked her.

Flora was eyeing it up and wondering why people kept asking her as if she knew everything, rather than, for example, Joel, who was standing right beside her and had actually built the damn thing.

Standing back, however, she liked it. She couldn't deny it. It was absurdly too huge and she couldn't imagine how much electricity it would use—thank goodness for the wind farms—and she knew some people were going to complain about it and possibly the civil aviation authority would ask them to take it down.

But it was, undeniably, a huge, bright, beautiful shining angel that had appeared in the middle of the village. And she liked it like that.

"What do you think?" said Joel.

"It's insane," said Flora. "But . . . in a good way."

"Do you think?"

Flora gestured. "Look how happy the kids are!"

And sure enough there was row upon row of excited upturned faces, and a large "Oooh" went out when the wings were extended.

KONSTANTIN HAD HIS head thrown back, laughing. Someone had put some music on, and he had gone over and stuck on Christmas carols on the speaker, fiddling with Spotify until it was playing "Silent Night" in Norwegian. He bellowed it loudly, and Isla looked at him, suddenly overcome.

She had thought he was such a callow, ignorant boy, rude and snotty and unpleasant.

But to build this was such an unforced, ridiculous thing to do. He couldn't be so up on himself after all; it was just lovely. And now he stood handing out shots from the bottle of aquavit the importer had left him; beaming broadly even if anyone made a rude remark about the Mure Angel, not minding in the slightest; pointing out the shiny bits for the smaller ones; agreeing solemnly with Agot that it was absolutely definitely a statue of her (she was wearing the angel costume now; someone must have given in).

Watching him, Isla felt her heart lurch suddenly. She realized, now that they were out of the confines of the kitchen, she was actually a little jealous. Iona was flocking around; so were lots of girls in fact. All the teasing that she had pretended not to listen to or had brushed off . . . well, suddenly she felt slightly annoyed that he was spreading it around, chatting to everyone. She was used, she realized, to having Konstantin to herself.

And as she looked at him, tall and silly and laughing in the bright light, as excited as any of the schoolchildren standing around, she realized something else.

She liked him.

She liked him a lot.

Oh God. She liked him and his stupid blond hair and his ridiculous dog and the way he couldn't get up in the morning and the puppy-dog look he gave her when he wanted her to do something for him.

And at first she'd found him pathetic, unable to do anything.

But he had worked with a will, dealt with his failures with good grace. He was improving every day. And he had definitely done this: this was all him. An achievement that was just him. Spoiled losers couldn't have managed this.

As if sensing what she was thinking, he glanced up and caught her eye.

She couldn't help it, she absolutely beamed at him. His eyes lit up almost comically and a smile split his face. He gave her a querying thumbs-up, and she replied with a double thumbs-up and got rewarded by that grin again.

She looked so pretty, he thought. Not overdone and Instagram-ready like so many of the girls he met at parties, with four inches of makeup and eyebrows plucked and stupid duck lips, wearing expensive clothes and talking about how bored they were with everything.

She was pink-cheeked and clear-eyed, her skin like roses and her lovely thick dark hair blowing around her, and her long scarf and coat concealing . . . well, who knew? It would be like unwrapping a parcel.

Even as the commotion continued all around him, he didn't drop her gaze. In response, she took a step toward him. The light was flaring out behind him; it was quite, quite dazzling.

He. He was quite, quite dazzling.

She took another step. His face had changed, was nervous now. His mouth was closed, a faint smile playing around his curled lips. God, thought Isla. He was so handsome. Had she really not noticed before? Or had she thought, *Stupid handsome tosser*?

Probably that one. She didn't think he was a tosser now. Not at all. She thought of those long hands and long fingers and suddenly felt a shiver go down her. This was something . . . this was something. She was sure of it. She took another step.

Perhaps, thought Konstantin. No. He already knew she didn't like him. She'd made it quite clear. Although . . . He licked his lips nervously.

Normally when he met women—and he met a lot of women—he had a lot of bolsters behind him. He had his money and his name. Most girls he met knew exactly who he was and absolutely fancied a shot at him.

More than that, he'd probably be drunk, and everyone else would be too, and it would just be a natural progression. The girl would do much of the chasing, and he'd be more or less happy to go along with it. For a little while at least.

This was different, and so, so new and strange.

He was standing in front of Isla with nothing—a kitchen boy, really, with no name and no money and not much except a dog who seemed to layer mud wherever he went. He hadn't been charming with her or deliberately flirtatious. Quite the opposite.

She knew him. She hadn't liked him . . . at first. But now . . . here she was, stepping forward, to him, with nothing at all. Could that have changed?

He felt a tug at his sleeve and glanced over, assuming it was Hamish wanting reassurance about how brilliant the statue was.

Instead, it was a blond woman with a pointed chin whom he didn't recognize.

"Uh, hi," he said, cross at being distracted.

"Hi there!" said the girl, exposing very white teeth. "I've heard this is your doing? Wow. Amazing. Candace Blunt. *Daily Post*."

As the children yelled and capered in front of the angel and Lorna started to massively downgrade the amount of her lesson plan she was going to get through the next day, she saw him.

Of course she'd known the boys would want to come down. It was absolutely part of the reason she was here in the first place. There was no point in lying to herself. She glanced around. Flora was looking at her in concern, which was ironic, seeing as it used to be Flora in the dodgy relationship and Lorna trying to be sympathetic. Now Flora was up in that beautiful house with a man and a baby, and she was . . .

Well. No point in feeling sorry for herself; it helped nothing. Saif edged toward her. Perfectly normal, just the village doctor having a brief conversation with the headmistress, business as usual—who could possibly suspect? If they were up to anything they certainly wouldn't be talking out in public like this, would they? No. So.

Nonetheless, she retreated a little into the shadows out of the great light the angel cast.

"Hello, Lorna," he said in that low gravelly voice she loved so very much.

"Uhm, hi," she said, as usual as casual as she could make it, which wasn't very. "Has this got anything to do with you?"

"No," said Saif. "But it explains all the electric shock burns in the surgery."

"Seriously?"

"Oh no, I am joking."

Saif didn't usually have to explain to Lorna when he was joking. Everyone else, yes.

"It's . . . I rather like it," said Lorna.

Saif nodded. "I saw it from the sky."

She nodded. "How was it?" she asked, in a voice of infinite tenderness.

He stopped short, realizing suddenly he was about to burst into tears if he talked any further. They could not be casual; they could not just chat about this.

Flora came over. She sensed something was up.

"You guys okay?" she said brightly. "I can watch the boys for half an hour if you like."

"We just . . . need to talk," said Lorna, glancing at Saif's stricken face.

"Sure, whatever," said Flora blithely, pointedly looking away. But Lorna couldn't worry about that just now. She glanced at Saif, who understood immediately—and could not, anyway, be there for any longer—and he slipped away to the entrance to her flat, just behind the museum. There were no other inhabitants of the building. Nobody saw him, and the flat was, as always, unlocked.

Chapter 46

Lorna found him there, sitting in front of the fire, his face buried in his knees, his hands clasping them to his chest. He looked like a statue; he wasn't rocking, or sobbing, or anything—almost anything would have made Lorna feel less nervous about him than she did.

She poured them both a little whisky and waited.

Eventually—because they never had time, never—he managed to raise his head. But he was still staring into the fire and would not look at her. She put the whisky in his hand and he took a small sip, then put it down and let out a huge sigh.

Her heart was pounding in her chest. A tiny bit of her—even now, even so—leaped at the simple fact that he was there, in her room, in front of her fire. The physical fact of him, to which she was so ridiculously and absolutely addicted. He was in front of her. Perhaps this was him telling her, telling her that he had decided—of course it would be sad—that he had made his decision, that they could be together.

The fact that this was absurd, unlikely, difficult . . .

Well. Difficult things happened all the time.

She couldn't bear it, almost. To sit still and wait for him to speak. Finally, she gently touched his shoulder, and his flinch cut her like a knife.

"Amena," he managed finally, and Lorna's heart dropped like a plummeting lift. Of course it wasn't him telling her things would be okay. Of course not. She bent over in pain. Soon, there would be nothing left of her, just a Lorna-shaped skin suit she would have to carry for the rest of her life.

"They . . . they found her?" she heard herself saying.

He nodded, tears coming to his eyes now, and still stubbornly, defiantly, he would not look at her.

She stroked his arm very gently, even as she felt as if she were being carved out by a cruel knife, to the gentle sound of nothing but the softly crackling fire and the distant oohs and ohs of more and more villagers coming to see the unearthly light.

He buried his face.

"She's . . . alive?"

Again the nod. But why was he so . . .

"What is it, Saif?" she said gently but firmly, drawing on all her years of dealing with recalcitrant children or shy little ones. "Tell me what it is."

CANDACE BLUNT WAS confused. She'd arrived to find no cabs, no transport, no nothing, except the airport manager had offered to give her a lift somewhere.

She'd informed him she wanted to go to the Rock without saying why, which was that she was down for the *Daily Post* to write an exposé on how dreadful it was, but he explained that it wasn't open for paying guests yet and dropped her at the Harbour's Rest instead. Which was, she had to admit, a bit peeling round the edges, and the glasses were a bit sticky, but the welcome, from a large, friendly Icelandic girl, was warm, the drinks were generous, and her bedroom was absolutely vast and overlooked the sea. There wasn't that much to complain about.

Hearing the commotion and listening to the voices in the bar discuss the angel, including at least one blaming the whisky, she had headed down to the scene, on the sniff for a story; she needed to justify this. One hit piece might not be enough.

It was freezing up here, good God. Her smart London mackintosh wasn't going to cut it at all. No wonder all the locals looked like they were going to join the British Antarctic Survey. The wind cut through her and she narrowed her eyes. How the hell could people live here?

It was even slightly spooky, all of them gathering around an enormous lit-up statue of an angel. At least she thought it was an angel; it was hard to tell. Modern art, she thought. Her readers absolutely hated modern art or anything that smacked of fancy concepts. If it had public funding, that would probably be another excellent take on things. "Island Wasting Taxpayers' Money on Crazy Modern Art" was definitely an angle that would work with this.

She asked the first person she met who was responsible, who nodded toward a tall, surprisingly good-looking blond boy who was laughing and looking at something over by the foot of the statue. Her eyes narrowed. He looked familiar, but she couldn't quite put her finger on it. Nonetheless, her journalistic instincts were tingling.

She marched up to him confidently. "Hi there! I've heard this is your doing?"

AT FIRST KONSTANTIN found it hard to break Isla's gaze. Why, he was thinking, had he not noticed before? How lovely she was. How sweet and shy and . . . just so different from the people he knew.

"Candace Blunt? *Daily Post*?"

The blond girl standing next to him was looking cross. He noticed she was wearing expensive high-heeled boots that could not have been less suitable for walking up a Mure hill at midnight. She stood confidently next to him, in no doubt she was about to claim his attention.

"Yes?" he said reluctantly.

"So is this your doing?"

"Well, I had a lot of help."

"And the council funded it?"

Konstantin wasn't really listening; he was looking for Isla, but she'd disappeared back into the crowd. He frowned. "The council?"

"Yes, the council."

Konstantin shrugged. He knew they'd had something to do with letting them have the space.

"Sure," he said, and Candace smiled happily.

"Wow, amazing," she said, jotting it down in her notebook. "You must be very proud."

"It's a great thing," said Konstantin. "It needs brightening up, *ja*?"

He meant, of course, the Christmas lights. This was not what it sounded like to Candace.

"Well, it's a pretty dark, cold, miserable place," she said, looking round.

"Hmm," said Konstantin. Isla had disappeared from his line of sight. Where on earth had she gone?

"And what's your name? You're Norwegian, right? What brings you here?"

"I'm just working in the hotel."

"The new hotel?"

"Yes. Excuse me, I have to go."

"Perhaps I can come talk to you there tomorrow? And can I just take a picture of you next to the . . . That's right," said Candace, bringing out her camera. She caught Konstantin mugging and sent it immediately to the pictures desk. They had people on there who were world experts at recognizing faces. If his rang a bell with anyone, they would let her know.

Chapter 47

B ut who . . . who is she married to?"
Saif shrugged.

"And they think he's . . . a jihadi? A terrorist?"

"Perhaps."

The silence sat between them. This was absolutely ridiculous, thought Lorna. She was a primary school teacher in a tiny village in the Scottish islands. She didn't get mixed up with horrific political situations in the Middle East.

She looked at Saif's head, still bowed. Nobody did, she thought. Nobody asked to get mixed up in this. But war could come and burst through the gates of peace; it could crawl in any window, sneak under the cracks of any door, just when you thought you were safe.

And they were safe. They were.

But oh: Amena.

"Will they let her come?"

Saif shrugged again.

"Do you want her to come?" she asked, more quietly this time.

He let out a muffled sound that was more howl than anything else.

Lorna drew closer to him and encircled his waist with her arms, sitting behind him, her knees on either side of him.

"There, there," she said.

"I have to get back to the boys."

"Not yet, my love," said Lorna, so quiet it was almost a whisper. "Stay awhile."

He took hold of her hands, lifted them to his face, which was wet with tears, and kissed her hand gently.

She shifted round to face him, so now she was crouching between his knees. Looking into his face, she felt suddenly, overwhelmingly filled with desire, desperate to feel his strong arms around her, his long body jolting against hers.

She moved closer toward him, gazing into his dark brown eyes.

"Stay awhile," she said again, and he closed his eyes and rested his entire face in her hair, breathing her in, trying to surround himself with her, the only thing that made him feel better. She moved even closer toward him, until he entirely engulfed her in front of the flickering firelight.

"Darling," she whispered, and moved in to kiss those sad, soft lips.

He pulled away, furious with himself, with the world, with everything. Shaking his head forcefully, he stood up. She stood up too, looking at him, their two bodies still touching.

"You can be angry," she said, barely recognizing herself, her voice cracked and hoarse. She had never been so desperate for someone, never in her life. It was absolutely crazy what he did to her, what he did to her body. "You can be angry. It's okay. You're safe. You're with me." She looked straight at him, full of desire, and said what she wanted out loud. "You can take it out on me."

He understood her meaning in a moment and grasped her on either side of her arms, staring fiercely down into her eyes and suddenly pushing her hard against the wall. He kissed her passionately, and she felt his long, lean body tightly pressed against her, every inch of him, and she felt herself melt into his hardness, pushed herself frantically against him, felt her breathing quicken and the blood rush to her head.

Then:

"*Al'ama,*" he swore at himself, shaking his head, tearing himself away, breathing heavily, clearly aroused.

This was not the kind of man he was. This was not the kind of man he wanted to be.

"I'm sorry. I'm sorry. I'm so sorry."

He half walked, half stumbled out of the flat, leaving Lorna breathing hard, furious, desolate, behind him.

Chapter 48

Isla's mum was waiting up for her when she got back.

"What's all that nonsense going on there?" she said accusingly.

"It's the Christmas lights," said Isla happily, even though she had taken flight when Konstantin had been distracted—of course he had, she told herself. Of course he'd wanted to go talk to someone else. Some gorgeous blonde she'd never seen before. She had scared herself and bolted.

But also, the intensity of it. The sheer hugeness of it had startled her, made her run off like a rabbit. This wasn't like getting drunk and pulling a Russian sailor. Or getting off with Nobby Parsons at every school disco for long enough that eventually they were kind of technically going out anyway, even if they didn't have much to say to each other and Nobby spent most of his life playing *FIFA*, talking about *FIFA*, and trying to explain *FIFA* to her.

This was completely different. He was so handsome, so fun, so full of life and ideas and nonsense. And tonight . . .

She wanted to clasp the idea to her heart, turn it over, enjoy thinking about it.

Her mother was looking out the window sourly. "Bloody waste of money if you ask me."

"Well, I think it was Colton's money," said Isla gingerly, which only made her mother sniff harder.

"You'd think he'd have something better to do with it than wasting it on that nonsense."

"I think he's done lots of other good things too," suggested Isla nervously, but that only got another sniff. "I'm going to bed."

"Nobody will get any sleep with that thing buzzing and giving off electricity," predicted Vera, who was half right: people got no sleep for many different reasons.

LORNA SOBBED HER heart out on her empty bed, once again feeling as if she was born to be ridiculous, to suffer. That love was meant to be something that people simply found—they found people they liked and they settled down. Look at Ealasaid and Anndra, the bank teller and her husband, who mended dry stone walls. They just seemed to rub on okay, have a bun together every so often, watch their children grown.

Had they ever collapsed fully forward onto the floor in despair of their love for each other? Had they spilled a river of tears? Had they yearned so hard that they were driven half mad with a confused and furious lust?

Perhaps they had.

SAIF GRABBED THE boys by the hands. They were cold and ready for cozy beds, a kiss on the head, and the absolute peace and security that they, he thought bitterly, had had to wait so long for, that had been so hard-won.

And now what? He stood for a long time at Ib's bed, watched the stern little face relax and untangle in the sweetness of a child's dream. Could he bring in more disruption—another man even? Another man.

His blood ran cold. What if she wanted to take them away? To live with her new family.

But no. Not his sweet Amena. Not his wife.

But she was not his wife anymore. And could anyone truly still be sweet after a war? After believing she had lost her own children?

Puzzled, he clicked on his Facebook once again. He had left it there, after he stopped checking it pathologically, religiously, all the time. Why, why had she never looked for him? Never found him? Was she being held, married against her will? The message was still there. But nothing more. He pulled down the poetry book, looked for answers, found none.

But she had looked happy. She looked happy in the photograph. She looked happy. How could she be happy?

KONSTANTIN COULDN'T HELP it, he was excited. For the first time he missed his phone. He'd have liked to look up some pictures of her. Remind himself. But what should he do? The problem was it was near impossible to ask her to something, given they had to stand next to each other at the sink all day long. What if she said no? Why had she run away?

He was so used to just having women show up, like taxis. Whereas with Isla . . . she was so quiet and shy, he was going to have to tempt her out. He wasn't even sure she liked him.

Although, that smile . . .

FINTAN LAY AWAKE, still worried about his betrayal of Colton, which had happened again—even if Colton wouldn't have minded, not in the slightest, had told him a million times that he was still young, that he had to get back out there.

Even so, it felt wrong. It felt like cheating, even if it was cheating on a dead person.

Fintan glanced downward. Under his arm, Gaspard slept the sleep of the dead, a heavily tattooed arm pulled over his eyes, his legs kicked out in front of him; fast asleep and utterly content in his own inked skin.

This was comforting in itself. Fintan thought back to their conversation earlier. He had tentatively asked Gaspard what he was getting out of this, and Gaspard had looked at him, incredulous at the question, then launched into a very complicated discussion about salmon heading upstream, which Fintan hadn't entirely understood.

"Ze feesh, he ees home, yes? But the water, eet ees *always moving.*"

"So, is this a good thing?" Fintan had ventured.

"*Bien sur,* of course! Day by day this is good, this is fresh, this has clear eyes."

"Do you mean me or the fish?"

"Today, you."

And just watching him, feeling his warm body, Fintan gradually drifted off.

Chapter 49

The Seaside Kitchen was insanely busy from the second it opened, with the Mure Angel still lighting the dark up the hill ahead.

"It's a scandal," said Mrs. Brodie.

"It's grand, aye," said Cuthbert McSquib, whose farm had gotten electricity only in 2002 and thought seeing the Mure Angel was a bit like what going to New York City must be like.

Already lots of people had taken pictures of it, and Iona could only assume that when it got light there'd be even more of them. She sold endless coffees and made a happy note to get out the angel cake cutters again to make gingerbread angels. She had a hunch they'd go down well.

The Mure Angel already had a crowd of spectators around it by dawn, and as Iona watched it did the most amazing thing. If you went to the southwest side of the structure, you could watch the very first of the sun's rays hit it. And as they did so, they bent and refracted in the glass—and a huge rainbow spilled out the other side.

There was an audible gasp from the children watching and even some of the adults. Iona had to yell at them to get out of the way so she could get a good shot, which she did, proclaiming herself the "official photographer." When you moved someone into the right position, it looked as if a rainbow were dancing off their head. The rest of the front of the statue glowed shining gold. It was undeniably magnificent.

Malcy arrived with the rest of the council—barring Marsali— to close it down at 9:05 A.M.

IT WAS ABSURD, thought Flora, that it was actually easier, in the middle of everything she had going on, to throw Agot a nativity party than usual. They had had one every year since forever; her mother had held them for them all, and gradually the entire village had very much co-opted it as an annual celebration, and Flora would have felt remiss for the MacKenzies not to carry on the tradition, but she outsourced it to the Rock to cater, figuring she might as well get a little recompense for her time and effort given she was doing Fintan's entire job. He had been less tearful recently, she noticed, and perhaps more thoughtful. As usual, any attempts on her part to get him to open up or talk about things or plan for the future were met with furious disdain.

Anyway. She popped in to find the kitchen at the Rock, for once, in perfect harmony; they were churning out scones and chopping sandwiches, and terrible French pop music was playing but the atmosphere on the whole seemed playful. She still wasn't 100 percent sure they should have a dog in the dining room but would leave that for another day.

"Drop them off around three-ish?" she said. "And please, do stay."

Konstantin snuck a glance at Isla. A party. It seemed like a pretty good opportunity, even though she had been pink and nervous all round him that morning. Although she was wearing lipstick, which was new. This was also a good sign. Then she noticed him staring at her lipstick and vanished, and the next time he saw her the lipstick had gone. That was a bad sign. Or was it? He wished it was just a little easier, like with girls who knew he lived in a palace. Or did he, though? He couldn't remember when he'd last felt so excited, so alive about something. The butterflies were in his tummy absolutely; he couldn't wait for four o'clock to come. His scones were light as air all of a sudden. He couldn't quite believe he now cared about the fluffiness of scones, but they reflected his mood and he ran around the kitchen like a puppy when the first lot came out, insisting everyone taste one and grinning his head off.

Isla had disappeared into the bathroom and was leaning her head against the cool wall tiles. How could she have been so stupid? He had spotted she was wearing lipstick straightaway and had looked like a wolf licking his chops. Oh God, was she making a terrible mistake? Was this a ridiculous thing to be doing? What if . . . what if he just wanted to get off with her then sod off back to Norway? He talked about Norway enough, didn't he? He would be desperate to get back there. He wouldn't want to be in a hotel kitchen forever—look how he'd organized the statue. He'd want to be with someone like that blond girl.

She looked at herself in the mirror. He was slumming it. She knew it. He was bored and looking for a dalliance. Of course he was. Then he'd go back to one of those nine-foot blond Scandinavian girls. It didn't matter how often Iona had told her that her dark auburn hair and brown eyes was witch coloring and beautiful. She was still five foot nothing in her stocking feet, and all circles from her round face to her curly hair, round breasts, round bum, and short legs. Her mother had once called her Chorlton, after the round cartoon character, which she hadn't understood until she was much older, and it had stung deeply ever since, though her mother had said, "Don't be so sensitive, darling, I'm only joking."

But here was her dilemma: if he was only messing about, and he almost certainly was . . . she still really, really liked him. *Really* liked him. So what would be the harm in going for it? Just this once?

She'd asked Iona in several frantic late-night WhatsApp chats so her mother couldn't overhear, but of course Iona had a very straightforward attitude toward all of this and firmly believed she should get off with him—at the very least—regardless.

Life is long, she had said, wise in her twenty-four years. Do you really want to look back in ten years' time when you're surrounded by ankle biters and your tits are hitting the floor and nobody ever even looks at you and you've got a mum tum and a long stare and you stay in every night with sick on you like Flora? Do you really want to look back and think, Well, everything sucks but thank GOD I never got off with that really hot bloke that Christmas but instead spent Christmas entirely by myself?

When you put it like that, said Isla weakly. But what if he only wants to take advantage of me?

Take advantage of him! said Iona, knowing Isla's weak spots irritatingly well. Think of it as practice!

Oh, said Isla, I don't know . . .

Well, I do, said Iona. He looks like he'd be massive fun. All that energy, for starters.

Isla squeezed her eyes shut. Even to think about him like that . . . Oh goodness, she said.

Well exactly, said Iona. That's what you want him to get you to say.

So Isla had washed her hair, even though that was pointless, as it had to be scraped back, and curled her eyelashes and put on makeup, and she'd seen him looking at her again and now it was just overwhelming. Could it . . . could it really be happening? She wiped the lipstick off. Then reapplied it. Then wiped it off again. Then absolutely fell out with herself. This was ridiculous.

She thought about her mother, who was always warning her about putting it about or showing off.

Oddly, this was the thing that steeled her resolve. She was an adult, not a child. And her mother's rules didn't seem to bring her much happiness. It was nearly Christmas, there was a party to go to, and a handsome man outside who wanted to take her. Did it have to be more complicated than that?

Yes, whispered her treacherous, terrified brain, but she resolved, just this once, to ignore it. Sometimes, being an introvert . . . it just got too much. That was all.

She reapplied a very thin layer indeed and blotted it so it was almost, but not quite, gone, then forced herself out of the bathroom and back into the raucous, warm, cheery kitchen, where even Gaspard, who was firmly of the belief that scones were not patisserie and never would be even vaguely acceptable, and questioned whether they were a sandwich or a cake or *quoi c'est quoi ça,* was tucking into one of Konstantin's scones piled high with local elderberry jam.

She smiled tentatively.

"Okay!" said Gaspard, as they loaded up the trays to put them in the van. "Thees ees a party for tiny children and old people, and I do not know who are the crazy people who leeve on this island so far from the theater because it is horrible and cold, you know, it is a bad, bad island."

He stopped himself suddenly, completely distracted. Outside, without anyone realizing, it had started to snow again. The whole world was a blur.

Delighted, everyone ran to the windows.

"Look how beautiful that is," said Konstantin.

"Like home?" said Isla a little nervously.

He turned, delighted she was talking to him again. "Not a bit," he said. "But I like it anyway."

"But!" said Gaspard, who hadn't finished. "It is still a party. In few days we start and we open.

"But today, you should be happy and have fun."

And they all rushed to the door and started pulling on their hats and coats, almost as excited as the children.

Chapter 50

Meanwhile, up at the school, the nativity was unfolding with its usual quota of tears, attention grabbing, and stupefied confusion, typified this year by Conal Feachan of primary one standing stock-still facing out at the audience throughout, one finger stoically up his nose as his horrified parents desperately tried to mime him to remove it, which only caused him to root around slightly harder.

Agot was having none of this.

"I bring tidings of great joy," she announced, looking less like a miniature angel and more like a fairy, her hair blow-dried for once rather than full of knots or pulled back in fierce braids that made her eyes water. Its near-white blondness rippled behind her like a wave; it was truly beautiful.

Her costume, ludicrously over the top, made her walk self-consciously, and having been entirely convinced that she was the star of the show, it took a lot to get her to stand behind and not in front of Mary, an affronted Effie-Jane McGhie. She and Agot would end up as lifelong enemies, Effie-Jane decided, clutching the doll and trying to catch her grandfather's eye round Agot's enormously wide skirts, not realizing that Agot already hated her with a deep and abiding passion because she got to hold the doll. Agot had argued furiously that the angel should bring the baby Jesus doll *"from God in heaven? You know? God? In the sky?"* pushing even kind Lorna's patience beyond endurance, and was therefore still making the most of her time in the spotlight.

Being at the front of the stage, she glanced at Conal Feachan, shepherding manfully still with a stout finger up his tiny nostril.

"I is Angel Gabriel. Stop picking your nose," announced Agot, to gales of laughter from the crowd. Realizing this would be a terrible spur to Agot to show off even more, Flora nudged Innes crossly, only to see him laughing along with everyone else—his daughter could do absolutely no wrong in his opinion—and it was down to Lorna to give her "the look" that sent her to the back of the stage, finally, where she could join Ash, who, after last year's debacle, when he'd played an innkeeper and Saif had gotten extremely upset about the wearing of tea towels, was safely playing a sheep. Ib, thankfully, was now too old to be in the nativity at all and was in the choir, mouthing the words so he didn't have to sing along, as he was eleven now and this was patently baby stuff and absolutely ridiculous.

Saif was planning on missing it—everything was too near the knuckle this year; work was still work and he had more than enough on his plate—but at the last minute, Ash's heartbreak that he might not be there had more than overcome his fundamental objections, and faced with an empty surgery—it was amazing just how much better everyone seemed to feel on the day of the MacKenzies' famous nativity party—he had closed up early and slipped in at the back, desperate not to attract attention. He made sure, though, that Ash could see him. The little boy instantly waved frantically, and Lorna, fatally, turned round to see him, then cursed herself for doing so.

She couldn't help remembering this time last year, when they had kissed for the first time. She knew he would be thinking about it too and swore to herself. She had thought things were complicated enough last year. This year it was a million times worse.

She focused back on the nativity play.

"The Wise Men arrived from afar," said the narrator, stolid Jimmy Donaghy. Good for him. They were going to get this thing done and dusted, then there were carols to sing and people to gouge for some very weak mulled wine, then everyone could go out . . . She peeped out the windows. It was nearing three, thus practically dark, and yes, there it was. Lit up again, you could make out the top of the angel's head over the crest of the hill. It was still surrounded by people—it had been all day. Frowning, mostly. But she loved it. She thought it was beautiful, even more so now as the snow settled all around.

AGOT WAS REFUSING to take off her costume because people kept saying, "Hello, Angel Gabriel," when she went up to them and this suited her very well, especially as Effie-Jane had had to take her Mary costume off so ha ha to her, an emotion that lasted right up until Effie-Jane smugly emerged from the girls' toilets in the stiffest, pinkest party dress Agot had ever seen. It had sequins that changed color when you pushed them over *and* an underskirt *and* a unicorn on the front, and Agot was instantly furious again at having to wait till she got home to change into her own party dress, which was not pink and did not have a unicorn on it. It was silver and had a bear on it, and she had absolutely begged for it the last time her mother had taken her to the mainland. She bitterly regretted that now.

But everything was forgotten as the children finished their final songs—as ever, they were "Paiste Am Bethlehem," the Gaelic carol that could and did make the entire hall weep, and, of course, "Caledonia." And then the children, bolting down their juice and biscuits, burst out of the school, screaming and yelling and delighting at the nearness of the Christmas holidays, at another exciting event ticked off toward the countdown to the most exciting day of all, their senses getting near hysterical as they met the snowflakes swirling in the playground as well as—most exciting of all—the incredible new angel that had appeared from nowhere to light their path.

As if of one mind, they all dashed toward it. After Malcy's failure to get the thing taken down that morning—the concrete had come as quite the surprise—he was convening an emergency meeting, so by the time the children got there, some loud grown-ups were already standing in front of it muttering things like "planning" and "you just can't barge in like this" and "completely illegal," and somebody was noting things down on a clipboard, and someone else was muttering crossly into a telephone, but of course, as far as the children were concerned, anything and everything grown-ups talked about at any time was irredeemably boring and to be completely ignored at every conceivable opportunity, so this didn't worry them in the slightest, and as the snow came down they danced ever closer, stunned by its size and beauty.

Taking a detour, Konstantin had been unable to resist going to take another look at his creation. He still couldn't believe they'd pulled it off. He absolutely loved it. Isla had been walking beside him, making small talk, occasionally sneaking glances at him from underneath her Fair Isle bonnet. Once their gloves brushed in the cold air and she had flinched, and he hadn't been able to tell if it was the good kind of flinch or the bad one.

Now, seeing all the children there, he ran up, more or less like an overgrown child himself.

"Do you like it?" he called out confidently.

Isla smiled; he wasn't the least bit nervous talking to anyone. Of course she had no idea how many trips he'd had to make with his father to children's hospitals and schools.

"Now, in Norway we have a song we sing going round the Christmas tree," he said. "It is called 'Jeg Er Så Glad Hver Julekveld.' Do you know it?"

The children all laughed and shouted, *"Noooo!"*

"Oh," said Konstantin. "Is there a song you know that would be good for running round a Christmas tree?"

"There's 'O Christmas Tree,'" said Effie-Jane, flouncing out her petticoats. Although she was only five she thought that Konstantin looked like the prince in *Frozen*. Okay, that prince had turned out to be bad, but he was still a prince, so she had decided to like him anyway.

"That's a really stupid idea," came an angel's voice from somewhere nearby, but rather more people were agreeing.

"Okay then," said Konstantin, keeping a weather eye on the grown-ups. He knew exactly what they were trying to do and it was very much in his interests to stop this happening, and showing them how much the children loved it could surely only help.

"Now if my glamorous assistant will join me . . ."

He meant Isla and held out his hand. She could barely believe it, but stepped forward and took his hand, and then the hand of the child next to her until everyone had linked hands all the way around the great sculpture. The adults were either pushed out of the way or reluctantly made to join in. Konstantin smiled like it was all a coincidence.

"Okay then!" He whispered to Isla: "I do not know this song. Please quickly help me with this song."

Isla smiled prettily. "Okay! *O Christmas tree, O Christmas tree . . .*"

She sounded a little tremulous at first, but the sweetness of her voice at the old melody soon broke through and sounded clear as a bell in the white afternoon, and it wasn't long before the children joined in.

"How lovely are your branches . . ."

"Oh!" said Konstantin in delight. "I know this!" and instantly joined in in a lovely German baritone: *"Wie treu sind deine blätter!"*

The children immediately laughed at him and he winked and they all carried on:

"O Christmas tree . . ."

"O Tannenbaum . . ."

Two of the older ladies with grandchildren in the show arrived and joined in loudly and querulously:

"O chraobh na Nollaige!"

And now they really had a party. Once they got to the end of the verse they started going round the tree, and nobody apart from Isla really knew the second verse anyway, so they just did the first one again and then again, as they got faster and faster, until they were whizzing round and round the brilliantly lit statue, singing faster and faster at the top of their lungs, and finally collapsed, all of them, giggling in the snow.

Which more or less started a snowball fight, which Konstantin and Isla got out of the way of as quickly as possible.

"I thought you would be good in a snowball fight," observed Isla as they marched down the hill, leaving it to the parents to intervene or join in, depending on the personality.

"I am," said Konstantin gravely. "Too good. I would kill every single one of those children."

Isla started laughing, she couldn't help it, as they trudged up the stony lane toward the MacKenzie farm. The van was already parked there, and Gaspard was looking at them crossly for not being there on time to help set up.

"*Venez, venez,* the lovebirds, come on," he grumbled, and suddenly neither of them could look at the other.

Chapter 51

The village descended on the scones and cakes and sandwiches like a plague of happy locusts. Hot mulled cider sat in pots on the oven, and people opened bottles and passed around whisky while the children ran riot over the farm, barely disturbing the beautiful sleepy cows, who eyed them without interest and went back to nosing about the snowy grass.

Flora took one look at Lorna, who came in late, as ever, after closing up the school, and instantly poured her a very large drink and dragged her into Flora's old childhood bedroom, now full of coats and scarves.

"Tell me everything," she said, and unable to help herself, Lorna told her everything.

"Oh my God," said Flora when she'd finished.

"I know," said Lorna.

"I mean that's just . . ."

"I know."

"On the other hand," said Flora, "it means you haven't done anything . . . technically wrong."

"Apart from sleep with a bigamist," said Lorna gloomily.

"You don't suppose it means . . . Does it mean he's free?"

"I don't think . . ." said Lorna. "I don't think he can ever be free."

And her voice cracked.

KONSTANTIN GRABBED ANOTHER two mugsful of the delicious hot cider and went and found Isla in a quiet corner of the kitchen. It wasn't exactly private, but people were more or less heavily involved with eating and drinking and discussing whether the weather would keep the boats away, deliveries being increasingly important this time of year, as were trips to the mainland for everything you couldn't necessarily get on Mure, which was, to be entirely fair, quite a lot of things. But Gaspard didn't like them hanging about for too long and soon sent them into the little lean-to pantry at the back to start washing up, and they rolled their eyes at each other but somehow, even washing up was kind of exciting, Isla thought, when it was with someone you desperately wanted to wash up next to.

Isla thought it was a good chance to ask him more about himself, but he skillfully deflected every question.

"No—tell me about you."

She shrugged. "There is nothing to tell about me. Well, I was born here. In the house my father was born in and his father and so on." She smiled.

"And is your father still there?"

Her face changed immediately. "No," she said. "He died. When I was small."

Suddenly she had his full attention. "How small?"

"Eight," she said, the very memory of it making her want to

roll up in a ball all over again. It had lessened, of course, a bit. But one of the massive benefits of living on Mure was that everyone knew her, and everyone had known Roddy too and liked him very much. And she never had to tell anyone why she was so quiet—she didn't used to be—and she didn't have to explain how her world had been torn apart, because everyone understood.

She hid her face a little, carried on drying in silence. She didn't want to see his pitying face.

But when she looked up, his face wasn't pitying at all. He was nodding.

"I was fourteen," he said, his voice sounding slightly strangulated.

"Your dad?" said Isla.

"My mum. Cancer."

Isla nodded. They were both quiet for a little while. It was, somehow, oddly relaxing to be able to tell people who understood. Because most people went, "Oh, I'm so sorry, that must have been terrible," which of course was true, but they didn't feel it, didn't *really* know what it was like to have your world cracked in two.

"How was your mum?" said Konstantin.

Isla bit her lip. She had to defend her mother. She knew other people had harsh words for how bitter Vera Donnelly had turned and how she'd taken it out on the wee lass. She wasn't stupid. And she would never ever have spoken to anyone on Mure about it, not even Iona.

But somehow, in the presence of someone from somewhere else—someone who understood, someone who, for all his annoying ways, was clearly and very simply kind—she felt something she hadn't felt for many years.

She wanted to talk. She wanted to speak.

"Very . . . very difficult," she stammered.

Konstantin nodded and didn't say anything, waiting for her to go on.

"I think," she said, "she was so very angry at him for dying. He died young, didn't leave us with much. And it was just me. I think she might have taken it out on me. I don't think she meant to," she added.

"Do you look like him?"

"Apparently yes," said Isla dryly. "But not in a way she likes."

Konstantin nodded again, adding more hot water to the suds. "Yeah," he said. "Your looks come out in all the ways they hate. It hardly seems fair, does it?"

"I can't help my stupid dad's face," said Isla, then laughed suddenly. "Sorry, that sounded so furious."

"I get it."

"Uh-huh."

"And I like your face. Very much."

There was a very long pause after that, as a flustered Isla dried and redried a cup because she had forgotten what she should do with it.

Konstantin found himself staring at the suds. "My dad sent me away," he said.

"You're kidding."

"I think he got sick of looking at me. I think I was quite annoying."

"He sent you here?"

"Well, I had to go somewhere. First away to school, then, when I still wouldn't be what he wanted . . . he sent me here . . ."

"He turned you out?"

Konstantin shrugged.

"Oh God," said Isla. This was her worst fear, that her mother would just tell her to go, because where would she go?

"Well, it could be worse," said Konstantin. "You know, I like the mince pies you have here."

"Oh my God," said Isla. "I can't believe . . . No wonder you were miserable."

"I sometimes think," said Konstantin, "that my mother was my only protector . . ."

"Yes! My dad, he just thought . . . he thought I was great. He thought everything I did was kind of cute and funny . . ."

". . . even when I was naughty . . ."

"Sometimes I think he liked it when I was naughty. Like we were ganging up against my mum . . ."

"Yes! We were a gang and then . . ."

There was a silence and Isla looked at the hurt and the pain in his eyes, and suddenly, without realizing it, he slammed his hand down hard, and it splashed into the water and sent white soapy bubbles everywhere, including onto Isla's nose. She looked at the mess for a second and he looked at her, worried about her reaction.

The next second, she too had splashed in the water, her hand sending a great big gout of foam up onto his hair.

Surprised, he laughed and immediately splashed back, and in two seconds they had gone from feeling miserable to laughing almost hysterically and having a massive foam fight.

As he rubbed some off her nose while trying to get some more of the foam down her neck, she found herself suddenly, willingly, drawn closer and closer to him, and she reached up a finger to wipe the big daub of suds off the tip of his nose, and suddenly he took her hand, gently this time, and put it on his cheek, looking at her, his blue eyes full of intent, his hand large and soft and warm. Color flooded to her cheeks, but she did not turn away, and instead turned and looked up at him, eyes wide.

He looked at her trusting face, eyes wide open, and got such a start. He brought his other hand up—still damp, but that didn't matter—took her little heart-shaped face in it, tilted it up toward him as she moved toward him, a little closer, a little closer, without either of them taking their eyes off of each other. There was noise, of course, outside from the party—fiddles and Nollaig songs—but here in the little back utility, it felt quiet suddenly, and everybody else seemed very far away.

Infinitely slowly, Konstantin bent his head toward her, while she found herself, almost involuntarily, creeping up on her tiptoes to meet him; the space between them grew smaller and smaller, and she found her eyes closing as she bent herself into him . . .

"Konstantin? Konstantin?"

The voice was loud, harsh, and English, and they both immediately, guiltily, jumped apart.

Chapter 52

Squeezing her hand tightly, Konstantin turned and vanished into the kitchen, not wanting whoever it was to spot them together, put two and two together, and make . . .

. . . well, four, he supposed. He smiled to himself and glanced back. Isla was still staring at him, a smile playing round her lips, those huge eyes staring at him. Christ, she gave him such a charge.

In the bright kitchen, full of people singing and carousing and flirting and eating their food, he was pleased to see, he came upon the young woman he'd met before at the statue. She leaned over to Isla—"You don't mind if I borrow him, do you?"—smiling and showing very white teeth.

Taken aback, Isla frowned. "Uhm, no, why would I?" she said, her voice a bit shaky.

"Oh, just looked like you were getting cozy! Not surprised, such a handsome chap!"

Candace couldn't help pushing buttons, and she was pleased to see Isla's face fall at the thought of being obvious.

"Oh, I'm only teasing you," she added meanly. "It's clearly nothing. Now come with me, you gorgeous hunk."

She threaded her arm through Konstantin's.

"Lovely to see you again."

Konstantin frowned. They were hardly friends. He turned round to look at Isla, but she was busying herself at the sink, desperately trying to hide her blushes had he but known it. Meanwhile, Candace was holding out her iPhone as if she was taping something.

"Listen, I just wondered how you felt about all the controversy about the statue?"

"What controversy?"

"From the council? They want it pulled down? Don't you think it looks like another calamity for Mure?"

"They want to pull it down?!"

INDEED, IT HADN'T taken Candace much time to talk to the people around the statue who were complaining, and she certainly didn't encourage them, no, not at all. But she might have asked them a little bit about whether they didn't feel very let down that nobody had properly consulted the council, and didn't this rather overrun planning, and well, what were they going to do about it, and wasn't it a disgrace?

"It is a disgrace." Malcy had nodded solemnly, being slightly bewitched by how pretty Candace was and failing to notice three of his granddaughters were running round the statue cheering and dancing.

And were they going to have a special committee meeting to figure out what they were going to do about it? They were, of course. The men in particular liked to look tough and decisive in front of the exceptionally pretty young woman from London.

Candace was amazed. This couldn't be going any better. Had none of them had any media training whatsoever?

But she still suspected she had a bigger prize on her hands. For a fishing expedition, Mure was certainly turning out to be absolutely chock-full of useful things.

"So," she said, turning all her attention toward Konstantin, who still looked worryingly distracted. Perhaps he was gay; there were a lot of gay men up here. On the other hand, if he was who she thought he was, then that wasn't it at all.

"So you must miss Norway living here."

Konstantin squinted. Why was she asking him all this stuff?

"Oh sure," he said. "But it has its compensations."

"It looks like you're cutting quite the swathe through the local girls!"

Konstantin eyed her suspiciously. "What?"

This reminded him, he should get back to speak to Isla.

"How long are you thinking of staying in this life?"

It was an oddly worded question, and if Konstantin had been paying closer attention he would have asked for clarification or had his suspicions about what, exactly, she was after. But he was desperate to get back to Isla, finish what he started. A smile played across his lips.

"Not long then?" said Candace pushily.

"What? No," said Konstantin, just as they both turned round at a commotion at the door.

"Where is that Scandi fellow?" someone was shouting.

The room turned round. Flora barreled up, cross that people were making a commotion at what was meant to be, excuse me, a children's party.

It was Malcy.

"We're having an emergency council meeting," he said. "You need to come and explain yourself."

"It's eight o'clock at night," said Flora, furious.

"That's why it's called an emergency meeting."

"Also I don't want to go," said Konstantin.

"Well . . ." The man hadn't really been anticipating this. "You have to."

"I don't. You're not the police."

"You have to come and explain yourself."

Konstantin waved his hands. "Yeah, no thank you."

Joel stepped forward, along with Ed, the young police officer who rarely had anything more to do than direct lost tourists and was looking slightly nervous.

"Excuse me?" said Joel. "I'm this man's lawyer."

"I don't need a lawyer!" said Konstantin.

"I'm the lawyer for the money spent by the Colton Foundation," Joel went on smoothly. "This is something you'll have to take up with me in the morning."

"Yeah, also you can't walk into people's houses like that," said policeman Ed. "I think." He screwed up his face. It had been a while since Tulliallan Police College, after all.

Malcy looked about in consternation. He was used to being pretty much a big man on Mure, and he wasn't used to being spoken to like this.

"Well, we'll sort it out tomorrow then."

"I'm afraid we got permission from the council," said Joel, "so it's going to be a bit of a fight."

"You have to take it down."

"We have to do nothing of the sort," said Joel.

"And it's beautiful," said Konstantin crossly. "You just have absolutely no taste, which is why you are wearing those trousers."

This was a bad move. Malcy was very proud of his tartan trews and wore them proudly to every smart occasion, which included the nativity play as far as he was concerned. He turned a very dark red, turned on his heel, and walked out, leaving the party slightly giggly and hysterical, the children running about wondering what had happened and Candace, who had filmed the entire thing, absolutely delighted.

There was a bit of quiet. Konstantin turned to Joel. "Seriously, I don't think . . . we need a lawyer?"

Joel shrugged. "I don't think the council budget could afford me. So hopefully they'll just have to let it go."

Around them the party was clearly winding down, and Flora was quite happy to see everyone go.

"*Allez allez!*" Gaspard was shouting, hurrying Isla out to the van with great trays of pans, empty except for the odd spare crumb. Everything had patently been an absolutely massive success.

"Still, you should probably go to a meeting," said Joel, unaware he was taking up valuable time Konstantin would much rather be using to chase Isla. She glanced back at him. "We could offer them a—"

"*Allez!!*" Gaspard was shouting. "Let's go, Konstantin! Isla, you can go home, *chérie*."

Everyone had gone.

With a desperate look at Konstantin, then at a beaming Candace, Isla slowly started pulling on her coat. Konstantin badly wanted to go to her, but how could he in a slowly emptying room with everyone looking at them both?

"Uhm, see you tomorrow," Isla said, feeling her voice pathetically weak.

KONSTANTIN DASHED OUT the back door of the farm and round to the front, where Isla was tramping away down the hill through the low-lying snow. The stars were gleaming overhead and it was absolutely freezing.

There were, to his utmost frustration, too many other people all heading the same way back into the village, sleepy children being carried piggyback, nodding over their parents' shoulders; buggies with babies wrapped up tighter than parcels; some people singing and breath everywhere showing on the frosty air. From up the hill, the statue was lighting all their way back home, a kindly glow over the moonlit road. Konstantin's brow furrowed again. How could they say it was horrible?

But he had to catch up to Isla. Normally in day-to-day life it would be nothing to shout at her, seeing as they worked together and knew each other. Nobody would think anything of it. Already she'd been engulfed in a crowd of people she knew.

But somehow now, everything had changed. He felt if he said her name—even worse, shouted it—the entire village would stand and stare and he could not, absolutely would not, be able to do what he wanted to do, which was take her in his arms and kiss her till he couldn't kiss her any more.

Meanwhile, Gaspard was calling his name from behind him. He thought about it for a second, then thought, *To hell with it, it's only a pot-washing job,* and, feeling faintly sinister for a moment, ran off down the hill behind her.

Chapter 53

It felt all kinds of wrong, following a woman, but Konstantin just wanted them to be alone, that was all.

He wondered where she lived and what it was like, but he didn't have to wait long. Up the second of the high cobbled streets in the village, behind the main street and the docks, Isla, with her friends carrying on, stopped at a tiny pretty cottage painted bright pink, with light glowing in the windows.

It was a small house, but cute as a button, and Konstantin smiled when he saw it; it suited her. Small and adorable, like a little mouse's house.

He meant to stop her before she got home, and he could see her glancing around, presumably for him, but just as he was trying to work out a way to do that without startling her, the door flung open, revealing a tiny, furious-looking woman.

"What time do you call this?"

"Mum," said Isla patiently, in that pretty voice he liked. "It was the MacKenzies' nativity party! You were invited! You should have come!"

"Waste of bloody time, parties."

"Well, anyway, I was working."

"Yup. As usual treating you like a bloody servant. You're meant for better than this, darling."

"Mum . . . can we talk about it later . . . ?"

She sounded conciliatory, soothing. Tired. He could see what her loss had done to her, to them. He thought of how his father had tried to do the right thing, had tried to be kind and how he had let him down. He found he had a lump in his throat.

"Did you bring me anything to eat?" Isla's mother sounded demanding.

"No, but I can make you an omelet if you like? We've got eggs."

"Go on then. If you're not tired?"

"No," said Isla, sounding exhausted.

And the door closed shut, and Konstantin turned away, sad for all the little things.

Chapter 54

The next morning, despite the threat of Mure civil war over the statue, and Christmas being two days away, Konstantin felt better. He was up early, playing with Bjårk out frolicking in the snow.

He contrived to be out throwing a ball on the side lawn near the entrance Isla always came in, despite the fact that it was both pitch black and minus 1 degree, which, though Konstantin could handle, Bjårk was very much not a fan of. Still, he had a plan that involved hot chocolate and some Norwegian ginger *boller* he'd baked before he went outside. He was ridiculously proud of himself: the idea that he could just go in and look up a recipe and then make it would have been, just a couple of months ago, as alien to him as flying in the air would have been. It was amazing, he thought, as he had left them to rise, that of all the things he would like doing in his life, working in a kitchen would be one of them.

But it was more than that. After a life entirely devoted to pleasure and fun, with as few difficult or intrusive things to do as he could bear, having to actually stick to things, to get up early, to work on dull, repetitive tasks until he got good at them—this was all very new to him. There was a physical satisfaction in it that he had simply never known before, and he was genuinely astonished.

He was therefore in a happy frame of mind when Isla slipped through the side gate and got quite the fright when Bjårk bounded up to her, barking in a way that suggested, *Get me out of this freezing nonsense immediately.* She smiled tentatively at first— there was a bit of her, once she'd had the dressing-down from her mother, that had wondered if she'd possibly dreamed the entire thing, or at the very least built it up in her head.

But now, seeing his blond head tilting toward her, she couldn't help but smile. "What are you doing out here? You're nuts!"

He shrugged. "Oh, this is nothing to Norwegians."

"I don't believe you!"

She bounced up to him, smiling, her eyes streaming with the cold. He reached out his gloved hand and took hers, then glanced around in case anyone could see them, something she couldn't help noticing. For once she put her insecure thoughts about other people—in this case, very much Candace—to rest and tried to let herself enjoy it. He was here now. Wasn't that enough?

"Venez venez!" a voice hollered at them from the kitchen door. *"Pas de* flirting in my kitchen, *please,"* and they giggled at each other and slipped into the luxuriant warmth.

It occurred suddenly to Isla that Konstantin, of course, actually lived in the hotel and had his bed upstairs. They were . . . well, more or less in his house. She blushed at the thought of it. Of course not. It was impossible. They were at work.

Konstantin glanced at her, wondering what she was thinking.

He needed to get away from the hotel; it was ludicrous, given that his bed was upstairs. That was definitely a problem in somewhere so small; he could hardly take her to the Seaside Kitchen on a date.

Which left the Harbour's Rest, he supposed. Well, maybe if they found a dark corner the sticky glasses wouldn't be quite so noticeable. Yes. They could do that later. It was a great shame, he reflected, that they couldn't go to one of the official rooms in the hotel, because he couldn't think of a more romantic place to take a girl, with the big picture windows framing the snow swirling around the little dock, with the toasty central heating and the immense blazing fire . . . A little of Gaspard's hidden stash of Bordeaux and everything would just be so nice.

Well. Alas. That absolutely wasn't going to happen. So he was pretty short of options. A picnic wasn't really on the agenda either.

"Uhm," he said as they were standing side by side again, both of them giggling at nothing and concentrating very hard on listening to the radio. "Uhm, so."

This was ridiculous. The confident Konstantin of a couple of months ago had entirely disappeared. He wondered, for an instant, if it was possible that the old Konstantin had been . . . a bit irritating and full of himself?

Isla couldn't keep her voice calm. "Yeah?"

Please, she thought. *Please let you not be about to suggest that we go upstairs. Please don't have plans for something absolutely sordid and not . . .* She was building it up, she knew. She had feelings for the pot boy. But at the end of the day he was still just a boy, a normal boy who . . . well. She held her breath.

"Uhm, would you like to go for a drink at that strange place on the harbor later?"

Isla could have burst with joy and relief. She knew she was supposed to play it cool and act like she wasn't bothered . . . but she was so happy, she couldn't keep a thing from her face.

"Uhm, yeah, all right," she said finally, trying to tamp down her smile, which was immediately matched next to her.

Chapter 55

Gala had gone through it with her and, to Flora's amazement, there were more and more bookings. Flora liked to think, possibly entirely optimistically, they could see past the silly headlines into the lovely rooms, the delicious dinners, the fabulous peace of the place. She wondered if people couldn't remember necessarily the story, just the hotel itself; the name had stuck in their head rather than whether it was good or bad. She hoped so. Christmas Day and Boxing Day were full, then they would close for a few days, then they had an absolutely full house for Hogmanae too, as well as a band and a full ceilidh. If people couldn't enjoy that, she thought, well, there was not much she could do about that.

Tonight was their last dry run: they were feeding all the people who went to the community day care—the very oldest residents of Mure and their carers. It was just a good chance to give the kitchen a last dress rehearsal with the waiters in place and make sure they were good to go for the big day. She couldn't deny: she was excited.

"This is getting ridiculous," Joel had said as she had collapsed into bed the previous evening as exhausted as only someone doing someone else's job with a six-month-old could be. Joel never had any trouble sleeping, and it made Flora jealous. Flora never knew how before he'd met her he had rarely slept more than four hours a night, jittery, anxious. Coming to Mure was the first time he'd slept all night in his adult life. The sweetness of the fresh cold air and the sheer ability to relax had transformed his life so entirely he got embarrassed even thinking about it. Waking up once or twice to pick up Dougie still hardly felt like a hardship of any kind.

"I know," groaned Flora, staring at some spreadsheets that were swimming in front of her eyes. "Innes says this should be easy to read, but I don't think Fintan even opened the message."

There was a silence.

"I mean, I can't *sack* him," said Flora. "It's his hotel."

"But you're doing everything! It's not right! You should be enjoying your baby!"

A bolt of fear went through Flora's heart. Did he know?

"I am!" protested Flora, even as Douglas was tugging on Joel's fingers. "I do! I love the baby."

"Uh, yeah, I know," said Joel, baffled.

Flora's eyes strayed back to her email. "I'll get him in tomorrow. If he can pull the old Fintan charm on the old ladies, that will be good for business."

The old Fintan charm hadn't shown itself for quite some time, but you could live in hope.

"Have I told you," said Joel, "how absolutely amazing and fabulous you've been and how proud of you I am?"

"For opening 'the worst hotel in the world'?" grumbled Flora.

"Oh, that's all over and done with now," said Joel, putting Douglas to bed and pulling her close to him.

He was completely and absolutely wrong.

Chapter 56

Candace couldn't believe it. Sometimes life depended on luck, she knew, and in this case, she liked to think that she'd made the luck on her own.

She stared at it again. Amazing. She'd talked to her friend on the picture desk, who was just as obsessive a reader of *Hello!* magazine as she was, and they'd tracked back through the pictures, knowing he was Norwegian, and—ta-da! With a bit of help from Google Translate they'd been able to easily put together "Tragedy of Young Norwegian of Noble Descent" with lots of pictures of his amazing castle and stories of the death of his beautiful mother.

Then, under his real name, racy stories of his dating models, pictures of him falling out of nightclubs, and a tabloid nickname, the Party Prince. There was also a small gossip item about him, speculating at his missing Christmas parties and wondering whether he was in rehab, as well as links to his social media accounts that proved the matter beyond doubt and were also full of ridiculous pictures she could easily pull, with him shooting deer and posing next to Ferraris. It was absolute gold. It was patently clear he'd been banished.

She had his quotes about Mure and how he couldn't wait to go; she had pictures—as well as the freeze-frame pulls from the video—and now it was absolutely up and ready to go. This was brilliant. She was going to get promoted for sure. It had absolutely everything: money, good-looking people, nobility, tragedy, shame, and, her readers' favorite thing, someone being punished ferociously. It couldn't fail. They'd have it up by the evening, clickbait of the finest order.

She emailed off the final copy for the page mock-ups with satisfaction. Then she headed out to get the last flight of the evening. God, she'd be pleased to shuck off this crap hole and get back to London. How could they handle being so far away and stuck in the middle of nowhere? It was absolutely freezing all the bloody time and there was nothing going on. Although to be fair, that statue wasn't bad.

Anyway, her work was done. She was out. She packed her neat little wheelie bag and headed through the snow to the airport.

Chapter 57

For once, the night of December 23, just for once at the Rock, everything went flawlessly. Well, as flawlessly as a dinner for quite a lot of extremely old people can go. There was some delicious lobster bisque, quite a lot of which made it onto the starched white tablecloths, and the waitstaff, many of whom were young recruits who knew or were related to absolutely everybody there, found themselves doing more cutting up of the meat than they might have expected in a normal service, and the noise levels reached an absolute cacophony even without the nice album of Christmas carols being played, so they took that off pretty sharpish.

The vast tree was beautifully decorated in scarlet and gold and gently twinkling lights, crowned with a huge golden star.

The salmon was delicious; the goose tender and pink and crispy on the outside.

Fintan didn't actually even bother turning up at all, to the point where Joel was going to go round the farmhouse and yell at him (or, more realistically, get Innes to yell at him), but apart from *that,* it was great. And the fact that Mrs. O'Brien got stuck crying in the toilets, because old Seoras, whom she'd been secretly in love with since 1954 and who had been widowed the previous year, on account of which she had gone all the way to the mainland to get her hair and makeup done professionally in Debenhams, which had been all right when she'd left but had gotten somewhat blown about on the ferry back, leaving her with mascara halfway across her cheeks and a definite slipping effect, but nobody had told her about it until she went to the bathroom, they'd all told her she looked lovely, which she might if you didn't have your glasses on, but when you could see properly she clearly looked like Haggis McBaggis, and anyway, Seoras was already cracking on, chatting to that blowsy Julie McSquire, who had always been a bit of a one, and here she was again, getting away with it, when Mrs. O'Brien had loved him for sixty-five years, so surely—*surely*—she had dibs.

That took a lot of talking down. But apart from *that*, it was flawless. Ish. Flora was a little concerned that a lot of raspberry juice from the light-as-air cranachan was adding to the lobster bisque and red wine on the tablecloths, making it look a little as if they'd been hosting a large selection of grizzly bears, but surely the laundry could cope.

In the kitchen, however, all was sweetness and light, apart from them having to occasionally turn back sweet Mrs. Piper, who had a tendency to wander, but everyone looked after her and was used to seeing her around and about, except Gaspard, who made the mistake the first time of giving her a biscuit, which meant they saw her seven or eight times. The carers from the old people's home were doing a brilliant job, but they had only so many hands, and, to be fair, they worked very long hours in what could be quite a challenging environment, so they deserved a glass of champagne and some good red wine on a very rare evening out and it was entirely explicable that they might slightly overpartake and, okay, it wasn't ideal that one of them had had to have a very small spew in the toilets, but other than *that* it was flawless.

Flora briefly thought she might sleep standing up. She found herself eyeing a spare wheelchair in the corner of the room and wondering if anyone would mind if she borrowed it for half an hour.

But to Isla and Konstantin, young and full of energy, and merry, and excited, and wildly, possibly on the brink of, well, who knew what, the evening flew in an exciting rush of suds and assembling food and washing up and dancing to music and giggling with each other, and when you were with the person you wanted to be with more than anyone in the world, work didn't really feel like work at all.

Chapter 58

W hat do you mean?!"

Candace banged her hand down on the top of the desk, which wobbled, as it wasn't a real desk, just a table set up in a small room.

Billy, who staffed the airport, looked up at her kindly. He was used to having to give this kind of news, but normally people were either accepting, if they were local, or genuinely quite pleased, if they were tourists, that they were going to have to take another day or two of holiday.

"I'm afraid the plane can't land tonight. Crosswinds."

"What do you mean?"

"Well. We have a wind from the north, aye, and a wind from the west, and they've kind of got themselves in quite the tizzy."

"No, I mean, how can I get back to Britain?"

"This is Britain, you know, even though it's actually closer to—"

"No, I mean, is there another plane tonight?"

Billy laughed. "Well, no, there would be but because of—"

"Crosswinds. When's the next plane?"

Billy shrugged. "Well, the weather forecast is not ideal, so it isn't."

"Can I get back on the ferry?"

"Well, you can ask them."

"When?"

"In the morning. They leave pretty early, you know."

"I don't care," said Candace furiously. She had a big Christmas planned, at her new boyfriend's mother's house in Fulham. His mother was absolutely terrifying, really a horrible scrawny old bat, and Candace had a lot of shopping to do to make a good impression. And she needed her nails fixed and her roots done, and she ought to have had plenty of time for this if she hadn't been chasing this stupid story . . . She'd like to tell herself that Dan loved her for her, he wouldn't care two shits if she had her nails done or not—nobody on this island, she'd noticed, cared about that kind of thing; nobody had their nails done—but she couldn't be entirely 100 percent sure that Dan didn't put quite a lot of store by his mother's opinion, and she had a reasonable suspicion as to what Dan's mother thought nails should be like, and it wasn't being chipped, standing in a ridiculous blizzard, banging a wobbly desk in the middle of absolutely bloody nowhere.

"Now, you have a place to stay?" said Billy kindly. More than a few people had slept on his sofa after an unfortunate mix-up or other. It was very much part of the job.

Candace sniffed. Oh Christ, how on earth was she meant to get back? She missed the old glory days of newspapers she'd read about, where people would hire helicopters and whatever it took to get them on a story. As it was, she was back to that grubby Harbour's Rest, which she was sure was far worse than the place she'd been sent up to do the actual exposé on.

"No thank you," she said snottily. "Can I ask you to contact me if a plane *does* decide to visit?"

Billy nodded as cheerfully as he could. Generally people didn't behave as rude as this on Mure, and he wasn't 100 percent sure how to handle it.

Candace had already turned around, remembering with a sigh that she would need to get the island's only taxi back and the driver had been nosy enough the first time. And she was going to have to call Dan. This was going to be tricky. Very tricky indeed.

Chapter 59

Isla tended to keep her makeup out of sight at home, as her mother would always have something to say about the cost and about it being a little tarty. Vera wasn't anything like old enough to have been to the dinner, Isla thought, but even there you could see groups of friends: ladies chatting with each other and having a laugh and even discussing a party as the group had carried on into the bar. She wished so dearly her mum had people like that.

But tonight, having cycled at top speed down the hill from the Rock into the village, then jumped into the shower, she was in too much of a hurry to be too bothered about what her mother thought. Even though they'd agreed to meet at Harbour's Rest following her shift, and even though he still had to mop the floor, and after all, where else was he going to go? what else was he going to do?—she still, nonetheless, felt slightly that if she were late she'd get there and he'd be gone. Ridiculous. But still.

Like he was something out of a fairy tale, a puff of smoke. She put on her prettiest dress that she'd bought for dancing at Colton's wedding the year before and never gotten to use. It was palest pink satin, pretty as anything and far too thin for the weather.

"Where are you going?"

"I'm going to meet a friend for a drink."

"Who?"

"Doesn't matter. Just a friend." Isla felt daring and nervous.

"That lipstick looks tarty."

"Good," said Isla.

Her mother looked stunned. "Don't answer me back," she said.

Isla rolled her eyes.

"And don't you roll your eyes at me. Are you going out to see some lad?"

"Maybe," said Isla.

"Is he good enough for you?"

"For *once*," said Isla. "For *once* would you let me be the judge of what is good enough for me?!"

There was silence. Isla felt terrified. But for once she wasn't going to be the conciliatory one, the one who tried to make everything better.

And she went straight back out the door and onto her bicycle, her hands trembling, before she even turned around and saw her mother's face, her hand still holding that damn teapot.

Chapter 60

There weren't really hours at the Harbour's Rest. Inge-Britt generally closed up when everyone was done, which could be very early in the winter, and January, she closed altogether and went to Iceland to sit in volcanic hot pools. More than once the people of Mure had suggested clubbing together to fumigate the place while she wasn't around—she normally left at least one fire exit propped open by mistake, it wouldn't be a problem to get in—but it hadn't happened so far.

In the summer, by contrast, when it didn't get dark, often people got rather carried away and could be found carousing until the early hours, which were also broad daylight, so everything could get a touch confusing.

So ten P.M. on a December night found the cozy bar warm and welcoming, full of jolly locals celebrating Christmas or farmers having a quiet pint, this being their quieter time of year before the havoc of spring and lambing. As usual they were talking about the disastrous work of farming, but nobody minded so much, as there had never been a year ever when farmers hadn't been talking about the disastrous work of farming.

Isla felt incredibly self-conscious as she walked in in her best dress. What if he wasn't there? What if he'd changed his mind? What if the bar was full of everyone she knew and they all had to watch her being stood up? Why couldn't there be at least one place to go where she didn't know every single person on earth? Normally she'd found that such a nice, comforting thing about living in a small community. Tonight it was utterly unbearable.

She had texted Iona en route, particularly to tell her her big news—that she was thinking of moving out! Iona had been on her to do this for ages, had visions of them sharing a flat together, but she'd known Isla would never leave that awful mother of hers. Iona's own mother was a riot, they would happily share a bottle of prosecco on a Saturday night watching *Strictly* together.

Isla glanced around the room and her heart leaped, as she suddenly forgot everyone else looking at her and saying hello, for there wasn't a soul on Mure who hadn't known Isla since she was a shy, wide-eyed bairn and barely a heart that hadn't broken for her when good, gentle Roddy had passed and left that mainland harridan to mother her.

But in the corner, looking more handsome than ever—he needed a haircut, and his blond hair was looking floppy and falling over his eyes, which, it turned out, was exactly how Isla liked it—Konstantin was already getting up, patently absolutely delighted to see her. A few of the older farmers smiled wryly at each other. Young love.

But Isla and Konstantin only had eyes for each other. They came toward each other and stopped just as he was about to grasp her hands, both giggly, each pink from rushed showers, the wintry chill, the excitement.

"Uhm, hello," said Konstantin, his eyes dancing. He glanced toward the bar, and winking broadly, Inge-Britt went to the slightly iced-up freezer and removed one of Mure's very few bottles of actual vintage champagne. Isla's eyes widened.

"How can you afford . . ."

"I have saved all my pot-boy wages," said Konstantin, shushing her, "and this is the only thing I could find to buy on the entire island."

He ushered her to the corner table, specially wiped down for the occasion with an almost new cloth, and Inge-Britt, smirking only very slightly, which was good of her under the circumstances, brought over the bottle and two glasses with some ceremony.

Konstantin was used to being watched pretty much everywhere he went, so he was completely oblivious to Isla's blushing awkwardness, but once they'd had a little fizz, everything seemed to settle down, and they were in the very darkest corner of the room, and finally they could talk.

"What's happening with the statue?" asked Isla anxiously. She'd passed it on the way down and thought it beautiful as ever.

"I don't know," said Konstantin, pensive. "The council is really cross, I don't know why."

"But people will come to see it! It'll be like the Angel of the North!"

"I think so. I think they're just cross we didn't ask them first and it didn't take five and a half years to get through nine committees and we didn't have a big ceremony and let them all make a very boring speech each."

Isla thought for a moment. "Well, couldn't we?"

"What do you mean?"

"Couldn't you name it after them?"

Konstantin blinked.

"You could call it the Malcom Marsali Aoghas Fraser William Bert Effie Angel," said Isla, tidily ticking off the committee members on her hand. "Put Malcy at the front; he's the biggest arsehole so he's the most likely to be happy if he's first. And let them all make a speech. Isn't that how Joel got it through in the first place?"

She smiled suddenly.

"They could do it at the Loony Dook!"

"In front of everyone naked?"

"They're not going to be naked, Konstantin! That's your stupid country! Here everyone is wearing swimming trunks."

"Getting in the sea wearing wet clothing on a winter's day is the stupidest thing I've ever heard," grumbled Konstantin.

"No, you're right, nothing better on a small island than everyone being familiar with everyone else's genitals," said Isla, rolling her eyes. "Trunks are fine."

Konstantin looked pensive. "Well . . . I mean . . . it might be worth a shot . . ."

"Have a grand opening. They'll have to make the speeches short, otherwise everyone will freeze to death."

Konstantin grinned. "Actually, Joel wants me to meet them all. That might not be a bad idea."

"I think it's a very good idea."

"Yeah," said Konstantin. "Making people feel important."

Isla looked at him mistily. "You . . . make me feel important."

"Well, because you are," said Konstantin. "You're the most important person I've met here. You've saved me loads of times."

Suddenly she was very conscious of his hand on the table and found hers moving toward his, just a little. Once again she had that oddest sense she only had when she was with him, that nothing else in her life mattered in the slightest.

Konstantin looked toward her, smiling. She was just so very lovely.

"We could . . ." she said, amazed at how bold she was about to be. But she suddenly, and very fiercely, did not want to do some of the things she very strongly now wanted to do in the full glare of the Harbour's Rest. "You know, we could maybe take that champagne up to the Rock," she said, rather quietly.

"Are you kidding?" said Konstantin, smiling. "If you'd told me that, we could have just stolen some of theirs."

But he saw from her face that she was very serious, and he stopped talking and gravely proffered her his arm. She emptied her glass for Dutch courage, then took it.

Just as they stood up, there was a commotion at the door.

CANDACE HAD BUMPED her expensive bag crossly back up the black-painted steps of the Harbour's Rest. This was absurd. She needed to get back and she was trapped here. It was cruel and unusual, like a punishment for breaking a fantastic story. Ridiculous. And Christ, here she was, trapped in this hellhole.

She left her bag in reception in the mistaken belief that there would be someone else to take it up for her and stared at the empty reception (although she noted there were keys hanging up behind it, so hopefully she'd get a bed for the night—the possibility of that not happening was just too awful to contemplate).

She would head into the bar, she decided, order a large GnT, check if the story was up yet, and then and only then decide what to type to Dan. Oh *God*. It had taken ten months to even get him to this point, of inviting her to have Christmas with his mother. And now she was going to not make their Christmas, and if there was a way that could be interpreted as not an actual snub, she had absolutely no idea what it was.

On the other hand, she was nothing if not goal-oriented. She clopped over to the bar in her heels, her feet absolutely freezing from standing in that ridiculous barn they called an airport. She pushed open the doors of the bar, feeling the not-unwelcome whoosh of warm, slightly fuggy air hit her, and strode inside. Oh good, Isla and Konstantin were right there. She wandered up to join them, her face taking on a curl that might pass for a smile.

"Hel-looo!" she said, sitting next to Isla. "So, how does it feel, I have to ask . . . to be dating the runaway prince?"

"The what?" said Isla, completely and utterly confused.

In answer Candace took out her phone, beaming. "I'm just going to tape your reactions," she said, and watched as Isla called up the link, stared at Konstantin, then back at the web page in disbelief.

Playboy Prince Slumming It in Britain's Worst Hotel

She blinked. There was a huge photo of Konstantin wearing some kind of weird military uniform with medals on it, next to the pic of Gaspard falling over with Bjårk.

Britain's Worst Hotel, the Rock, on the tiny island of Mure, will be further "rocked" by the revelation today that their kitchen junior is none other than the playboy son of one of Norway's richest and most aristocratic families . . .

Beneath this there was a picture of Konstantin looking drunk and frazzled at a party, surrounded by scantily clad models.

Isla's hand flew to her mouth. What on earth was happening? She scanned the following paragraphs, as phrases leaped out at her: "not going to stay long in this life . . . really misses Norway," and "Mure is a dark, cold, miserable place . . . 'it needs brightening up.'"

It made reference to his illegal "eyesore" (a direct quote from a "senior council source" who spoke of planning to "pull it down as soon as they had the chance") and talked about how he had been banished from Norway for his appalling behavior: "Close friends have been asking when he's coming back from his time with the 'little people,' so they can all have fun again."

So what is next for the Island of Calamity when the Prince finishes his little session of "slumming it" with the locals?—he's been reported as cutting quite a swathe.

And to her horror, there was a picture of him with Isla, taken on Candace's traitorous iPhone, Konstantin looking handsome, her wearing the ridiculous kitchen hat, looking pathetic and hungry and utterly stupid.

Isla jumped up, just as someone burst through the bar doors. It was Iona.

"Have you seen this *shite*?" She pointed at Konstantin. "You bloody bastard! You leave my friend alone. And *you*!"

It struck Candace forcibly that she'd have much rather been circling into Heathrow about now. "Just doing my job," she said smoothly.

Isla came up to stand next to her friend Iona, who put a supportive arm around her.

"Look at the two of you," said Iona. "Well suited. Come on, Isla. Let's leave them to it."

And she helped her speechless friend out the door as the rest of the bar looked on. They hadn't had quite such an entertaining evening since Wullie Stevenson had gotten his false teeth stuck bobbing for apples at Halloween and scared the living death out of all the children by taking them out, apple and all.

Chapter 61

Isla stumbled out into the snow with Iona, her thoughts blurring.

Oh, she was such an idiot. He was slumming it. Literally flirting with her because she was standing right next to him; he couldn't even be bothered to take a look around the island. She was right there, she would do. Her face flamed brighter than ever as she remembered the pictures of Norwegian supermodels and actresses and of him at premieres and parties. Oh God, how could she have been so dumb?

As if. As if she would ever have been more than a plaything for someone like him. And worse than that, he was obviously horrible. Imagine being sent away by your own father. She thought back to her fight with her mother. Oh God. Everything was so awful.

Oh God. And she had been about to . . . Her blood ran cold. Would he have made fun of her with all his rich Norwegian friends when he went home?

So much made sense now. His lack of phone. His patently decent clothes. The way he had absolutely no idea of the value of money. Even the stupid bottle of champagne, now sitting nearly empty on the corner table.

Iona didn't even pause; she took her straight to her house and opened up a bottle of whisky.

Chapter 62

Lorna sat by herself, staring at the box and wondering whether to wrap it. She was going to the MacKenzies' on Christmas Day, so she had a massive pile there, including far too much for Agot, as usual, even though she knew fine well spoiling her didn't help.

But she had one gift—very small, something easily concealed, nothing anyone would ask about. She had hemmed and hawed and wondered about it, but in the end had decided what now did she possibly have to lose?

They hadn't been in contact at all, and she had absolutely no idea what was going on with him, but the boys, she noticed with some satisfaction, seemed happy and well, hadn't become withdrawn or difficult. Ash was looking forward to Christmas as much as any of them; Ib was still out there in the most freezing weather kicking a ball at playtime with his chums. If there had been some major upset at home, she'd have seen it through the behavior of the children. Teachers always did. So nothing had changed. Yet.

She wanted to take him a gift. But she knew she shouldn't. If he was free she'd have seen him.

She walked out into the swirling snow, past the Mure Angel. Looking at it made her smile. It was amazing how quickly it had become part of the landscape. She rather loved it. It gave her light and courage somehow, and suddenly, feeling the parcel in her pocket, she became emboldened. She would take it to him. She made a mental note also to turn up to the emergency council meeting on Boxing Day, make sure to add her voice to the people who wanted to keep it.

She had gotten almost as far as the surgery, then turned round and gone home again. Maybe tomorrow.

IONA FOR ONCE didn't start gabbling, but came over and put her arms round her friend. "I'm sorry," she said. "I honestly didn't realize. I didn't know you liked him so much."

She poured two large measures of the medicinal whisky she'd found downstairs.

"I miss you," she said simply.

"I miss you too," said Isla. "If you'd been about, I probably wouldn't have made such a fool of myself."

"You haven't made a fool of yourself! He's a dickhead!"

In response, Isla pulled down the top of the pink dress, exposing a bright red bra strap, something she'd ordered specially from the mainland.

There was a moment's silence, then both girls burst out laughing, Isla's bordering slightly on hysteria.

"Oh lord," said Iona. "Well, he's missing out."

"You'd have steered me clear, told me to leave him alone," said Isla.

"No, I wouldn't have," said Iona. "I think he's a ride. I'd have been even worse. You'd have been with him a million times by now."

Isla let out a big sigh. "I really liked him," she said. "What an idiot."

"Why?" said Iona. "He looked really cut up about it."

Isla sniffed. "Yeah, he'll just have to get off with a million super-models. Or that stupid journalist."

"She *is* stupid," said Iona, and refilled their glasses.

Isla glanced around Iona's little bedroom, filled with Highland dancing trophies and old pony books. Not unlike hers in fact.

"He had no interest in involving me in his life at all. I was just a bit of fun."

"Well," said Iona defiantly. "We *are* going to have fun."

"What do you mean?"

"There's a flat coming up on the high street. I miss you, you miss me. We *could* rent it together."

"Oh," said Isla. "But I'd have to leave Mum."

"You're going to have to leave her sometime!" said Iona. "She was always trying to push you to university or something anyway. 'Don't you think you could do better, Isla?'" Iona made a passable stab at Vera's voice. Isla sighed again.

"She means well."

"But it makes you miserable."

Isla shrugged. "It's just not my day."

"Don't be daft. You're famous and in the paper!"

"For being an idiot!"

"We'll have fun, I promise. Come on. It's Christmas, Loony Dook, Hogmanae, Burns Night, Valentine's, and then it'll be spring and all the tourists will be here, and you can enchant one of them to fall in love with you and he'll stay forever and all will be well, because! We'll have our own place and you won't have to skulk about to get a lumber."

Isla couldn't help smiling at that. "You're such an optimist."

"That's because we live on top of the world. Stay over?"

Iona was already pulling out the little trundle they'd used when they had sleepovers at eight and nine, talking excitedly about *How to Train Your Dragon,* and at thirteen, talking the same but about Justin Bieber and the fourth-year boys, and now, it was strangely incredibly comforting that here they were again, looking for the spare toothbrush, trying not to wake Iona's mum, hushing each other, giggling, and to her great surprise, Isla slept.

Chapter 63

Konstantin did not sleep. Quite the contrary. As Candace stood at the bar, he considered going over to Isla's, but remembered Iona's ferocity and considered it a good idea not to. He was also very, very pleased he didn't have a phone; the last thing he needed right now was to hear from his father about how he had somehow managed to bring even more disgrace on the family. Oh God. That was hellish in itself. It would be everywhere.

He'd just ignore it all. Presumably Gaspard wasn't going to fire him—or even if he did, he thought defiantly, he could wash pots. He could find another job. Go out and seek his fortune. It hadn't been bad here, not at all.

In fact, he thought sadly, he'd been enjoying it. Learning how to do something properly for the first time in his life. People liking him, really liking him, for himself, not for his money or his ridiculous house. He thought back to the camaraderie of the garage when they had built the statue, the patience (albeit laced with shouting) of Gaspard, taking him from knowing nothing to being actually reasonably useful. He'd been looking forward to the Christmas service, the first time to really stretch themselves at full mettle, to make a roomful of disparate people happy and warm and content. It seemed to him a rather fine way to live your life.

But now everyone was going to despise him, thinking he was just using their island to play Marie Antoinette, to pretend to be poor.

He hadn't felt poor. But he felt every stare in the bar, every aggressive glance, as more and more people read and whispered about how he'd brought the island down.

In fact, here came the first person now. He stiffened, ready to defend himself, or if he couldn't, at least take it.

It was Innes, whom he'd built the statue with.

"Well," said Innes in his slow, careful way. "I see you've been shaking things up a bit."

Konstantin winced. "I'm sorry," he said.

"What about?" said Innes. "I don't care that you live in a castle. Looks nice, if anything. And the statue is brilliant, so screw them."

"But this might be really bad news for the hotel."

Innes snorted. "I wouldn't care about that. I don't think Fintan wants anything to do with it and it's killing Flora. I'd be happy if it fell in the sea."

Konstantin smiled. "I like the way you think."

They chinked glasses.

"How is Agot?" asked Konstantin. "Does she still hate me?"

Innes sniffed. "She hates everyone who tells her she can't skate."

"Have you got her ice skates?"

"There's nothing to skate on, is there? All the water here is salt! Eilidh sent for some from Aberdeen, but they'll be wasted."

"It's a bad Christmas for everyone," said Konstantin, and they chinked glasses again sadly.

KONSTANTIN SMILED AT his kind friend, then got up himself and made his lonely way out into the dark, made miserable by how unhappy he had made his lovely little Isla, how the look on her face had cut him to the quick, how much he missed her, how everything was in ruins.

"Come on, angel," he whispered in his native tongue as he crossed the great figure beaming out brightly across the water, as he trudged up against the wind to the northernmost point of the island and into his little aerie at the Rock, very happy to have Bjårk's shaggy company. "Now I need a miracle."

And it occurred to him that he would have to make an offering to the angel before he could receive anything, which was a strange thing to think, but it crossed his mind nevertheless. It had something to do with this place: the interdependence, the kindness of the people.

It struck him forcibly that it was December 23, the day he would have been celebrating Christmas back home in Norway.

The last few years had been stiff affairs: long dinners of lutefisk and ribs, often with worthy charity leaders of the region.

But he remembered long ago when Christmas was still the most exciting thing in the world, when his mother made a treasure hunt through the palace for him and all the local children, excitedly hiding wrapped gifts in every crevice. He remembered her singing, her happy pleasure as she went to parties, looking and smelling magnificent. The palace had been filled with what felt like thousands and thousands of sparkling lights.

Christmas was on the twenty-fifth here, and nobody had so much as known to mention that today was the real thing for him. Nobody knew.

And of course he hadn't heard from his father   wouldn't, now that he'd brought down even more disgrace on the family name.

He had come; he had done everything he had been told to do. He could even, grudgingly, accept that his father was right. And now, he had been forgotten.

It hurt, formidably.

On the empty road, as the angel faded behind him, he had never felt lonelier in his entire life, like the only man in a world that had turned very, very cold toward him.

Chapter 64

The next day was the prep day for Christmas, and Isla, though waking up with a sore head, arranged with Gaspard that she would come in early for the first shift so she could leave early too and she wouldn't overlap with Konstantin. When Konstantin came down the stairs, he was slightly terrified not to see her there, even after Kerry reassured him she had just worked an earlier shift, which wasn't ideal either.

Chopping and prepping in a cold kitchen wasn't remotely as much fun without his little companion by his side. Konstantin had the sinking feeling that nothing would.

He vowed to go find her after he'd finished. Explain to her . . . or at least try.

But it wasn't all false, that was the problem. He had hated it here. He hadn't wanted to stay.

Until he'd met her. But would she believe that? He thought again of those awful pictures of him and the models. Okay, he'd thought it was pretty funny at the time. But that wasn't who he was now, wasn't how he felt, not at all. Isla was special. He just needed to figure out how to show that.

LORNA WOKE, DETERMINED to do better today. Or at least finish it.

The surgery was empty, many people miraculously finding their symptoms improving as they prepared to stay indoors for a few days fortified with Quality Street sweets, telly, and the fire on. Jeannie was tidying up and trying to ignore the many, many boxes of chocolate that had landed there—Saif was ridiculously popular, but he didn't want to take the sweets home, seeing as he neither had a sweet tooth nor had ever gotten used to the amount of sugar Scottish children ate and being keen to spare his children a similar fate—so now they littered the place up. Jeannie had been pressing boxes on people as they'd come in for being "good customers," but unsurprisingly that had gone down very badly indeed, so she was going to swing past the community hall.

"Oh, hello, Lorna," she said shrewdly, looking her up and down. There was patently not a thing wrong with the pretty teacher. "He's not here."

She realized immediately she'd said the wrong thing.

"Dr. Hussein, I mean," she said, using his surname, which nobody ever did. "He's just finishing up his last rounds before the holiday, topping up prescriptions, that kind of thing."

"Of course," said Lorna, her courage suddenly deserting her. She couldn't bear looking foolish in front of Jeannie; she was terrified of giving herself away.

Jeannie, likewise, couldn't bear the fact that she had guessed, seeing Lorna away every time Saif had booked leave, and busied herself with paperwork. Then something occurred to her. "Everyone's been dropping off doctor presents! Have you got one too? Is it from the school?"

"Uh, yes," said Lorna, grateful for a way out. "Sorry . . . we should have got you something."

Jeannie gestured dryly to the piles of chocolates. "I'm fine, thanks."

Lorna smiled. "Oh yes."

She also had plenty of boxes piled up, along with some really not very helpful personally made artwork from children and— thank God—a bottle of island-made gin from the kind family at Rubhan Taigh, who had to make up for their five naughty red-headed chaps somehow.

SAIF SAT IN the car in the shadow of the parking lot, watching her leave. It took everything he had not to jump up, run out. When he saw her face as she left, so sad, and her hands deep in the pockets of her long student-y coat, and the red hair under a black velvet cap that made her look so young, so lovely, so undeserving to be so sad when happiness was always circling and never in reach, he wanted to run to her, grab her, who cares what the world saw.

He looked again at his phone. On his Facebook. Nothing.

WHEN HE FINALLY got back in, Jeannie handed over the little parcel from Lorna with a kind look that bypassed Saif completely. He held on to it as he went home, heated up the lasagna kind Mrs. Laird had left for him, and tried, completely unsuccessfully, to calm down a highly overexcited Ash. There would be presents tomorrow, then they were booked in to the Rock; Flora wouldn't hear of them having Christmas on their own and had absolutely insisted. Of course it wasn't entirely unselfish; she wanted the place filled with people she knew would appreciate it, plus Ash could keep Agot distracted, which could only be a good thing.

He looked at the sparkly tree in the corner, smiling again at the joy Ash had gotten out of it. Sighing as it marked another year without . . .

Well. He had driven himself crazy for so long. And she now . . . Had she had the baby? She must have. Or perhaps that photograph had been old, perhaps that child was growing up. Did he look like her other children? he wondered.

After the boys were finally asleep, he sat downstairs, feeling the silence weighing heavily on him.

He held Lorna's parcel in his hands, found himself opening it, his heart heavy. He wished, more than anything . . . Well, what did he wish for? He was in love with two different people: one who was there, one who was not, and could never be again, but was still his wife, his legal wife. Sworn to him before God. Mother of his children.

At first he couldn't quite believe what he was looking at. It wasn't possible.

It was the same—the exact same edition—of the book he had looked up online, for the message that may or may not have come from Amena.

This couldn't be true. It couldn't be real. How could she know? Could she have sent it? No, of course not, how could she have known about the crocodile? How could she have known? And Nizar Qabbani was a very famous poet, of course he was. Of course.

It was a coincidence, that was all.

The volume was beautiful, gold and bright blue. There was a

bookmark in it, placed as if it could have been almost put in at random. But he knew, of course, that it had not been.

إذا كنت صديقي
ساعدني لأتركك
أو إذا كنت حبيبتي
ساعدني حتى أتمكن من الشفاء منك
لو كنت اعلم
أن المحيط عميق جدا . . . لن أسبح

If you are my friend
Help me to leave you
Or if you are my lover
Help me so I can be healed of you
If I knew
That the ocean is very deep . . . I would not have swam.

Saif sighed heavily. He got up and stared out the window. Just at the very edge of his vision he could see the beam of the angel statue light up the sky. He looked at it for a very long time.

Then he picked up the phone.

IN THE DEEP quiet of Christmas Eve, there were clusters of drinkers in the Harbour's Rest still, mostly the young people home from the mainland to see their families, laughing loudly and boasting madly about their new lives in Inverness and Aberdeen, London and Edinburgh, while in homes mums and dads wrapped and lost Sellotape and begged excited children to sleep and cursed themselves for hiding gifts months ago and forgetting exactly where, and checked anxiously again to make sure they had enough roasted potatoes and tried to make their mothers-in-law comfortable in their beds while they arranged themselves on pullout sofas, and tried to hide the sherry from Auntie Morag, who got a bit maudlin this time of year, which was completely understandable, what with everything she'd been through, but even so, for the sixth year on the trot it was really bringing everybody down, and oh my *God,* did you see that thing in the *Post* online, what on earth were the MacKenzies going to do? And families rolled on with Christmas, some with the mixture of the sad and the sublime, and several hardy fellows made it to midnight mass and the Reverend Janey gave a lovely low sermon about never making the perfect the enemy of the good, which wasn't strictly speaking in the Bible, but she always found it a very useful sentiment anyway at this time of year.

Nobody noticed a small redheaded figure slip out the flat door tucked behind the tiny museum, hop into the little hatchback, steal up the back road to the old manse (Reverend Janey *much* preferred her modern flat next to the church, with its triple glazing and gas central heating), park round the back rather than out the front, and steal, softly, to the back door, where she did not have to knock, because someone was waiting for her, had been waiting for her for a very long time, who said nothing but pulled her into the warmth of his body and the dark sweetness of his eyes, and in the quiet beating of their two hearts, they shared the deepest gift two people can share.

Chapter 65

*B*ang! Bang! Bang!!!
    "*It is Christmas and everything is terrible!*"

Flora and Joel had woken up very early, of course, to check on Douglas, and they had brought him into the bed and exchanged gifts, which were, in Joel's case, the most beautiful diamond bracelet for Flora because he thought she deserved something beautiful, and she nearly cried because she wanted to wear it to more beautiful places, and Joel said, "As soon as you knock sense into Fintan I am taking you to the Bahamas," and then she burst into tears again because she couldn't imagine a day when that might be the case and that made her sad all over again, even as she assured Joel she loved everything and gave him a Folio Society–bound set of Dickens's novels, which she had thought he might like, correctly.

Then they attempted to give Dougie his gift—a beautiful rocking horse—and they both realized immediately that he was far too young to get Christmas at all in any way and they were completely wasting their time, but to his credit he made a fair stab at eating the tail, which was fairly impressive.

They loaded up the car with food and gifts, even though they were going less than a kilometer. It wasn't really walking weather anyway; the snow had settled and it was treacherous for buggies, although there was no doubt about it: the angel beacon was incredibly helpful. It was amazing, thought Flora as she loaded the boot, how quickly she'd gotten used to it, always checking to see where it was—you could see it from almost anywhere. It was absurd, she knew, to feel like it was looking out for you, looking after them all, huddled together on this little rock. But it made her smile to see it.

Everyone was already up in the farmhouse, Eck by the fire with his morning tea, Hamish running up and down excitedly and buzzing about his new train set they'd all chipped in for, Innes and Eilidh sighing and trying to calm down Agot, who was banging spoons very hard everywhere and saying, *"Everything is terrible."*

"It's not terrible!" said Flora, giving her beloved niece a big kiss. Agot instantly wriggled away.

"It's a terrible, terrible Christmas."

Flora looked inquiringly at Innes.

"She is being the brattiest brat in the history of terrible brats," he said quietly, as Eilidh poured coffee. She looked like she'd been having a very stressful morning. "Would you like another kid? You've already got one, it shouldn't be too much trouble."

"Most people wait till after eight A.M. on Christmas morning to try to give their children away," said Flora. "Oh dear. We have some lovely presents for you, darling!"

"Is there ice skates?"

Flora blinked. "No . . ." she said. "There *might* be Shopkins."

Agot sighed and her chin trembled. "I *haaate* Shopkins."

"This is something of a change from her birthday," whispered Flora.

"I know," said Innes.

"When she loved Shopkins more than anything on earth."

"I know."

"That was only two months ago."

"Seriously, you don't even have to keep her, you can sell her to pirates," said Eilidh, looking a tad too longingly at the champagne Joel was unloading into the fridge.

Agot looked around at the adults, then ran out of the room.

SHE HAD GONE to Flora's room, her favorite, because it still had Flora's old Highland dancing trophies and ribbons. Agot had just started dancing, but Flora had found her, on occasion, holding up Flora's gold medal and announcing, "I would like to thank everyone for this award."

Flora followed her now, leaving Joel to start breakfast while Eilidh cuddled Douglas and made lots of cooing noises about how nice it was to remember what it was like to have a lovely baby.

Agot was lying facedown on the duvet. She wasn't doing performative crying, making a big loud fuss about everything so people would hear. Instead, she was sobbing gently, like a real child, rather than the changeling she sometimes resembled.

"Hey," said Flora. "What's gone so wrong?"

"Miss Lorna said . . ." sniffed the child. "Miss Lorna said if we were good and wrote to Santa Claus, we would get the thing that we wanted. And I was *so very good*."

"Were you?" said Flora doubtfully.

"I did not shout in class! And I did not do chatting chatting

chatting, and when Miss Lorna said, 'Agot, no chatting,' *I did not do chatting*. And I took hands with Hamish when it was time to take hands, and I did not say yuck yuck yuck. I was very, very good—ask Miss Lorna!"

"I will do that," said Flora.

"Everyone says, 'Agot is very naughty,'" said Agot, looking heartbroken.

"They don't say that," said Flora, stroking the girl's long pale hair.

"Yes," said Agot, with a resigned look. "'Agot, she is very naughty and spoiled.'"

"Oh, sweetie." Flora took the small body in her arms. "Well. You're still one of the very favorite people I've ever met."

"You love Bugglas now. Everyone loves Bugglas now."

"There is room," said Flora. "There is room to love everyone."

"My mummy and daddy didn't have room. Then they did."

Flora hugged the little girl harder. "Grown-ups are complicated," she said. "And they are very sorry about that. But everything is all right now, isn't it?"

"But! I did try," wept Agot. "I did try to be good for Santa. So I could go ice-skating. But he brought me . . ."

And her voice wobbled, on the brink of total collapse.

"Stuuuupppiidddd Shoppppppkinnnnnnnsss."

FLORA STAYED WITH her until, to her surprise, Agot actually dozed off on the bed, having been up at regular intervals till midnight and from two A.M. onward. Flora rather fancied joining her, but it was a very busy day. She tucked the child in and went back to the sitting room, where the pleasant smell of scrambled eggs from the yard and locally smoked salmon was filling the room. Eilidh had given in to temptation and poured everyone a mimosa, which Flora reluctantly refused.

"There's nowhere for her to skate!" Eilidh was trying to explain. "If I'd given her the stupid skates, there would just be a big tantrum after that!"

"Well, she's having a sleep," said Flora. "I'm sure she'll feel better after she's woken up."

"Ready for the big day?" said Innes.

Flora grimaced. It had seemed such a good idea at the time. "You're asking the *wrong person,*" she said.

Chapter 66

Fintan woke up curled in the strong arms of Gaspard, snoring gently beside him. It took him a moment to remember, just as he was waking, that they were sleeping in the hotel Colton had paid for, that he had funded and built. That he was betraying the man he loved.

Who was dead.

Suddenly Gaspard's tattooed arms felt like a trap, felt too heavy on him. He stared at the handsome, scruffy, dissolute Frenchman, whose face, unfurled from its customary snarl, looked younger and softer in the clear white light. Fintan looked at it for a moment . . . then thought of his day ahead, and his heart sank.

No. He did not want to walk the halls of Colton's great dream. Did not want to oversee the kitchen that had been Colton's pride and joy, look around the ridiculously over-tartaned dining room and remember Colton's absurd tartan outfits (he had liked nothing better than dressing up as monarch of the glen, stag feather in his cap and all).

He hated the Rock, hated everything about it. It was a mill-stone, nothing else. He got up crossly to get ready to head to the farmhouse first and see his family before pulling himself up to play the jolly host at their grand opening lunch. He assumed everything was ready; Flora had been sticking her nose in all over the place. And Gaspard had told him not to worry, although that was also when Gaspard was trying to get him into bed, so he may or may not be able to take that as gospel. There were almost certainly issues involved in guiltily sleeping with your chef, but Fintan pushed those onto the huge pile of problems he had that couldn't get any higher and slinked off to Gaspard's en suite shower, the weight of the world on his shoulders.

Gaspard sat up. *"You are sad!"* he shouted, but it wasn't really a question.

Fintan turned back. "I don't know what's going to happen," he said.

"Nobody know what going to 'appen."

"I hate the hotel."

"So walk away. Whenever I am sad, I walk away."

"Are you sad now?"

Gaspard eyed him up seriously. *"Non."*

JOEL WATCHED FLORA carefully when Fintan came in, trying to smile as he handed over another huge gift for Douglas. "You'd better try to dress him," she said. "I'm crap at it."

Joel went over to her. "You're not," he said, surprised. "Of course you aren't."

Douglas was already waking up from his morning nap and

preparing to make a wail. Joel looked at Flora's face—she was almost flinching—and suddenly something dawned on him.

"Darling," he said. "Can I take you next door for a second?"

IN FLORA'S OLD bedroom, beside a snoring Agot, Joel took Flora's hands in his.

"All this time," he said quietly. "All this time. I didn't realize."

"What?" said Flora, anxious to get on to the Rock.

"Darling," said Joel. "Have you had trouble staying at home with the baby?"

"No!" whispered Flora loudly. "I love him!"

"I know you love him," said Joel with infinite patience. "I mean, have you found it difficult?"

Flora froze. He knew. He had seen it. She had tried so hard to make it look like she could do everything, when it was obvious that she couldn't. That she was failing Douglas. Pam was right. She barely saw him. It was awful.

She burst into tears.

"He doesn't love me!" she whispered. "He prefers you! I'm shit at it! I get bored and frustrated and distracted, and he cries *all the time* with me! *All the time!!* He loves you and I'm shit at it!"

Joel wanted to laugh, although sensed, correctly, that this perhaps wasn't the time. "He cries all the time with me too," he said soothingly. "He's a baby."

"But you're so patient with him."

Joel looked at her. "But this is all new to me," he said, astonished it wasn't as clear to her as it was to him. "I've never had a family before. You've been surrounded by brothers and children and relations and so many people your whole life you don't even realize it! I've had nobody. Nobody ever. And then I had you and now I have Douglas, and oh my God, Flora. Oh my God."

They were both crying now.

"But . . . you don't think I'm a terrible mother? For doing other things?"

"God no," said Joel. "You're great. And wanting to run the Rock . . . it's okay. I'm not sure, between you and me, and I'm sure absolutely nobody else has noticed . . . I'm not sure Fintan is quite cut out for it."

Flora swallowed a half-gulping half laugh. "You mean that?"

"I take absolutely no responsibility for interfering in Mac-Kenzie business," said Joel. "But I am happy, Douglas is happy, everything is well. Fintan is miserable, and as for you . . . you'll be fine, my darling."

He hadn't been planning to do it *quite* at that moment, but suddenly, it seemed fitting.

"I'm not sure if this is the time, because you are very, very tear-stained, but . . . I brought you something to go with that diamond necklace . . ."

And he took a small box out of his coat pocket.

"If you can get enough time off between shifts . . ."

Now he was going down on one knee. Flora was just staring at him, astounded. Then she wiped her face furiously.

"Oh my God, this is *so* unfair," she said.

"I know," said Joel.

"Oh my God."

"In your own time."

He smiled up at her widely and she returned his grin.

"Oh my God."

"I know, Mark and Marsha are going to kill us for not doing it when they were here."

She flung her arms around him. *"Yes please! Yes please!! Yes please!!!"*

"Shh," said Joel. "You'll wake him."

But it was too late. She heard the familiar wail from the sitting room. But somehow—somehow—it wasn't as hard as it usually was. Just knowing that Joel understood . . . and omg, she was engaged!

She danced into the sitting room.

"Where are you, my darling little man?" she crooned.

Joel stayed behind in the bedroom for a moment, slightly stunned with himself.

"I knew that was a bad baby Bugglas," came an unrepentant voice from under Flora's old duvet.

Chapter 67

It had been a hard night's work, but a hard night's work was exactly what Konstantin didn't mind anything like as much as he'd always thought he might, and he couldn't sleep anyway so it had made sense.

Now he was hovering, waiting for sunup. He couldn't help it; he wanted to see her face. However alone he felt, there was someone who might be happy to see him.

Also he was dreading going back to the Rock. Having to face Isla. Knowing she felt he'd let her down, that she hated him, thought him some sleazy, lying player. It had taken so long to break down her defenses so she felt she could trust him, like a little bird, in a funny way. And then just as he'd thought they had reached an understanding, and as he was getting to know someone better than he ever had before—certainly better than any of the girls he'd been with—well . . .

He could see it from her point of view. But he had wanted to get away, desperately at first.

Now, though, as Christmas Day dawned bright and frosty, the

ice crackling over the fields with the short, shaggy cows with their big horns mooing enthusiastically; the beautiful, endlessly long beach with the clear blue sea to the horizon; the little painted houses huddled round the harbor; the fresh air with the scent of warm baking—he could see why people loved it too. He didn't mind it at all, in fact, as he strode through it, warm in his darned jacket.

As he reached the MacKenzie farmyard, he saw that the family was up, could see smoke billowing from the chimney and figures moving inside the low windows.

Taking a quick breath, he knocked at the door.

"It's the prince," said Fintan uninterestedly, when he opened it up.

"I am not a prince," said Konstantin awkwardly.

"Is everything okay at the hotel?" said Flora immediately, taking two seconds off from looking at her beautiful new ring from every angle and waking Mark and Marsha at four A.M. in New York, as was traditional.

"Why should he care? He's only passing through," said Fintan.

"I wish you cared as much as he does," shot back Flora, then remembered what Joel had said and held her fire.

"Actually . . ." said Konstantin politely.

"Come in, come in, it's freezing," said Innes, who knew exactly what was up, beckoning him in and handing him a cup of tea, which left both Flora and Fintan feeling rather ashamed of their lack of goodwill.

"Happy Christmas," said Flora. "Sorry."

"She was just shouting at me," said Fintan.

"Well, I like your local Scottish traditions," said Konstantin, taking a sip of the tea, which was disgusting to him. He had never gotten used to it.

"I have coffee too," said Flora hastily.

"I was actually looking for Miss Agot," said Konstantin gravely. Agot had in fact woken up when the knock at the door had come and stood rubbing her eyes at the hall entrance. "I owe her something."

"Are you really a prince?" she said.

Konstantin shrugged. "Oh well, for you, why not?"

Agot took a look at Douglas's pile of presents by the wall, all wrapped in blue animal paper.

"And who are they for?" she said suspiciously.

"I have brought you something," said Konstantin quickly.

Agot blinked. "Did you bring anything for Bugglas?"

"I brought nothing for Bugglas."

"Okay."

Konstantin winked at Innes, who vanished obediently.

"What's going on?" said Eilidh suspiciously.

Presently, Innes arrived back, bearing a white box.

"But!" said Eilidh, but Innes hushed her and handed it over to Agot.

Eyes wide, she opened it.

Inside were the most perfectly beautiful little pair of skates, white and trimmed with white fake fur, with pink laces.

Agot gasped. *"Nooooo!!"*

She lifted them out of the tissue paper wrapping as if they were the most stunningly lovely things she'd ever seen. The silver blades caught the light, flashing and glinting in the early winter sun.

"But where is she . . ." started Eilidh.

"Shh," said Innes.

"And you see here," said Konstantin, pulling out a pair of skates. "I too have my skates."

"You brought your skates from your palace in Norway," said Flora.

"Of course," said Konstantin, looking confused.

He lent the little girl his arm.

"Would you like to come skating with me?"

And he led her out into the farmyard, to a sight that provoked a gasp from all the others too.

On a flat piece of grassy ground, out by the cowshed, Konstantin had done something very simple. With Innes's help, he had built a small wooden fence in a rectangle, about fifteen centimeters high. He and Innes had had a conversation the day before and had met in the night. Then they had used an old tarpaulin as a liner, filled it half full with water, waited overnight—and now, Konstantin was using a kettle and a broom to carefully smooth it flat.

It was a perfect little rink.

Agot's eyes were wide as saucers.

"Now," he said. "You have to be careful not to trip over the ends. That is why you have to hold my arm."

"I would like to hold the arm of a prince going around an ice rink," said Agot gravely, and she sat up in the tractor seat while he tied her laces carefully, and then, after he'd bundled her into her warm clothes, he took her hand and Innes took another, and slowly and steadily, they led the little girl round and round the rink.

Chapter 68

Everybody laughed and cheered as she went round and round, until she finally found the courage to go off by herself, her low center of gravity helping, her tiny knees knocking together.

"I have to get *all my friends! For skating!*" she shouted, her cheeks pink in the cold and her eyes bright with happiness and desperate to share it.

The others gradually retreated inside as Eilidh took endless hours of footage, and Flora took Fintan's arm. He was resistant at first, but she dragged him back over to the dairy, normally busy turning out the island's sensational butter and with the milk suppliers turning up to take the milk, but quiet today.

Fintan spent no time in here these days; it was run by a lad from the village. But he missed the happy days he had spent in here, experimenting with cheese—fabulous, some of it—tinkering and working and simply being his own man.

"What are you showing me this for?"

"I was wondering," said Flora shyly. "If . . . if you would like it as a gift?"

Fintan frowned. "What are you talking about?"

"Look. Me and Joel have discussed it. I'm useless on maternity leave. It's not that I don't love Douglas . . ." she added fiercely.

"Uh, nobody said that," said Fintan.

". . . but I love the Rock too, Fintan. I loved what Colton was trying to do, right from the start. It's where I met Joel. Where I fell in love. Where everyone fell in love. It's where I've had more fun than I can remember. I want his legacy to be right. I want to do it, Fintan. I can do it. If you like . . . I could take over the Rock. As a real job. And you could go back to making cheese."

He looked at her suspiciously. "What's the catch?"

"There's no catch," said Flora. "The only catch would be if you desperately wanted to keep doing the Rock and didn't want me to do it."

"Oh *God*," said Fintan, his face brightening suddenly. "*I'd love* you to do it! Then I wouldn't feel like I was letting down Colton by selling it or giving it away."

"You'll need to pay me," said Flora.

"No, I realize that. But I don't . . . I mean, this is . . . this is . . ." He looked at her, eyes red. "Thank you!" he said. "I thought you were just interfering to be a putz."

"And I thought you were being lazy because you too are a putz," said Flora.

They grinned at each other and hugged in the freezing dairy.

"I miss him," said Fintan, starting to cry. "I can't believe I still miss him so damn much."

"Because you're not an idiot," said Flora. "Of course you do.

Make the best cheese you can in his memory. That's what made him fall for you in the first place."

"Actually, I think it was my fabulous butt," said Fintan.

"Yeah yeah, whatevs," said Flora. And properly arm in arm this time, both beaming, they made their way back to the house.

Chapter 69

Well, Isla couldn't say she was surprised to find him gone. Heartsore, sick, and tired. But not surprised. She didn't even know where Bjårk was. So. He didn't care. It was all true. He was probably in his room, back to his long lie-ins, planning his return to Norway, famous once again, and doing media interviews and talking about his terrible banishment. They'd probably sent for him.

On Christmas morning, Isla had scampered back to her mother's, leaving Iona looking forward to a full day of her and her mother drinking prosecco, eating sausage sandwiches and Quality Street, and watching TV in their pajamas.

Isla had come down to a silent kitchen and her wounded-looking mother being passive aggressive, hoarding the teapot at her end of the table and making her disgruntlement very clear.

"Happy Christmas," she'd tried, and her mother had har-rumphed.

"For you maybe," she'd said inaccurately. There were presents under the tree, but for once, neither of them was interested in looking at them. It was heartbreaking.

"Well," said Isla finally. "I'll see you at lunchtime? I think Flora's put you next to Mrs. Laird and that nice Dr. Saif."

"Will he eat the food? They eat weird stuff."

"Uhm, he's fine, Mum."

Vera sniffed. Although the doctor might enjoy hearing about her rare symptoms. That might be something. Other people had common or garden-variety complaints, but she was a medical mystery.

"Mum," said Isla. "I need to talk. I think I'm going to move out after the New Year. In with Iona."

Her mother's hand went to her throat. "You're moving?"

"I don't think . . . I don't think we're making each other very happy."

"You're getting a flat! You're growing up! That's *wonderful*!"

Isla was completely and utterly taken aback.

"I don't need you here fussing round me!" said Vera. "That's just . . . I'm so pleased for you, my darling. Your life needs to move on."

Isla was slightly astounded as they hugged.

GASPARD CAME DOWN to the kitchen looking uncharacteristically happy for once and, even more surprisingly, kissed them and handed out large tins of mystery duck, which made no sense to anyone, and announced, "Today will be *huge* success. And those who hope it will be *poor success* will be so wrong they shall cry into their steam horse pudding thing you like."

Gaspard had never gotten the point of mincemeat, and he wasn't about to start now.

"Where is the young prince?"

"He's not a prince," said Isla automatically, then wondered why she was defending him. "I don't know. He might be gone."

"He is not gone. There are no planes, no boats, nothing. He is lazy. Go wake him up."

Isla flushed. "I don't think—"

"*Allez! Allez!* Now! We have much to do! Go!!"

Isla slinked out of the kitchen, despondent, and mounted the beautiful stairs. Everything looked even more spotless than usual. Gala on the desk was already busy, checking in the very first customers with a broad smile. It was actually happening! After three years, the doors of the Rock were finally open! Bertie the boatman was bringing people round from the village. There was a mix of people who were genuinely interested, people who were there for an ironic break, and, after all the fuss in the papers, some Norwegian star spotters, locals, and even, which would have surprised Joel, some of his old party friends, who were tiring themselves of the London lifestyle and wanted to see what the big draw was up here. The ferry had come in—a special service—but, to Candace's pure annoyance, wasn't going back again. The captain was staying for his Christmas lunch too. There was a small group of old friends of Colton's: graying, fit-looking men who smiled ruefully at one another and traded sad anecdotes. And there was Candace, standing crossly in the middle of the foyer, her plans in ruins. The fact that she had had an unbelievably comfortable bed last night was just irritating.

The waitstaff was already fetching coffee and shortbread for the drawing room as people waited to get checked in to brand-new rooms. There was a palpable air of excitement.

All the way up in the eaves, everything was quiet, the rooms empty. Isla remembered the very first morning she had come here, how shocking she had found him. Well, now it all made sense, she supposed. She hadn't liked him then. She shouldn't like him now.

But even so. She remembered his face as the statue went up, the boyish enthusiasm he'd allowed to run riot. Even how nifty he'd gotten with a knife. The look of concentration when his too-long hair flopped over his face. The way his hand had felt in hers . . .

She almost let out a groan. The room was empty. Of course it was. He had gone.

And she was alone, but it was worse than before. Because before, she hadn't known what she was missing, hadn't realized there was something bigger out there, hadn't ever—she hated to admit it to herself—hadn't ever fallen in love, even if it was with a cad.

Almost out of habit, she glanced at her social media, even though she was terrified of seeing anything about herself in it. Konstantin was in loads of papers, but she ignored it all.

Then she saw one thing, on Eilidh's Facebook account. It looked impossible, but it was true. A picture of two blonds: Konstantin holding Agot's hand as they . . . Were they *skating*? The clear winter light was hitting their hair; it was beautiful.

Underneath Eilidh had written, The prince built us an ice rink!

Isla stared at it for a long time. He had really gone and made an ice rink. He had really gone and done something for someone else, no thought to himself, just so that Agot would be happy on Christmas Day. This wasn't something she would ever have thought him capable of before. She blinked, stared at the photograph for a long time.

As she finally turned away from his door, suddenly she heard boots. It couldn't be. She steeled herself. He was coming back to pick up his stuff, that was all.

He walked slowly: after the excitement of seeing Agot, all his miseries were back. His face was sad, his back stooped, as he got to the top of the stairs. Even Bjårk looked disconsolate next to him. Then he glanced up and saw her, and his face changed completely.

"Were you . . . looking for me?" he asked.

There was a long pause.

"Gaspard was—was wondering where you are," stuttered Isla.

"But not you."

Isla shrugged. "I thought you'd be heading back."

"Where?" said Konstantin instantly. "Where? You know the truth about me. I got thrown out of my own country. Thrown out. And I have heard nothing. Not from my dad, not from anyone. They were more than happy to see the back of me. And now everybody here thinks the same. You'll all be happy to see the back of me too. So it hardly matters where I go, does it?"

He walked straight past her.

"But you have loads of friends! Everyone knows you," Isla found herself saying.

"Everyone knows me," came the voice heading into the room, "and nobody gives a damn."

And he pushed the door shut behind him.

"I do," said Isla in a very small voice. "I give a damn."

There was a squeak as the door pulled open again.

"What?" said Konstantin. "What did you just say?"

Isla was flushed.

"Tell me!"

"I said I give a damn," she said very quietly.

"You didn't when you stormed off."

"I didn't say I don't think you're a jerk."

He looked deep into her eyes. "But you make me not want to be a jerk," he said.

"Well, I'm not sure it's working."

In response he took her face in his hands.

"I need to ask you," he said gently, as the mood instantly changed. "I need to check and I need to tell you that my intentions with you . . . are not exactly pure. But. Can I say good? Or at least better. But you make me want to be—"

Before he got to the end of the sentence, she grabbed him and kissed him, hard.

Chapter 70

Of course Gaspard was yelling for them before thirty seconds were up, and no, it couldn't possibly be, but—was that a smile? A tiny hint of a smile on his face as they catapulted down the back stairs. Surely not.

Isla pulled Konstantin back just as they were preparing to enter the kitchen, flushed.

"I—I just wanted to say I don't care. If you're here forever or if you're just passing through or . . . well. I've decided. I don't care."

He turned to her, hands outstretched. "Darling, I have nowhere else to go. I'm here."

She looked back at him. "That's not very flattering."

He leaned over and kissed her. "And there's nowhere else I'd rather be. Happy Christmas."

She watched him go into the kitchen, put on the freshly laundered whites, and pick up his knife and swish it round, cheerfully and confidently, and her heart blossomed suddenly, full of excitement and thoughts and plans. Maybe . . . Could this happen? She scuttled after him into the kitchen.

FLORA ARRIVED IN her best red dress, the diamond bracelet, and the brand-new ring and with a smile the size of the Endless Beach, because after all it wasn't every day you got engaged *and* became the manager of the loveliest hotel for miles around *and* stood in the foyer smiling and welcoming everyone in.

She'd tell the kitchen later. And also have some quite strong words with them about how they spoke on the record about the business.

There was an empty table vacated by the councilors, led by Malcy, with Pam and Charlie out in solidarity, but she'd managed to fill it, so the boycott was hardly going to cause them too much trouble.

Because otherwise it was such an interesting group of people: hipsters, possibly looking for a giggle; proper, serious-looking foodies with guidebooks, including one or two who followed Gaspard wherever he went; locals, of course; some older people from the mainland who had seen past the daftness of the videos and into the loveliness of the remote surroundings; and, she even noticed, some old flames of Konstantin's, looking around for the "prince."

She smiled. He may not be a prince, and he may have done some pretty questionable things, but she couldn't help smiling, thinking about how happy Agot had been that morning.

At 12:45 P.M., all the MacKenzies turned up, Douglas resplendent in a ridiculous baby-shaped full tartan outfit, courtesy of Marsha and Mark, of course, but gurgling happily in his increasingly heavy car seat. Fintan had changed back into a paisley shirt and soft jumper, and his face looked a decade younger. He shot straight off into the kitchen, for possibly the first time ever. Joel and Flora looked after him, confused.

"Okay, what's going on?"

Joel laughed.

"What??" said Flora.

He shrugged. "It's just . . . we always thought I was the type A in this relationship, Mrs. Booker."

"People change," she said, kissing him and closing her eyes with happiness just being near him, as she always did, because she always was.

"NO *FALLING DOWN*," Gaspard was saying severely. Bjårk Bjårkensson was imprisoned upstairs just in case, which he was dealing with by steadily ripping apart every single one of Konstantin's socks, which was going to make it slightly ironic that he wouldn't be able to complain about getting socks for Christmas this year, because he wasn't getting anything that year. Everyone was lined up ready to go. Kerry was looking more furious than ever as Fintan came into the kitchen.

"Hello, stranger," said Konstantin, but Fintan didn't look the same at all. He looked exuberant if anything.

"Happy Christmas, everyone," he said jovially. "I know you'll be wonderful today."

They glanced at one another.

"But also . . . I wanted to announce that Flora is taking over as the proprietor of the Rock!"

They looked at one another.

"What, she wasn't?" said Konstantin.

"She recruited me," said Isla. "I thought she was."

"Who are you?" said Kerry.

In response, Fintan went up and kissed Gaspard in front of everyone.

"I'm just some guy," he said. "I might have some cheese to sell you."

Gaspard beamed. Only Isla saw Kerry's face fall even further and realized, finally, why the silent, stolid girl had followed the mercurial chef when all those around him had tired of it, and her heart went out to her.

"Okay, *allez allez allez*," said Gaspard finally, glancing at the clock. "Starters, please."

AT ONE P.M. precisely, everyone was seated in the dining room, drinks in hand, canapés circulating, and finally the blessed lutefisk (with smoked salmon, if you'd rather) starter was plated up, and there was a moment, just before service, when Gaspard got them all together and held their hands.

"Well," he said finally.

Isla was acutely conscious of Konstantin's hand in hers. She waited for some inspirational words.

"You've all been completely, my God, so very, very *not useful* for so long. But now! Please let us say this will not be another terreeble deesaster. Bless you all!"

And no one said anything, then Konstantin kind of said, "Uh . . . amen?"

And they laughed, and Gaspard rang the bell, and service began.

EVERYWHERE WERE HAPPY faces, thought Flora, looking around as the courses came out, seamlessly and delicious. There were, miraculously, vegan options for the fussy people from London, but good hearty dishes for the older people too: a splendid local beef; goose, of course, delicious; an absolutely stunning lutefisk made in Konstantin's honor; a chestnut soup of glorious lightness.

The cellar was cheerfully emptied; the new young waitstaff, if not always immaculate, cheerful and sweet. Flora kept looking fairly ferociously at Candace, who rolled her eyes at her. Yes, it was amazing. Yes, she was being chatted up by two frankly incredibly hot men to either side of her, Ed the policeman and Fionn the fisherman, neither of whom she could understand a word of, but really, did it matter when there was this much good food and laughter and quiet music and jollity? Dan had sent a couple of very strangulated, passive-aggressive text messages that had very much made her wonder if someone so uptight was quite right for her, and for God's sake, she had barely meant to upset his mother. What, she thought, about all the times when she would deliberately want to irritate her in the future? That would be awful. And yes, okay, so she was going to have to file something—that irritating flea Iona was already taking pictures of her. And she didn't normally eat carbs of any sort, of course, but was that why the roasted potatoes were so good? And "World's Worst Hotel Comes Up Trumps" wasn't a bad headline anyway.

BY THE TIME the Christmas pudding had been served, and they were on to coffee and liqueurs, and the band was setting up for a ceilidh, Flora couldn't have been happier. The Rock was alive, brimming with cheery, well-fed people, and you could hear it in the buzz of noise and laughter; the children running around the huge tree, brandishing their best new toys; the women giggling in the lovely bathrooms, reapplying lipstick and glancing at their hair. For the first time ever the place felt fully lived in, properly doing what it was supposed to do. She wished so very much Colton were here to see it. She looked over at Fintan and realized that of course he felt exactly the same. She got up and squeezed his shoulders.

"He'd love it."

"He'd wish I'd done it."

"He wouldn't give a rat's ass," she said, using one of Colton's favorite expressions, which made him smile.

"I think he liked quite a lot of MacKenzies."

She passed on, thanking the waitstaff and heading into the kitchen.

"I think people want to see you," she said to Gaspard, who had disappeared outside for a cigarette.

"*Vraiment?*" said Gaspard, but he wasn't unused to this. He'd always known he could cook. He just hadn't thought there'd be a kitchen that could hold him.

GASPARD DRAGGED THEM all out in front of the room, which erupted into a loud round of applause (drink had been taken at this point).

Konstantin, to his surprise, found himself a little overcome. Service had been fast and intense, and he'd amazed himself by how hard he could work, how much he could do when he tried, when he really tried. He found himself turning a little pink as he faced the clapping, even though it was silly, it was only lunch.

Then one table stood up, and he froze.

Chapter 71

It couldn't be. He dropped Isla's hand immediately even as she turned to look at him, puzzled. Then he stepped forward.

The short man at the table stepped forward also, beaming.

"Pappa?" said Konstantin in a very small voice.

He looked at the rest of the table. It wasn't just his father: his aunts, his friends, omg, even Anders, his dreaded nemesis. He felt like he was sleepwalking. Isla's face suddenly dropped as she realized who was there.

"We thought we'd surprise you," said his father in Norwegian. "But you have surprised us. And I am so proud of you."

"But . . . in the papers . . . I looked like such an idiot."

"That is when we decided to come!" said his father. "When we saw you with the dog! We did not think *idiot*. We thought . . . Look at my boy. He is *working*! And we are so proud of you. Your chef said you were doing so well."

"I deed not, you are eediot!" came a voice from far off, but Gaspard couldn't possibly understand Norwegian, so they both ignored it.

And, completely in opposition to everything he had once

thought he would do when he saw his father again—the harsh truths he would unveil; the cold, disdainful words he would give to the family who had banished him—Konstantin found himself burying himself in his father's arms, like a child again.

"*And he makes ice rinks,*" announced a small voice loudly. "Are you the king? When I am bigger I am going to marry him. Maybe *next year.*"

The older Konstantin looked faintly perplexed. "Well, thank you for the advance warning, miss," he answered formally, as Konstantin buried his head in his father's shoulder in order to hide his tears.

GASPARD LED THE rest of them back to the kitchen as the wait-staff was pouring back in with crockery, and there was still much to be done as the tables were cleared for dancing.

Isla, stony-faced, stood by the sink alone. It was ridiculous; two hours before she had been building castles in the air, fantasizing about the two of them, just the two of them, going out properly, making a life together, working in the hotel, enjoying the spring that lay ahead and the long summer months, celebrating Hogmanae and Burns Night.

And now it was all over. His rich family—she had seen the way they were all dressed—his rich family was back and of course he was going to want to go with them, off to where all his bloody trees were and all his great fun and sleigh bells and skiing and parties and all those skinny rich blondes.

And she'd be left behind, as she'd always been.

She scrubbed a pot particularly hard. Kerry came over.

"They're not worth it," she said dully.

Isla looked up at her, wondering if there was more wisdom coming.

"Men," said Kerry slowly, "are all minky-manky spinky-spanking copper-bottomed bollock-wobbling *fucking dickheads*."

Then she shut her mouth, turned round, and went back to tidying up her station and helping with the mountain of plates coming through.

Isla put her ugly hat back on, got her elbows soaking wet in the suds. She should be wearing her gloves, but who even cared now if her hands got red and chapped working in the water and with knives all day? What did it matter if she grew careworn and old back here, hidden away—well, yes, just like a scullery maid, while the young dukes and princes lorded it around outside, just as it had always been, just as it was always ordered to be.

"Only at Christmastime" came on the radio, which was just what she didn't need right now, and she was very close to tears by the time the kitchen swing door banged open once more.

One of the waiters yelped. "A dog in the kitchen!" he howled, as Bjårk immediately turned round, stupid doggie eyes shining brightly as he smelled the many delicious scents of the forbidden area, and he jumped up with two paws on the kitchen unit and started licking down the dirty plates.

"Oh, *Bjårk*," said Isla, then she looked at him. "Well, I suppose you're being helpful for once." She caressed the stupid animal's big pointy ears as he panted appreciatively.

"Bjårk!" came another voice, rushing in. "I brought you down to say hello to your *family*, not *eat the kitchen*."

He stopped at Isla.

"And you too," he said. "Aren't you coming to say hello?"

Isla looked at him. "Not like this," she pleaded. Her apron was dirty, her hands filthy and soaking wet.

Konstantin came over, unpinned her cap, then carefully pulled the pins out of her hair, which came tumbling down. She looked up at him, scared.

"Let me kiss your mouth rosy," he said, then proceeded to do so. "Okay. Now you're perfect. Come on."

And he tossed the cap to the side and led her out through the swinging doors.

Bjårk stayed behind and dealt very efficiently with the gravy.

Chapter 72

The dancing was in full swing in the dining room, with an energetic Strip the Willow going on. The usual lines of four or eight couples appeared to have morphed into all sorts of numbers, and Agot and Ash were racing hand in hand through every archway whether it was their turn or not, so it was pretty much business as usual.

Isla could never have known how delighted Konstantin Senior was to meet, for the first ever time, a friend of Konstantin's, properly introduced, who didn't look like an overindulged party girl or behave like a spoiled brat. Someone sweet, pretty, normal, kind. She was just conscious, still, of her apron and her damp hands.

"It's lovely to meet you," said the old man genuinely, and, feeling slightly ridiculous to be meeting a strange white-bearded man with rosy cheeks and a Scandinavian accent on Christmas Day, Isla smiled back and managed not to accidentally curtsy.

"Ahem."

There was a clearing of throat behind them, and Isla turned round. There sat her mother, refusing to get up, clutching her handbag.

"Ah," said Isla. "And this is my mother."

"Enchanted," said Konstantin with all the charm he could muster.

Please don't be rude to them, thought Isla with all her might. *Please don't be off with them.*

Vera stood up to her full height, extending a hand as if she herself were royalty. "I see your son has had the very good fortune to meet my daughter," she said calmly.

Chapter 73

Boxing Day dawned clear and bright. Breakfast was tasty and done quickly; there would be no further meal services that day. Konstantin looked nervous, Isla realized. He had stayed up late, speaking Norwegian to everyone, and she had taken her mother home, the pair of them getting in and opening their presents. One of Isla's was a new, cool Cath Kidston teapot.

"I thought you might like it," said her mother shyly. "For the new place."

"I do," said Isla. "Very much. But not as much as yours."

THEY STILL HAD the emergency council meeting at ten A.M.

"What's the worst they can do?" she said.

"Just the idea that people hate it makes me sad. They could tear it down," said Konstantin, frowning.

"I know."

"I just wanted to do something nice. I thought it would be nice."

"You don't know who hates it."

"All the powerful people who run everything," said Konstantin, gloomily munching a sausage.

Isla plucked up the courage to ask, "And then . . . are you going back? With your dad?"

"Yes," said Konstantin, and Isla's heart dropped. "For a visit. Can you come? There's no more meals till Hogmanae."

"What?"

"I mean, we could go for a few days? I could show you around."

"And then come back?"

"Well, for now, yes. I've got a job. I like it. I'm trying to get a girlfriend, although I will tell you up until now it is going very, *very* slowly."

Isla smiled in delight. "And then what?"

Konstantin screwed up his face. "Come on. I've barely got my first job started, don't ask me my five-year plan. Also, I'm in some danger of getting banished from here too. Two countries in one year would be quite good going, I think."

"Even for a playboy."

"Even for a playboy."

Although in fact the papers, desperate for copy, were already running Candace's glowing review of the beautiful Christmas lunch. Candace herself was staying on a couple of extra days; Fionn had promised to take her out on his boat and catch her a lobster, and she was absolutely feeling rather up for it.

At 9:45, they looked round the empty kitchen, then, nervously, headed toward the town hall. The angel towered above them, glinting in the sun. It was as beautiful as ever. But today the glow gave it a sinister cast, as if it knew it might have to come down.

Hand in hand, they walked to the doorway, where they saw the most amazing thing. They'd noticed a lot of people around the village but assumed everyone was heading for the Loony Dook at eleven. Many were carrying blankets and flasks, and Mrs. Brodie was rattling the tin for the school fund as usual.

But as they reached the door, they heard a great swell of people and a noise. *"Now!"* came a voice, and everyone took hands.

"What's going on?" said Konstantin.

Malcy, arriving at the same time, looked around crossly. "What the hell is this?"

Right up the street from the town hall, leading to the statue, was a human chain: Billy from the airport, all the children more or less from the school, Lorna, and Giorgio, the pilot who had flown in to speak for all the pilots who loved it for navigation, with a message from the ship captains likewise.

The councilman harrumphed, following the other members in, including poor, slightly terrorized Marsali.

Then everyone from the chain came behind Konstantin and Isla and took up every single space in the hall.

"We are here to vote upon the removal of a nonplanning permission object on the island," said Malcy. But every time he tried to get people to be quiet, they started up again, chanting, *"Keep the angel! Keep the angel!"*

Malcy spoke at some length about how it was an eyesore and completely illegal, and there was some harrumphing. Then Konstantin looked at Isla and winked. He stood up.

"May I speak? I wish to name the angel the Malcom Marsali Aoghas Fraser Bert William Effie Angel," he announced grandly. "And I personally will pay for a plaque to commemorate the full name, to be placed at the base," he added.

There was some silence over this. People started cheering and shouting, "Vote, vote, vote!"

Obviously Malcy did not want a vote he did not know he could win. There was some private conferring.

Eventually he returned.

"The provision is this: the statue will stay as long as Konstantin undertakes to keep it in good order and to return and tend to it. And make the plaque with all our names on it."

Everybody cheered.

"Thank you," said Konstantin gravely. "I realize you are an important man in this town."

He turned to Isla delightedly.

"I'm not sure you can get rid of me that easily. It's the law now."

Chapter 74

The visiting Norwegians were well used to getting in extremely cold water and only had to be reminded, yet again, that here it was done with swimming trunks on, so they were all up for the Loony Dook.

The children were doing it because it was fun and naughty, and it meant their parents had to do it too so as not to look like wusses.

Candace decided to do it because she had a fabulous figure in a bikini, so any excuse. Also the light and the color of the water and the pale, pale white sand on the Endless Beach made it look like she was actually in the Bahamas, if the temperature hadn't been 3 degrees Celsius, so she could take lots of excellent pictures for her Instagram. She was getting quite the following. She noticed Iona taking selfies in a particularly fetching spot and copied them exactly, to Iona's stone-cold fury.

By eleven there was a piper burling up and down the beach and much laughing and bantering and remarks and swearing about how cold it was just to take your jumper off, but there was nobody there—apart from the older members of the community, who stood with warm towels and blankets and coats, and flasks full of hot coffee laced with whisky, and bacon sandwiches wrapped in silver foil—who wasn't ready to get in.

At eleven sharp, the entire island lined up along the sand. There was a great horn blown—by Agot, naturally—and hand in hand, the entire long line ran down the Endless Beach screaming their heads off and into the freezing, churning water.

Several words were heard that would not have truly passed muster in front of the children, but it was only once a year. There was much shrieking, and most of the children ran in only up to their waists, figured that was enough, and immediately turned and charged back the other way, to be scooped up by adoring grannies and rubbed fresh pink.

The others, bolder, swam.

Konstantin loved the cold water and took Isla with him, deeper and deeper, and when he thought no one was looking, finally kissed her flushed face full-on, and laughed at her shock and joy as she wrapped herself around him.

Flora and Joel held hands, and Flora jumped up and down screaming while he endured the freezing water with complete and utter calmness, and she burst out laughing and said, "I am sure this is a metaphor for something about the two of us," and he laughed too and grabbed her close, and they ran back out together, heading for Douglas, who was laughing and giggling in the blanketed lap of his doting grandfather, to swing him up between them.

Saif and Lorna swam out farther and farther and moved just close enough so their toes could entwine in the water, for it was not deep, and the sand that joins the world flowed over their numb toes. They couldn't feel each other but they were still together: because sometimes even when we cannot feel each other we are still together.

And the town laughed as one and ran back in, glowing and jolly, feeling refreshed and cleansed and alive, under the watchful eye of the great Mure Angel, bright in the winter sun, lighting the way, keeping them safe.

لذلك سوف أميل دائما قلبي
أقرب إلى روحك
كما استطيع.

So I will always lean my heart
As close to your soul
As I can.

—Ḥāfeẓ, "The Woman I Love"

Eg stansa vel uviss, utan svar,
Som framfor eit ukjend land,
Om ikkje min kjærleik til deg var
For meg som ei lykt i mi hand.
I paused uncertainly without answer,
Finding myself set against an unknown land,
To see whether or not my love for you,
Was a lantern in my hand.

—Halldis Moren Vesaas, "Lyset"

Tha caoin-shlios mo leannain mar eal' air a' chuan,
Nas gile nan fhaoileann air aodann nan stuadh,
Mar shneachd air na beannaibh, mar chanach nam bruach,
'S i furasta, suairc na giùlan.

My love is a swan on the ocean,
Brighter than gulls on the waves,
Like snow on the mountains, like wild cotton,
It is easy, and I shout aloud with joy.
                    —Dòmhnall MacLeòid, "An Cluinn Thu Leannain,
                                                    An Cluinn Thu?"

Acknowledgments

Thanks: Kjersti Herland Jonson, my Norwegian publisher, who answered all my Norwegian questions so helpfully and kindly; Layla Al Ammar, Tom Holland, and M. Lynx Qualey for their help with Nizar Qabbani; Nicole Moore at Lynne Rienner Publishers, and Guri Vesaas.

Huge thanks to: Jo Unwin, Lucy Malagoni, Milly Reilly, Donna Greaves, Joanna Kramer, Charlie King, David Shelley, Stephanie Melrose, Gemma Shelley, and all at Little, Brown; Deborah Schneider, Rachel Kahan, Jennifer Hart, and all at William Morrow; Alexander Cochran, Jake Smith-Bosanquet, and Kate Burton.

ALSO BY JENNY COLGAN

AMANDA'S WEDDING

MY VERY '90S ROMANCE

THE BOOKSHOP ON THE SHORE

CHRISTMAS ON THE ISLAND

THE ENDLESS BEACH

CHRISTMAS AT LITTLE
BEACH STREET BAKERY

THE CAFÉ BY THE SEA

THE BOOKSHOP ON THE CORNER

SUMMER AT LITTLE BEACH
STREET BAKERY

LITTLE BEACH STREET BAKERY

THE CHRISTMAS SURPRISE

CHRISTMAS AT ROSIE HOPKINS'
SWEETSHOP

CHRISTMAS AT THE CUPCAKE CAFÉ

WHERE HAVE ALL THE BOYS GONE?

DIAMONDS ARE A GIRL'S BEST FRIEND

500 MILES FROM YOU

CHRISTMAS AT THE ISLAND HOTEL

WWW.JENNYCOLGAN.COM